ANCIENT SAGAS
OF AMERICA

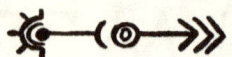

THE PETROGLYPH SERIES

ANCIENT SAGAS OF AMERICA

THE NETHERWEIR

Chris Hegg

Rowe Publishing

ISBN: 978-1-64446-024-5 (hardcover)
ISBN: 978-1-64446-025-2 (softcover)

Visit the author's website for more information about his ongoing research, follow him on social media, sign up for his blog, and contact information for speaking arrangements.

AuthorChrisHegg.com

1 3 5 7 9 8 6 4 2

Printed in the United States of America
Published by

Rowe Publishing
www.rowepub.com

DEDICATION

For all your support and nurturing,
we love and miss you Willow!

To my family,
I offer within these pages a
piece of my lifelong research findings.

CONTENTS

INTRODUCTION

The arid desert of the American Northwest we see today was not always
how it was! In paleolithic times, the west coast of America was teaming with life. Mega beasts roamed the lands; wooly rhinos, mammoths, and
sloths ten feet high grazed in the presence of giant predators like Dire Wolves
and Saber Tooth Cats. They lived along massive lakes between mountain
ranges that looked like islands. From Oregon to Arizona, these lakes filled
the valley floors, now parched and covered by dry playas, which once connected to the Gulf of California.

The freshwater lakes once teemed with giant fish and creatures like the
Ichthyosaurus, a toothy, whale-like beast fifty feet long. Timber rose hundreds of feet high, and snow covered the mountains with active volcanos,
always threatening destruction. The lands were indeed a utopia, raw and untouched, but it wasn't to last. There was a time twenty-five thousand years
ago when man traveled to North America by sea; traces of his existence are
only now being revealed to science.

Their saga is based on actual events told by firsthand accounts carved in
stone as symbols known as petroglyphs. These symbols were the Ancient's
Universal Language, capable of bypassing the spoken language barriers of
the world to provide trade and a world peace not realized before or after.
These remote panels continue to be painstakingly hunted down and deciphered by the author in his lifetime of research.

Thousands of petroglyph panels are spread across North America and
tell fantastic stories of exploration and the hostile environments the first
people faced as they entered the untouched land. These stories define strange
acts of nature, contact with others who came, and great cataclysms that
shaped today's land. These firsthand accounts, forgotten by time, are again
revealed from the stony surfaces that have survived eternity.

Thrust yourself into this ancient saga of the newly discovered Netherweir, which we now call America. See it through the eyes of Seldik, a young
boy who is ripped from his humble beginnings out at sea near the Gulf of

California and lunged into the perilous Netherweir, the land of death described by their elders. Follow along to see how he became the first to gain the knowledge needed to conquer this new world and discover his true path as a unique Soul Type, ensuring his people survive another ten thousand years.

Seldik and his band of explorers must sail up the ancient lakes covering California to land near Mount Shasta. From there, they must continue a dangerous quest into a more hostile land where many have already perished. They must cross the Sierra Nevada Mountains, discovering Lake Tahoe, where they encounter another group of people displaced into these wild lands. Will this new contact between cultures be the key to conquering the Netherweir or spell their demise?

Chapter One

DAWN BEFORE

The sharp dagger of first light fought through the swaying dried-kelp blinds of Seldik's window. A warm ocean breeze mixed, aligning the city perfectly so that the sun's rays cast dazzling prisms of colors upon Seldik's closed eyes—Mother Earth's attempt to enter Seldik's mind while in his dream world to offer a dire warning of his future—a future that would change his life forever. The warning went unheeded as the colors dancing through his eyelids only combined with his wonderful otherworld dreams of swimming with the giant fish in the ocean under a full moon's light.

Slowly waking into yet another beginning in the repeated ritual of returning to the living, Seldik slipped from his bed and slapped the swaying kelp blinds in disgust. As he listened to the pleasurable, crunchy sound of fracturing along the dead plant's lengths, he noticed a piece of parchment fall from the window's ledge onto the ground. He reached down to pick it up, and through squinting morning eyes, he read his father's handwriting. "*Seldik, when you wake, meet me at the center spire. There is someone I would like you to meet.*"

Discarding the note with a sigh, Seldik let out a yawning stretch and dressed before grabbing some dried fish meat from the hut's tiny table bag. After stuffing a piece in his mouth, he went to relieve himself in the open toilet thatched into the room's corner before setting out to meet his father.

The bright blue sky had no clouds, and the dampness was already burning off, leaving a layer of fog miles away on the eastern horizon. The ocean before him appeared wakeless, with no measurable waves, as it had remained for weeks. This time of year is most pleasurable to him, as the city requires little upkeep, meaning much play will be in store after he visits his father.

Seldik headed between the many thatched huts to the city center, greeting familiar faces as he went. He passed down a row of thatched, round-peaked huts that look identical to outsiders, but for those who live on CED, each home possesses its own unique charm. Some are adorned with ornate seashells strung between bird bones and various charms; others have elaborate

entrance husks of bright reds and blues bearing symbols painted in black relief to ward off sea spirits. Even entryway rugs sometimes have ornate, woven
symbols to protect against tiny sea sprites who try to sneak in under them.

Waving, he politely acknowledged the older women who sat chatting
and singing on thatch perches, playing foot games as they ground various
grains or meat on stone metates, pulling the heavy rolling pestles or banging
them along the smooth stone surfaces. Speaking only ancient tongues, they
rarely chatted with younger ones, but they gave him a warm smile as he continued. Despite the language barrier, he had grown to appreciate the older
members of his community. They do what they can to contribute, mainly
fishing, preparing food, and weaving the never-ending repairs needed to
keep the city intact.

When he arrived at the wide rows dividing the central axis of the
housing, much activity was taking place. Giant fish-drying areas were being
laid out in squares so tenders could flip and pinch for moisture determina-
tion, and folks were walking past in rows carrying burden baskets on their
backs or heads to take supplies to various storage huts. As Seldik continued,
he passed the water-drying vats lined with animal skins covered with pitch
for the slow cooking of seawater. These are used to mine the salts, as the
slow process allows for the constant accumulation of raw crystals, which are
then harvested from the brine. Seldik snapped off an old salt crystal clump
hanging off the edge and began licking it as he moved along.

Stretching for several Megarthy[1], CED blossomed out from the towering
spires on the main circle to the edge, comprising three massive concentric
living rings tethered to the gigantic central circle by twenty-four wide, spoke
walkways jutting out like a wheel with a dot in the middle. The significant
gaps opened with the ocean lapping between, set between the rings along
the center circular area, allowing flexibility for strength, like a fabric. Seldik
could not help but think of the fantastic technology his empire possessed to
build such a vast city.

Riding the inner currents of the gap's ocean surface were hundreds of
paddle tail boats whipping along the causeway, delivering goods and people
efficiently without using the top ring surface, minimizing the overcrowding
of walkways. He watched as skiffs and paddle tail boats docked along both
sides of the gaps' edges while supplies were moved into or out of tunnel en-
trances within the rings where products were stored.

Seldik hoped to be exploring these storage caverns with his friends later in the day, as he had done many times before. Oftentimes, they would
sneak into so many labyrinth-like passageways they got lost, emerging on

---

1   Megarthy: One Megarthy is equivalent to one mile.

the opposite side of the city and having to walk back farther than expected, resulting in a mild scolding when they turned up late for dinner.

Today's adventure will have to wait, Seldik thought as he used his foot to flip a heavy stone. This is a practice that all on CED maintained, as these stones, if flipped throughout the day, soak up the sun and omit light once it has set. They have been placed throughout each circle, allowing light to be had without fires deep into the night—a fortunate trade from a mainland far around the curve of Mother Earth. Passing along the rings at night is always a sight to behold. As the stones begin to glow, the whole of CED lights up as if it is covered in a blanket of starlight from above.

CED, though massive, is built entirely of plant-based matter. Winding within the tall layers of harvested and thatched matter are long, exotic veins of rooting vegetation that feeds on the decay and bind everything tightly together, creating a harmonious living structure. Though the vines are harvested once they are overgrown, their deep roots remain beneath the city, releasing gases as they decay to keep the city buoyant. Many living plants layer the city's foundation, but the upper living levels along the ring sides are made of hollow bamboo and Toole swamplands plants, like the cat-tail variety without the sharp top bulb.

Many plants grow within gaps along the rings' walls where wicking cords suck up water while filtering off the salt so the plants don't suffocate. Spiking out around the rings on net trays are shelves that provide a renewable source of materials plus a windbreak from the winds at sea. Small boats move along the causeways and traverse the narrower gaps to harvest and grow the crops mixed between the woody jungles.

Sea water is filtered into drinking water by using a high-tech process involving melted light-colored sand that forms into a thick, nearly transparent glass-like material that transfers sunlight into square, sea water-filled tanks, not unlike the brine harvesting ones. The angled top glass brings water drops upon the underside, which continually builds up and sheds the clean water down to the bottom surface until it drips into bamboo canals that flow to the bladders held within depressions along the causeways. Catchments are also installed everywhere that allow rainwater to flow into similar collections along the rings' surfaces. The city lost little clean water over its edges without being captured for use. As Seldik looked around the city, he saw a landscape that stretched beyond his eyes plane of the most magnificent floating jungle.

He focused his eyes out from the spoke he was crossing and imagined the many races he competed in with the empire's youth training program. He loves to run and is just as good at swimming. In fact, his favorite place to practice his speed and strokes is in the causeway, swimming by each region. Several segregation zones developed naturally among their empire, creating unique cultural variations in the whole of CED. Within these regions is where the best of the empire rose, be it Vision-Souls, War-Souls, or Knowledge-Souls. He hoped that, someday, his side of the ring would make him a great leader, too, just like his dad.

Seldik paused on the massive walkway before he stepped off onto the center circle and looked back over the living rings. Staring down the tall walls of stacked and woven matter that comprised the great city, he thought of all the ongoing upkeep over the decades to sustain the great body below that kept CED afloat. As far as his eyes could follow around the distant curvature of the ring's edge along the causeway, he could hardly see the border. He let his eyes follow the mass as it stretched to the horizon before being lost around the center circle's edge. Some 35 hands tall of exposed matter meant that over seventy-five hands lay underwater, too. The thought of many tons of plants able to sway in the ocean's fury is daunting to him. He could see massive oil-soaked ropes rising from deep along the circle's brim, anchored with other ropes jutting out of the intricately woven mat fibers comprising the structure. Thousands of huts and structures along the living rings help to hold the frame together, which is mended and maintained by adding new material under the water instead of on the rings' top surface, mitigating the need to lift huts when adding new mats thanks to the technology designed by their ancestors.

On the outer perimeter are docks, bays, and hidden cavities where his city thrived with trade. Invisible holes within the outer edge hold enclosed war ports where vessels are stored fully ready to set sail, though nobody has had a reason to fight them, as the empire is peaceful, wishing only to trade.

No one else, he was taught, could construct a design of this magnitude. CED is a self-reliant floating empire that holds a quarter million people with technology so grand that it can navigate the oceans by water power and the knowledge within the empire to navigate currents that take them around the globe to the shores of the latest discovery and the most hostile land ever discovered—the great Netherweir.

The Netherweir, Seldik thought on, a shivery feeling going down his spine just thinking the name, is a massive continent of the most inhospitable environments and is home to some of the most fierce animals ever encountered by man. Seldik looked toward the elusive Western shore and felt a dark, looming fear that reached miles across the open water to his very soul. He tried to imagine what it looked like, but all he could see was a horizon of fog above the water and the mass of CED that stretched before him. He felt so small in the presence of the giant that loomed just over the horizon, like an ant standing before a volcano.

Seldik made haste now to the center spire in search of his dad. At over half-Megarthy in size, or Meg for short, the center circle was teaming with activity. Trading of goods was taking place at almost elbow distance everywhere, and the streets were filled with wagons, creating traffic in all directions as the freight was delivered from one side to the other. Seldik skipped along happily, watching goods swap with loud arguments sounding here and there as he moved between the great spiral street edges, heading to the distant spire looming before him.

Everyone on CED was dressed in bright, alarming colors. Women wore elegant, embodied layers of material that flowed over dresses with jumper pants died from exotic pigments from the Homegath region, and men wore tunics and pants with less frill but not fewer colors, signifying the dawning of the new wave of enlightenment that was upon them, never witnessed by man before this Great Year. Next year is considered the start of the Golden Age, an age when man will peak his knowledge by learning the universe's ways held secret until now. Such is the reason for the color changes, permanently erasing the dark times of the empire's past.

Finally arriving at the capital, Seldik stared up at the center spire that led up like a curved peak from the flat single-layer shops and buildings that spread throughout the center ring. Surrounded by other less massive spires composing the different factions of the empire's ruling bodies, the center spire loomed ten stories high. Some towers had rock-carved stone pillars holding their lower-level entrance in a smooth, angled transition. Atop them sat intricately woven bamboo that curved upward to a single point covered in gold. These intricately decorated exotic blue basement stones were also from Homegath, the native home of the first enlightened land-dwelling peoples over six thousand Megarthy to the east called the Easterlies. CED discovered the continent before the written record, and a trading kinship remains between them.

Being magnificent rock workers, the Easterlies built many temple pillars, which CED incorporated into their central structures. Floating the giant megalithic stones around the globe was a feat no other society, living or gone, could achieve, so the pillars were erected with great pride in the heart of the empire.

Land-dwellers have vast resources, often brutally fought over by many as no barriers exist. Rugged mountain ranges with huge rivers are the only places where one cannot cross to raid others. In the mighty oceans, no such issue exists. Despite the abundance of resources, there are no other known solely waterborne civilizations.

Like himself, many in the empire have never stepped foot on land, having lived generations upon the waters of the world. Those who remain on the ground use only occasional boats to visit the seas for fishing or travel, but none except the shore cultures to the east live upon the waters similar to Seldik's kind.

For thousands of years, the great circle of man was living on land or water, but not until the Great Peace foretells will there ever be a merger of those kinds—a destiny the Future-Soul predicts will occur within this great Golden Age. It is said that when a mighty Aquarionite finds true love, there will be great peace around the world, and all will gain from the knowledge of each other. Seldik didn't believe in the hype that was always passed along in the story and doubted other's Souls differed much from his.

He walked between the great pillars of Homegath into the center spire. A tapestry of the finest cloths and hides of animals from around the globe lined the thatched walls within. Technologies like sailing, fishing, navigating, war, planting, and astronomy were all embellished within the confines of walls meant to awe anyone inside them. Hereupon, his ancestors' writings were painted throughout, displaying sacred scripts in what is considered the first written language. As he passed each panel, he was taken aback by the thin gold and silver layering of symbols that designated the beauty of an empire rising from the ashes of old to become the knowledge center of the world.

Rare artifacts hung beside these stories. There is a tusk from a mythical sea creature killed by Sea'Cedric of the clan Char, as well as the simple flesh of the mighty white bear Brim, who first brought man his wisdom atop a magic floating ice sheet. Together, they crossed the sea for the first time and arrived upon the shore of Netherweir—the lost continent of the world. Brim was a more modern tail than the others. History is said to be an absolute fact now that they possess the ability to write and preserve it, and the great Knowledge Soul Nasok still actively seeks the one who first discovered Netherweir, the great War-Soul Skag~Nether, given the mythical distinction upon his name for the world in which he discovered. Seldik pondered that teaching as he climbed the many stairs to his destination.

If Skag~Nether is still alive, he would be of the first blood, living some 3,000 years! Seldik thought. *Could that be? An ancient who is still alive today? What of Brim, the mighty white bear of knowledge? Could he be alive?*

"Seldik!" came his dad's voice, snapping him from his daydream.

"Yes, father?" Seldik said at once, stopping halfway up the stairway.

"Keep coming! You're late, as usual," Cedrin said with a sigh.

"Yes, sir!" said Seldik, racing up the remaining steps.

Chapter Two

DECLARATION OF CHANGE

"Seldik, I want you to meet someone," Cedrin said, pointing toward his workroom. Seldik marched toward the charge without delay. Cedrin followed and led him to the balcony where a man was waiting, back turned to him.

Seldik immediately became uncomfortable when he saw the colossal statue of a man before him. His bare, brawny arms exposed brisk lines of muscles and scars mixed with vast tattoos—*a Warring Soul*, Seldik thought, shocked.

Cedrin didn't pause as he made introductions. "Kolkesh, meet my son Seldik." The behemoth of a man turned like a cat on a ball so fast that Seldik stopped dead in his tracks, staring.

"Well met, young warrior! Well met indeed!" Kolkesh immediately went to Seldik's frozen form and shook his arm in greeting.

"Your great father sure knows how to make legends, Seldik, and you will be a destiny-seeking, ravage-taking, globe-shaking kind you will! I know it!" Though he spoke quickly with no evident gaps for air, there was a shudder in his voice that twanged the skin with each syllable that rolled off his tongue. Seldik attempted all forms of composure and decorum like he was taught, but the untangled mess he was simply transferred to an "Ahh," expelling from his lungs as he realized his mouth must have been hanging open during the entire exchange. Kolkesh gently slapped his jaw shut and shook his head.

"No need to speak, boy. Cedrin has told me all about you and your lessons." Kolkesh now leaned his hand, pointing a finger toward him as he continued. "A pupil worth investing in, Cedrin." Seldik felt himself relax slightly now that the giant man was addressing his father.

"Thank you, Kolkesh. You can see the boy is star-struck by your presence and size." Cedrin said, pointing out the obvious. "Ahhh," Kolkesh mustered as he waved his words off and headed for the table of drinks already heavily broken into by the looks of it.

"Come. We will drink together," Kolkesh said as he summoned Seldik and his father to join him.

"He is old enough to partake in more than thirst drinking now," Cedrin said, slapping a hand on his son's shoulder before grabbing a glass. Kolkesh poured himself an overflowing amount and swallowed it in a giant gulp. "Drink! It tastes better than the sea!" Kolkesh roared, then let out an amused laugh at his own well-rehearsed catchphrase.

Seldik had never partaken in the mass drinking of alcohol by purpose. Since seawater isn't consumable, and the filtering process is lengthy, alcohol was the drink of choice for those who lived at sea. Children were only allowed small amounts unless it was mealtime, so Seldik never indulged in the habit his father and Kolkesh now displayed. He took slow, small sips in a confused and still-scared attempt to look the part of a lord's grown son.

"Seldik's first real taste of the bad stuff, eh?" Kolkesh belched after consuming another full glass of the juice.

"He is your responsibility now, Kolkesh. There is much to teach him," His father stated after drinking what appeared to be an entire glass himself. Seldik rehearsed the words his father said in his now bubbly brain. *Did I hear him correctly?*

"I see the shock on his face!" Kolkesh said, looking at Cedrin, puzzled.

Cedrin lowered his glass carefully while moving his troubled gaze from Seldik to Kolkesh. "I have not told him of his future. This is his first knowledge..." his father's worried voice trailed off. "Oh!" Kolkesh said, putting his cup down.

"I'll be waiting at the north docks, then. Take your time," he said, nodding to Cedrin and Seldik with much reverence before excusing himself. Father and son watched as Kolkesh's giant form moved ghost-like and silent through the hall and vanished down the stairs.

"Seldik, Son of Cedrin, I am Chief of our mighty CED!" Cedrin proclaimed, staring past his son. "I have approved your disciplines at the school. They graduated you to my care yesterday, and I now send you on a journey of Soul, which I pray will lead you back to me when it is over!" He turned to look at his son, shoulders slumped, and took a seat on his throne.

Seldik's mind was reeling, spinning out of control. *What has today brought me? Calamity? A secret destiny?*

"Father?" was all Seldik could muster. What started as a frightful encounter with a living hero had turned into a nightmare of change he could not wrap his head around.

"I know you have questions. I kept what I would do with you a secret, but I was given the vision not a year ago. I have carried that vision in sorrow and joy until today. Today, you begin your journey toward your Soul's destiny, a divine right of your soul that neither you nor I can stop." His words cut into Seldik like a knife against bone.

"I don't understand. I have continued teachings in two days. My teachers say these advanced…"

"You are done with school, son!" his father barked.

Seldik stood dazed and confused at his father's abrupt interruption.

Cedrin stood and approached his son, draping a gentle arm around his shoulder. "This destiny will complete you. You will go with Kolkesh and learn the world's ways away from CED." He said, lifting his son's chin to look into his eyes.

"I… I will miss you until your return," Cedrin continued with problematic attempts to control his sorrow. "I will gaze upon the stars, knowing they will shine upon you no matter where you are. I will love you as I always have, but this quest is yours alone now, son." Awaiting any motion from his child, he continued softer.

"This quest will take you from a child to a man and will change our world!" Cedrin stood back to show his son the importance of his words. "I have been shown that this is the future. A vision brought your old father a gift of unprecedented meaning, you understand?" he asked, now intently looking into the unbelieving and bewildered eyes of his son.

"I don't understand, father. You… you had a vision about me?" Seldik asked uncertainly. But his father only nodded the way he does when teaching a lesson before continuing.

"This is a destiny of the body that will open your mind to the enlightenment of this Golden Age!"

Seldik looked back, stunned, knowing those words but unable to place them in his fragile mind.

"You have heard those words in your teachings, right?" His father asked royally.

"You have been chosen as that herald of the age! You, Son of Cedrin, Son of the mighty CED, you are that man who will bring peace upon the world!"

Seldik was beside himself in anguish. *What is happening? Am I being kicked out of CED? What about my plans? This is my home! Is he really sending me out into the ocean to train with a warrior?* The excitement was not as shattering as the sheer terror now focused on Seldik's mind.

"Father, I do not want to leave CED. It is my home, my chosen place to grow and do great things!" He pleaded, but his father was already shaking his head.

"You are royalty. You have been taught the ways of your ancestors, and I have done my best since your mother passed on during your birth." Cedrin said, driving another sharp stake into the mix. He continued but lowered his tone. "I knew that sometime during your growth, a change would surface, a scary change for us both." Seldik looked at him with strange eyes.

"You do not believe I, too, am not scared of you leaving? Of sending you off into the unknown, my only child, my only connection to your mo…" His father's words bit off sharp as the pain of loss surfaced in visible anguish.

Seldik was in a panic now. Never has his father shown a weakness of this kind. Seldik feared he was becoming a letdown, a refuser of Soul!

"Father, I… I can be what you want. I can be strong in this face of change," he said, stepping toward his father, who instantly stood up straight in response to his words.

"I do not want you to be strong, son, not strong for me. I want you to be true to your destiny and have the forethought to follow it as your Soul requires you to do, son." Seldik knew his words were true but slowly realized that neither wanted this path. His father was given a gift, and Seldik was chosen to do great things. *Is this not what I have craved?* Seldik thought. *Somewhere deep, I have dreamed about becoming enlightened in what I can do that no others have accomplished, to walk in my father's footsteps and become "the one" who will bring some… enlightenment to the world!* He was staring intently now, deep in thought, when his father noticed the change on his son's face.

"You have visioned something, my son. What is it?"

"I realized this path was coming, and I wanted it to, but was uncertain it would, I suppose?" Seldik said, questioning his logic.

His father placed his hand firmly on his shoulder. "I believe telling you sooner would have distracted us both. I had no idea when Kolkesh would get my summons or if he was still alive. His life is somewhat perilous." Cedrin finished, making Seldik uneasy, knowing he would be going with him.

"Father, why is Kolkesh always in peril?" he asked, though he didn't actually want to know.

"Because, son, Kolkesh is the War-Soul," he said, looking Seldik square on before continuing. "…of Netherweir!"

Chapter Three

NO REAL GOODBYE

Seldik remained uneasy as he spent the night packing, stuffing items into an old sack, then pulling them out again, unsure of what such an adventure would require. Knowing he had to be on board with Kolkesh before first light, he tried to push the stories of the Netherweir's creatures and barren lands away, but a neighbor's words echoed in his mind. *"No one from CED who dared to venture to the Netherweir has returned alive. Sleeping unprepared will get you killed!"* He felt his heart jump as he rubbed at his eyes. *But Kolkesh returned,* he thought, *and he looked just fine, except for all those scars etched across his body. What could the Netherweir have that other lands don't? Bad weather?* Seldik pondered his future as he tied up his bag and set out toward the ship, making time to say his goodbyes and to accept the parting gifts craftsmen had fashioned to aid in his survival within the Netherweir.

Seldik took the warning of his people to heart, but his education let him know otherwise; at least, he thought it did. *Surely, I wouldn't be sent away on this journey if it was as truly horrible as they say, so why the panic? It's only land, anyway. Sure, the weather is sometimes harsh. Even CED has been ripped open by a storm once and drifted too far north. But it healed with time, and life continued*

At age 14, Seldik was well-tuned to the natural world and the changes it was making. He had heard of the mighty landquakes and believed the myth that Mother Earth rose in relief of unknown forces ripping against her surface so that life could remain without the fire rock consuming all. Even in his life, the dusty, drowsy skies of ash from some far-off volcano erupting long ago had been slowly settling out of the air, and light and heat entered the surface to warm it more each year. The seasons of famine and feast were reversing, and the Great Spirit shined down for all to enjoy more prosperity worldwide. *Maybe the Netherweir is getting less harsh, too?*

Seldik was at the last ring and made his way onto the docks just as the twilight of morning began to creep across the horizon. The silence of the early hour and the distant glow of a full moon were all that accompanied him.

His father had an unusual call in the middle of the night and was dispatched to observe warships off the western rim, forcing him to wish his son farewell by whale oil flames dancing in the window of his hut. Strange auroras and unusual dancing balls of light were standard sometimes, and as the head of defense, his father was usually up late or dealing with false alarms in the early hours. There has been no war on the sea for thousands of years, but the recent storms have brought CED closer to the shore of Netherweir, and the legends have increased false sightings exponentially. Seldik knew his father and city defenders were more than a match for anything, so he relaxed his concerns to focus on the journey ahead of him.

Kolkesh's tall form cast a shadow even in the moonlight, and Seldik recognized his voice giving orders, and he immediately made hast to the dock. Kolkesh saw him before coming aboard and yelled down to him from the top deck of the large vessel.

"Welcome aboard, prodigy!" Kolkesh laughed.

Seldik gave him a nervous wave under the strain of his bag.

"Can't see you well, but let us depart fast. We have quite the journey ahead."

Seldik boarded, and a shipmate showed him to a sleeping hammock below deck. After pointing out the specifics of the ship layout, the mate left Seldik to find his way around and to the topside, where ropes were already being thrown off for departure. He could hear a commotion arising from across the city toward the sea. Kolkesh was on the topsail mast nearly two-thirds up with a scope at his eye, looking in toward the noise.

Soon, a most brilliant flare of fire arose from the commotion along the outside ring of the city, and then two more followed beside it. Large plumes rose as fire spread through the city. Seldik rushed to Kolkesh's side, who hurriedly waved for the boy to lower him by rope back down the mast as he shouted for the crew to get under sail.

The docks cleared, and the mighty warship lurched forward under sail with a quickness that shocked Seldik. As the morning light grew to witness the actual size of the ship, Seldik realized, looking over her port side, that the vessel was some 300 hands[2] long, very wide, and possessed a wooden exterior with no grasses, bamboo, or other small materials. It was like nothing he had ever seen before, and based on the exterior's construct, he wondered if the vessel was entirely made of solid wood. He quickly noticed that the ship was not sailing toward the fires and found Kolkesh at the rear helm to ask when they were turning.

---

2   One hand is equal to six inches.

"Kolkesh, we have never been attacked at sea. Is that fire from attacks my father was called to this morning?" Kolkesh remained looking through his scope at the fires.

"It is the same, Seldik, the same!" Kolkesh said, handing Seldik the scope. He held the device to his eye, mimicking Kolkesh. The shocking, zoomed-in image of the event was instantly before his eyes. The far-off attackers' black ships were just off the outer ring's bank, and much fire was being delivered back and forth from both sides.

"An attack on my home!" Seldik shouted, looking to Kolkesh for wisdom.

"It is true!" Kolkesh said matter-of-factly, placing his scope back in its box. "We have encountered others we call the Sea People, who are a bit... un-tame."

"We need to help! My father is there!" Seldik said in a panic.

"No, we won't be helping, Seldik. Your father has forbidden it!" Kolkesh watched as the boy's brow furrowed.

"He informed me they were coming, a massive wave of them, and you were to be gone by the time they arrived. The currents must have favored them to be this early." Seldik listened while he headed for the tower's ladder.

"My father knew of this, and there were no preparations for it made?" he demanded, biting back, knowing well that it wasn't his father's way.

"Oh! Preparations were made alright, just not where you were concerned." Kolkesh said and left him alone on the deck as he tended to other tasks. Seldik was in shock, struggling to understand why his father did not want him to know a raid was upon the city. He must have known he would demand to stay. *He certainly kept it a secret when Kolkesh showed up earlier than anticipated*, he thought. Then he saw the outline of the ships attacking from afar—thin, long, dark ships with short sails and oars with giant outriggers likely for balance and seemed of high technological construction. The group was more than un-tamed, he thought; they were barbaric. He watched the fire with great worry that he might never see his father again, but soon, they were dancing under full sail, and the mighty ship began to glide farther away atop the waves into the unknown.

Seldik kept his worries on his father's unknown situation back on CED but settled into a routine of training on the ship that Kolkesh set up the first night. He paired him with two seemingly mute individuals who seemed ignorant but did repetitive tasks in the queue. Seldik quickly fell in line, hauling rope, checking mast lines, and tugging constant sail adjustment. On open seas, Seldik was at home, recalling the many week-long fishing trips he used to take. Though he was comfortable with small skiffs, he was unfamiliar with the workings of a ship this strong, heavy, and full of unusual sails, but he knew the general principles applied.

"How goes your training?" Kolkesh asked as he caught up to me at the bow. "Eyyy!" shouted the hilarious pair. "I don't think they like Seldik, Kolkesh!" he said, knowing they probably didn't understand his words.

"They'd have already thrown you overboard if they didn't!" Kolkesh laughed. "Have you seen how few sailors we have? Ask them why," he said, walking over to the side.

"You notice the design of this ship?" Kolkesh asked as he slapped the wooden side rail.

"I did. Never knew we had such strong ships." Seldik had puzzled for days over the construction, having never heard of such technology.

"She is a beauty!" Kolkesh took out his knife and waved Seldik over to kneel with him by the railing.

Seldik complied quickly. "See these pieces and how they lap together so tight?" Kolkesh continued with his knife dug into it. "That is a lap seam, an angled seam where chinking isn't required. It swells and bends together, joined by our newest invention of steel pins at the brows coming up from the bottom keel!" He pointed to the many vertical beams popping up through the floor planks to support the lap wood siding.

"Steel?" Seldik asked, confused by the name.

"Iron is made by melting and pouring mined rock to create a substance stronger than anything known to exist." He then pointed to an unusually round, flat end in the wood. Seldik came close and clinked it with the knife he borrowed for inspection.

"Knives are made of a copper mix. This metal is ten times as strong as copper but a thousand times harder to work with." Kolkesh showed Seldik the end under his knifepoint. "See the dark center? Iron is black, so is the ore, a new resource we get from deep within the lands, same as this strong new wood." Seldik tapped it again to hear the complex, unusual sound before handing Kolkesh his knife back. "Just one more technology we discovered from the Netherweir," he said, looking off into the distance over a horizon of water. We are still many Megarthy out, but a long day may get us there by tonight.

"Here is the wood type we use—a solid white oak. The way it is split along its grain, it will become the future of all ships that sail open waters." Kolkesh took him atop the tall center mast, far higher than Seldik had ever climbed.

"And here you see why that strong oak is needed. Unlike bamboo and flexibles, this stuff is heavy and strong, allowing ships to carry huge payloads, the purpose they were designed for," Kolkesh said, pointing to open stows in the now blazing sun's light.

"Can they be rowed?" Seldik asked, indicating the sides with no oars protruding.

"The oars are stored interior, and ports are closed until needed. We only have a small rowing party onboard now; we will pick up more at the beach camp when we hit land."

Seldik instinctively looked toward the ominous horizon hiding the inevitable land of the Netherweir that awaited him. He felt deep despair well up inside for the future challenges he will face. Just a week ago, he and his friends discussed spending the summer months on long voyages out fishing and deep diving. But now, his life had been yanked from him to finish within the confines of the glorious yet terrifying Netherweir.

"Are the stories of the Netherweir true, Kolkesh?" He asked, finally facing what kept him preoccupied on this voyage.

"You bet your ass they are a true, boy!" Roared Kolkesh. "It's that and a lot more! From here on, though, you must look the part. We all simply call it The Nether, or just Nether…" His voice trailed off as he walked along the ship's edge, now bored with the topic. "You'll learn it all fast. I have faith," he finished, gazing out over the sea. "There she is! The Nether!"

The shoreline manifested seemingly out of magic and now lay visible along the horizon in sharp detail, much closer than Seldik imagined possible. It looked like Hell's gate was about to open and swallow them whole!

Chapter Four

ENCOUNTER BLACK

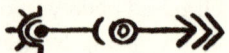

Seldik ate and talked the rest of the afternoon but never once took his eyes off the fantastic display of land before him, growing larger and looming heavier in his mind. At moments, he thought of jumping from the ship and swimming away into the sea just to get away. But the terror rising inside him kept breaking his resolve. He felt like screaming.

He was lost in thought, unsure what teachings of this place were authentic. *Are the dreaded beasts the worst? No, it must be the wild men who are said to be among the lands that attack and eat you if defeated.* Yet, the environment was the natural killer, said to be like the sea but with freezing temperatures and torrents of flood waters and winds every day sometimes. None of it sounded good. No matter what the legends boasted was the worst, there were too many ways to die here.

Off in the distance, a giant of a bird dove into the lapping waves of the ocean after some sought-after prey. Its wings were bent into razor-sharp edges that looked like arrow tips, and its long beak was like a spear point longer than a man. He had never seen its kind before and wondered if it lived above and below water or if one would dive on him while doing chores on this ship's deck, giving him pause to keep an eye skyward, just in case.

Kolkesh spouted orders after their meal, and everyone attended to their tasks, swinging ropes this way and that, clear to the great bow of the ship. The moves were unusual on open water, and Kolkesh knew it, sending Seldik immediately to the front bow to help others. Seldik discovered the reality of shoreline sailing at once, and shallow waters were ahead. He was given the pull-up ropes, having to yank them in as fast as possible as soon as he got them. They dropped sounding readers, rocks tied to the end of long ropes, overboard until the bottom or the end of the rope was hit, whichever came first. When the reader hit the bottom, excited shouts rang out all around the ship. "Thirty fathoms! Twenty-five!" shouted a mate. More readers were dumped overboard on each side. Loud cries came from all around as Kolkesh responded with quick orders, sending the entire crew scampering from one side to the other, directing sails that turned the ship left and right. And rather than slowing the ship as expected, they charged ahead.

"War-Soul!" cried a mate from the lookout perch, "enemy ship rear!" Kolkesh spun around and pulled out his scope at once. There, on the horizon, poked up the clear image of a slick black ship with strange outriggers bearing down on them. All mates now put their hands above their eyes and squinted out over the horizon in dismay. Kolkesh yelled in an undistinguishable language and ordered at his officers beside him as everyone ran from the bridge to their posts in urgent haste.

"Faster soundings! Raise all sails!" Kolkesh commanded, and the onlookers immediately returned to their tasks post-haste with new enthusiasm. Seldik did the same, now deeply concerned. He was headed to Hell; he just knew it. *Who are these sailors, and what do they want? There is no way these are the same barbarians who attacked CED!* Seldik could think of no one outside of CED who knew of this secret place, but his heart sank when he realized that they were, in fact, the same vessels that had attacked his home.

"Fifteen! Twenty-five! Good! Left!" The crew shouted out the soundings as they moved along the shore. The retrieval of the readers was sped along by Seldik's hasty recovery of the rocks from the deep. One after another, they read, pitching that way, and this, all the while, the black ship in the distance laid a straight course onward, growing closer each minute. Seldik watched the other commanders direct tiny escort rowers into formations and stuck long, thin rows out of the ports on each side. Only ten per side were cast, and Seldik wondered how many more the giant ship would need in order to use them effectively. The crew was busy hauling various items from below onto the sides of the deck: ropes with attached hooks or metal, weapons, and armfuls of garments, some of which were thrown against the backs of his legs. At a glance, he noticed the garments to be thickly padded. While maintaining his tasks, he could see the crew was quickly layering them on, so he followed suit, assuming it must be some form of armor. *Does this mean combat with the oncoming ship?* Seldik swallowed hard, suppressing the fear creeping up in his throat.

"We make for land as fast as we can! Any delay with this small crew may make us fight a battle unprepared, you rats!" Kolkesh's voice carried clearly across the entire ship.

"Send up Seldik," Kolkesh ordered, not needing to tell others; Seldik heard it himself and took off for the bridge perched at the rear. Coming up the stairs, Seldik was growing more worried about his future, but unlike the hells awaiting him, it was a more immediate thought of being gutted and killed by an unknown foe where his empire rained dominant.

"Boy, you may get some target practice today on living people. You up for that?" Kolkesh asked, but without hesitating, he continued. "Didn't think so, but reality has called upon it anyway." Kolkesh reached for the other weapons handed to him, draping them this way and that over his entire body.

"I'm always ready. As you know, I am a War-Soul, born to kill those wanting the same of me, and I'm planning on opening up a few of those who may change their minds to be racing me down out here!" His matter-of-fact statements made Seldik feel like he was in the presence of his father.

"They didn't get to feel me on CED, but I guarantee they felt your father's discord before running our way!" Kolkesh quickly analyzed a short dagger of beautiful obsidian with an antler handle. "Here, this is your death seeker. It will find and kill anyone on that ship you go pointing it at; it just needs you to get it there, and it will do the rest!" He said, handing it straight to Seldik, who accepted any form of defense with great thanks.

"You've been hand-to-hand trained, and though we do not know what your Soul is yet, it may just be a War-Soul too, so we might as well find out today!" Kolkesh held his hand across his heart to point to the inner Soul's location.

Seldik kept sternward of Kolkesh, continuing to belch orders and keeping an eye rearward of the fast-approaching, jet-black ship. It was sleek but not near as tall nor wide as Kolkesh's, though it still had an ominous trait of death attached to it and appeared to have red and yellow dots... *no... eyes!* painted on its bow just above an unsettling set of teeth.

"Light the fire, crow!" Kolkesh yelled to the nest. The lookout high up began sparking a fire, and soon, a giant plume of smoke bellowed continuously from his perch, covering him in choking black smoke, causing him to abandon the nest and perch lower on the horizontal sail support.

"It'll let our friends ashore know to be ready," Kolkesh said through a half-smirk. Seldik hoped this meant reinforcements were waiting, a little tactic Kolkesh had withheld from sharing in his battle plan.

"Do you know how they fight, Kolkesh?" Seldik couldn't resist now, knowing what their odds were.

"Well, I know few of our empire's ships have survived an attack from them, and we better get smarter quick, or we might be next." Seldik felt a chill run down his spine. There was no help and no plan. These were survival steps, pure and simple.

"But then again, boy," Kolkesh turned to face him, "they have never run into me either." A laugh left Kolkesh that was loud and much more resolved than his others. This laugh, Seldik noticed, sounded like it originated from deep within his Soul—a war cry.

The mighty ship lurched, rocked, and swayed in great arcs as they fast-tracked the depths of the Nether's looming shoreline. Due to the ship's wider girth, they were able to keep to waters at least twelve feet deep. It was unlikely that land people could compete with such abilities, as you must live on the water and float the seas to understand their fury.

But the black ship in pursuit was of another fantastic design, and Seldik noticed the various techniques employed in its creation were for objectives other than their own. The long, sleek prowess meant it could move quickly in a straight line, and the outriggers provided buoyancy and stability in shallows and strong waves. The similar yet different features gave him pause as he realized their ship could perform nearly as well as theirs but had been engineered differently, leaving him to ponder if this race lived upon the water as well, and feared they might try to rival those from CED.

"Unless you got any better ideas, boy, I am going to swing us around, and we are going to duke it out with them. We can't get away without getting beached, which would leave us open to an attack with no defense. We have but two thin skiffs aboard to launch." Kolkesh left his words to hang in the air as Seldik puzzled over what he assumed was a question or request for war advice.

"Didn't think so," Kolkesh said, turning to give the order to drop sail and begin turning the shop once they hit an open patch.

"I... I might, Kolkesh," Seldik said, surprising himself. Kolkesh turned and stared at him inquisitively, but the long look soon turned to despair as Seldik only stared back quietly.

"Still nothing," Kolkesh replied, beginning to turn again.

"They have speed but no turning ability," Seldik said, finally managing to put his thought to good use. Kolkesh looked back, surprised, waving his hand to encourage him to share more.

"It's too long and sleek to turn. The side pylons add to that inability. It can't turn like our swing sails and shorter bow can." He now realized he knew more about sailing than he previously thought. He had actual, honest knowledge.

"You know, you just might be right, water boy!" Kolkesh said, spinning around and summoning his crew. He developed a quick plan of tasks to follow and sent them to their stations within minutes. The sounding charts they were navigating were discussed, and quickly, they chose the perfect spot.

Kolkesh returned to the rudder and yelled his first commands. long and narrow sails began popping out along the entire edge of the larger sails as they were being drawn in and tied off. Soon, groups of thin three-sided sails blew strong, with even the slightest breezes coming inland off the sea. The light was fading fast, and the day was about to end in a race of wits so near to hell that Seldik could begin to smell the sands and plants awaiting him in the Nether.

Finally, the sleek black ship was beginning to slow, appearing to hit sandbars. What looked like the ships commander shouted and pointed to avoid more shallow traps as their sails fell slack and crowded the edges of their vessel. Seldik informed Kolkesh immediately upon realizing he was right. The ship isn't any lighter than their own and likely possesses a deeper draft as well.

Suddenly, a yell rang out from above as the lookout pointed toward land. In the air was black smoke rising. Kolkesh smiled, gesturing toward the signal. They see us! He shouted. "They've seen our distress call!" But Seldik quickly recalled Kolkesh mentioning that their friends on land had no ships to aid them, and his short-lived relief subsided, knowing his plan was their only chance at survival.

The cry of the enemy ship was now audible, and the staged crew with weapons shouted back furiously, and suddenly Seldik realized that a battle was going to happen, that his brilliance was nothing more than too little too late. He gripped his weapon firmly, relieved not only that he had one but that it was chosen by the War-Soul he aspired to be. Kolkesh, still at this moment, loomed as a great hero standing just in front of him like everyone aboard was no match for him. His presence could induce a shudder, causing your worth to zero out in an instant. Everyone respected him, and Seldik's only courage to hold fast was Kolkesh's presence and resolve. Though Seldik didn't believe this should be the day he discovered if he was a War-Soul, he realized he better act like it quickly.

Who am I kidding? Seldik thought, having never fought in combat before. *I'm not even that big of a fella.* He knew he might die this evening, never to reach the shores of the Nether or be killed by its hellish creatures. And as far as he knew, his father may already be dead. He wished desperately now to return to his simple life on CED.

Screaming with a mass of warriors upon its deck, the black ship bared down upon their slower, taller ship as Kolkesh and Seldik looked down upon it. The terrifying sounds of giant spears and bolas swished through the air in all directions, but the sails were taking the most hits. Kolkesh yelled a battle cry of death and decay upon them, then raised a tall hand to his crew, causing them to scatter at once to fulfill their tasks. All sails went slack, massive anchors were thrown from the left side opposite the enemy ship, and everyone rallied to the right to await the enemy alongside. At once, the wind-driven force of the ship's forward momentum stopped, and Seldik had to take a step forward to balance. The black ship came upon their side fast, still under sail and skimming effortlessly on the surface. The large outriggers hindered rail-to-rail contact but hit the ship's side, creating a sizeable snapping sound as its supports broke from the momentum against the solid oak. Yells went unchanging from the ship. Nobody could hear their captain give the command, and all were ready to fight with weapons in hand. Seldik noticed their ship's thick oak lap siding held firm, but the events happened so fast that Seldik could only watch with awe.

At once, the enemy crew threw claws with ropes attached to their vessel, catching both railing and sailors alike, quickly drawing them taunt to the bar of Kolkesh's ship before climbing across the just as fast, dropping weapons, or falling in the water, from the fever pitch of close combat. Kolkesh made no other orders except an upraised hand to the left where his commanders were now operating the keel. They swung the arm hard right, instantly lurching the ship into a breakneck left turn. Lines across the ships snapped, taking with it large parts of the enemy's railing, being vastly thinner than the oak skeleton-supported railings of their own.

At that exact moment, the anchors started catching and helped turn the vessel and slow it considerably more, throwing Seldik against the rail so fast he almost went overboard. Seldik witnessed a large cluster of snaps as the ropes, one by one, pulled at the enemy's ship with the turn. Entire sections of siding were ripped away, causing a mass of the enemy crew to fall overboard. As he watched the calamity before him, he noticed an enemy mate light a throwing pot on the top deck of the vessel, but before he could launch it across, the sudden snapping of their vessel caused it to fall from his hands and roll across the deck. At once, the black ship was ablaze. Seldik could hear the creaks and moans of the ship's oak timbers as they flexed under his feet, taking the abuse of force from the instant turn. He was sure the ship would suffer the same fate as the enemies, and they would be forced to fight in the water as both sank to the bottom. But the ship held, and the turn was called as quickly as it began. Now they were headed away from the enemy at a right angle. The anchor lines were axed, sails were ordered full taunt, and the ship launched forward again through an alternate byway. Some hundred feet from the fast-sinking black ship, the screams and commotion heard were no longer that of war but of pain and the coming realization of swimming for their lives. They abandoned their burning ship before it sank in the fading twilight of dusk. Still far from land, they would need some resolve to make it to shore before the night current turned on them and they were swept out to sea. The tide, already beginning to turn, didn't favor them getting to land, Seldik realized, but he was grateful that the most frightful day in his life had closed without him in one-on-one combat.

"You are not a War-Soul, young Seldik!" Kolkesh's voice came from behind him, breaking his fascination with the enemy's survival, now only known by sound and not by sight. Seldik spun around, surprised to see everyone piled up the steps behind Kolkesh, all staring at him.

"Seldik of CED City, Son of Cedrin, Chief of CED, the hero of today's battle!" Before Kolkesh could say more, the entire ship rang out in cheer and rushed young Seldik where he stood. They hoisted him above their shoulders and paraded him down the steps and around the ship to return him to Kolkesh's side once more. Kolkesh laughed and praised the while of Seldik's position.

"See, you are someone great," he said, motioning to the crowd for silence. "This man, I proclaim, will be known as the Hero of Netherweir!" Without pause, the crowd yelled and chanted the title for minutes more in such thunder the enemy swimming behind them could hear it in the now-dark waters.

The ship steadied into shore, bustling with action until the night fires on the beaches were lined up as navigation beacons in the shallow mooring. Anchors were dropped when the ship touched the shallow sandy bottom, and everyone piled over except the guards and went ashore to the large group awaiting them in the fire's shadows. Shouts of conflict chants and the day win spread to all on land. Healthy portions of beer flowed for Kolkesh's victory before they even walked up to the campsite.

When the initial torrent of cheers had settled back to a lull, the fires raged brightly in the night sky as others set out on small skiffs to see if they could kill or capture some enemies still bobbing around the water. Some of Kolkesh's best trackers were on the prowl, so nobody would get past them. Others combed the beaches for signs anyone had made it ashore.

Seldik sat by the sizeable oblong fire where most of the group lingered. Kolkesh pulled up a dead wood stump and invited Seldik to sit with him. Once all settled close, Kolkesh greeted everyone and informed them of the raid on CED as predicted by Cedrin, then pointed at Seldik sitting alone on the perch.

"Bear witness to Seldik, son of Cedrin, Chief of CED!" Kolkesh continued without pause,

"After today's glorious battle and victory by Seldik, Son of Cedrin, I pronounce he is no more!" A large gasp fell across the gathering, hushed in reverence and confusion.

Kolkesh paused with his arm still raised while pointing to Seldik as he maneuvered slowly until he lay vision on the entire circumference of the crowd. Once the impact was sufficient, Kolkesh spoke with words loud enough to make some in the front rows fumble back a step when he started.

"He will now be known forever as Seldik, Hero of Netherweir!" Kolkesh could not finish his long-drawn words fast enough before the crowd jumped to their feet, screaming and chanting the words in succession, "Hero of Nether! Hero of Nether!" Seldik enjoyed his night of hero status, but the anguish of the events still left him raw with feelings of a near disaster. Thoughts of his father and what had become of his home swirled in his mind as he wondered if the enemies on the black ship had killed them all. The crashing waves behind him cut through his thoughts, no matter how much he tried to force them away.

After disappearing for some time, Kolkesh finally returned, bringing with him a group of strangers to Seldik's log seat.

"Seldik, I want you to meet the rest of CED's magnificent Souls," Kolkesh said as Seldik rose from his seat.

"This is Edeldon, Vision-Soul!" Kolkesh was said to be taking a royal rank, which Seldik met with shock and awe at the fellow standing before him. *Edeldon! The only seer of the future, the one predicting the Netherweir's finding and direct commandant of my father.*

"I am so excited to finally meet you, Vision-Soul!" Seldik said with much unbridled excitement.

"As am I you, Seldik!" Edeldon said with reciprocated excitement.

"You have turned out a fine young boy, Seldik. Your father was right to adhere to the Soul's wish to send you on this journey." He said, calculating Seldik's response. Seldik was unsure if he had lost his nerve over that stark reality or if he had passed Edeldon's test.

"I believe Father was choosing the Soul's needs, but I am unsure if I am truly ready for such a quest," Seldik said, accidentally voicing his thoughts.

"You are ready. Just look at the enemy rats swimming out there in the bay," Kolkesh said again, referencing what Seldik viewed as only a thought, not a successfully executed war plan.

"You know, boy, what you think of war and what is reality are two different things. The reality is nothing goes as planned, everything is dynamic and changing in conflict, and the mind comes out the winner." Kolkesh continued unbridled. "It could be that you didn't know why you were generating those thoughts, but the reality is that your soul was on the job of spotting what you could not see and gave you that information to act on."

Seldik was visualizing his training in Soul knowledge, that part of every human that guides from the beyond. His people believe a Soul is connected to the unknown layer of reality nobody can see or touch. But the Soul lives in both and can be guided by time and space, the space of a planet and the time covering birth to death. It is a destiny that awaits each person.

Some Souls are interconnected, and some are of the highest level of achieved understanding, possibly being returned to the human world repeatedly. These Souls are unique and sought out. If a pupil shows signs of this higher level, other training is required to flush out the Soul's type. There are many Souls, some rarer than others. The mightiest are Chief-Souls, born to lead and one of the rarest. His father is a Chief-Soul, given command of CED. There are also the pre-dawn Souls, born of the Skaggs, pre-human giants who lived for hundreds of years. They are mythical and supposedly the ones who found the Netherweir. The lesser but still significant Souls of power are the Vision-Souls, who see the future; Knowledge-Souls, who design and create technology and have a deep understanding of nature; and War-Souls, like Kolkesh, who are entirely warring.

Seldik returned to Kolkesh's introductions just as a tall, slender man, even for their stature, stepped forward.

"This is Nasok, Knowledge-Soul." Kolkesh knew it would excite Seldik to meet these individuals, though a grimace was now on his face.

"Hello, Seldik, well met!" Nasok extended an arm in greeting, now very pleased he was in such a high-ranking company.

"Very nice to meet you, Knowledge-Soul!" Seldik said, keeping with his training of royalty manors by using only titles as an introduction.

"Please, I'm not like this stuffy guy. Call me Nasok. I piss like everyone else here." His comment made Seldik break character and let out an audible laugh before catching himself and reeling it in.

Seldik then turned to meet the third, somewhat shorter, individual Kolkesh had fetched. This figure was positively dashing in stance and appearance. His eyes were blazing green behind long, bright red hair, and his skin was much lighter than the dark red the rest of his civilization displayed. A shorter version of all, but still looked the part of a hero unto his own. Though his form was thin, he was in excellent condition with no visible fat on his body, just lean muscles flowing everywhere like a beast in a compact form, ready to spring at a moment's notice. Seldik noticed the unique bounce to his step that carried him quickly in whichever direction he guided them.

"This unique fella is Sylic, a warrior tracker of mine from Homegath. He is of half Aquarionite blood and half Homegath blood. He is a royal prince in his homeland!" Kolkesh said, again posturing in his royal greeting stance, but he always appeared a bit bored.

Seldik shook his arm Sylic's arm, though the unique man said nothing in return and only bowed slightly at the shake. Despite Sylic's hesitance, Seldik remained taken aback by the natural, honest Homegath person standing before him. *A land individual, not of the sea!* Seldik thought, having never met anyone from Homegath, let alone land. *If we all consist of CED Souls and have included Homegath blood, what is the reason for us being on the sands of the Nether?* He was deeply intrigued. Being of high blood on CED, he had learned of each of these Souls, but none had been present in the city. *Which means they must have been within the Nether this whole time,* he thought.

"You have questions, I can tell. We will cover everything over dinner," Kolkesh said as he and the group of Souls left, leaving Seldik to ponder the remark.

Chapter Five

DAY ONE, HELL AWAITS

Seldik joined the Souls in a tent at the beach camp. Kolkesh was busy finishing his report to them when Seldik arrived within. There was an empty seat reserved for him, so he sat and listened to the remaining talk, wondering what he had missed. Kolkesh finally cleared the wall's edge of beer vesicles and unrolled a map over the tent's horizontal beam so it draped downward. The map was drawn on a large, tattered hide with many markings outlining the Netherweir's perimeter. The ancient language of his tribe was written all over its edge, indicating travel routes.

"Here we are, on the outer edge of the Nether, and here is where we head in the morning." Kolkesh sought a designed ruin listed to one side and began again.

"Here is the mythical land of the Skagg; this inland passage exists somewhere, and we are to find it, exploit it, and see what we run into!" Kolkesh stopped to face everyone.

"Last attempts inward were slow, but we have the navigation logged and a new defense and support city afloat here," he said, pointing to a spot at the end of the waterway far inland, some four to five days sailing from where they were at the beach.

"And another here," he continues, pointing just over a land region to another waterway. Seldik presumed it was a lake as it had no connection with the ocean. The remainder of the map was blank except for features far above and below the region in the center.

"We are to find the unfindable, using unknown direction in unknown lands then?" Nasok spoke up.

"Yes, that is our mission from our beloved Chief-Soul," Kolkesh replied, nodding toward Seldik as if not ignoring the fact that the Chief's son was sitting in the tent.

"That is why all of us Souls are present, including a new one." He pointed at Seldik.

"We are all going into the Nether, and we will succeed where others have failed...." Kolkesh trailed off before voicing a realization.

Seldik knew their journey would be challenging. They were to conquer the Nether and seek the legendary Skagg. "We may even find them out there!" Kolkesh finished, and the realization was then clear to Seldik—the legend may be true of the mythical Skagg, the legendary first beings.

Dinner was consumed as warm greetings to Seldik continued, and the conversation quickly fell on the topic of the enemy he was credited with defeating, so he gained no more knowledge about why the journey must include them or where the myths originated. He eventually had a moment at his place of rest and sat, realizing so much had happened. He reeled at the idea that they could have died. Just days ago, he was carefree swimming, playing, and schooling with his friends, but now it seemed like a lifetime ago. He was utterly tired and was asleep the second he hit his bed roll.

The clattering of goods awoke Seldik the next morning as the camp was packed. The early morning sun barely cast enough light to do so as Seldik wrapped up his roll and headed out. The skiffs were already packed and making trips to the ship as Kolkesh, along with the other Souls, were gathered around a morning fire. Seldik met and ate with them, and they boarded the last skiffs out to begin sailing. A complement of over 30 rowers was present that Seldik had not seen the night prior. It was impressive to see them scurry aboard the now fully staffed vessel. Seldik and Kolkesh were last up to the ropes, and the boats were yanked out of the water. Anchors were pulled, and the large ores paddled backward in a cadence unison until the boat unbeached itself and backed out to sea. Sails were then set, and paddling commenced, turning the great bow deeper into the Nether.

Once an hour passed, portions of land appeared on the horizon on one side of the vessel. Seldik used the Kolkesh's scope the entire time, looking this way and that and occasionally checking behind for the enemy he was now consumed with. Kolkesh told him they had two captured below, but they would see them soon enough. They had to hit the morning tide to get toward the inward guts of the Nether. Seldik heard nothing from below but worried that a raging charge would come out of the hatch any second as he saw the black enemy ship approaching. He kept his obsidian weapon at his side just in case.

After an hour, the tide settled, and they were floating the calm, transparent sea waters in a large inlet of the Nether's interior. Soundings were not needed until sometime at nightfall when the waters would narrow. Kolkesh summoned the Souls to the deck as the crew lined the ship's rim to await them. It was time to reveal the enemy captured during the night.

Seldik remained on the steps up to the bridge with Kolkesh and the other Souls as the hostages, gagged and tied, were dragged backward up the lower stairs onto the deck and thrown down on the central sailing box, leaving their filthy, bloody, naked bodies on full display. Whether from the sinking or the night's beatings, they were in rough shape. Their limp, slung heads and drooping limbs showed they were brought to the edge of death.

"Ungag the filth," Kolkesh ordered, and a crewmember pulled the rags from their mouths. Each slowly spat out a block of wood, an additional form of torture.

"Raise that one to his feet," Kolkesh ordered as he walked toward the leftmost hostage. He motioned Seldik to follow him. He was immediately alarmed, not wanting to be near the enemy he had pondered in terror all night. But his fear of Kolkesh triumphed, so he followed diligently.

"You, you speak?" Kolkesh asked, pointing to his lips and then the prisoner's. The prisoner just bobbed his head around as Kolkesh repeated several more times, his voice growing louder as he gestured, wanting him to speak. Finally, the prisoner mumbled a few words in an indiscernible tongue. Kolkesh looked back, shocked.

"You filth! You do speak! Who are you?" Kolkesh demanded but got nothing else from him. Frustrated, he turned and bowed to Seldik, silently commanding him to take over the effort as he walked away discouraged. Seldik stared at the prisoners, who were blankly staring back at him. *What am I supposed to do?* He thought. He knew nothing of these people and was certainly not a linguist. Edeldon spent some time doing what looked to be deep thinking in the background, but alas, he washed his hands of the attempt, crossed his arms, and watched the interrogation. Nasok was studying a long strip on a string for some time during Kolkesh's attempt but soon wandered a distance back to the railing and stared with a staunch gaze.

Finally, Seldik felt compelled to repeat Kolkesh's initial moves and words, but to no avail. He studied the prisoners' long black hair for a moment, noticing their braids and lengths of painted wooden beads clanking and thudding together as their heads bobbed to the sway of the ship and the guards strong-arming them. They were thin and tall, but not as tall as his kind, and resembled ocean-going types with lean muscles for enduring long bouts of rowing. They were covered with black ink tattoos of designs unlike their language. Still, they seemed to mean something, swirls and dots coalescing into intricate decorations in harmony along their arms and under their ribs until they merged together on their chests. Ship designs also covered their chests in what looked like voyage marks or remembrance. Seldik could not touch the man, still fearful of him, so he used the end of his weapon shaft to indicate the shipping mark.

"What of this mark?" Seldik managed to say as he poked the man's chest. The prisoner flew into a rage, yelling unrecognizable words, causing Seldik to jump back. The guards wrestled him to his knees again and secured him. Within the altercation, Seldik noticed something.

"Raise him again, please," he asked the guards instead of ordering, then requested water for him, which the crewmates reluctantly produced in a dirty cup. But the prisoner drank it down without pause. He had the other one watered as well. Seldik waited for them to finish their fill, then approached again, trying to repeat the words he heard while pointing to the man's chest more honorably.

"You said Derra…Mass, or Deerahass?" Seldik pushed. The man cleared his throat and spoke clearer, "Dera~sah. De Dera~sah engol," and said nothing more.

Seldik then requested a skin and char stick as he had them both sit but kept his distance from them. He drew the ship tattoo and pointed out where they had battled him. "Dera~sah?" he asked as he pointed to each, and the prisoner shook his head no. The man then raised his head and looked skyward, using his eyes as a pointer.

"Dera~sah" *means heaven?* Seldik confirmed that by several more gestures as the rest of the crew, including Kolkesh, stared in disbelief. Seldik showed them his empire's version in drawn form and repeated the name.

"Edenic! Edenic is Dera~sah!" The prisoner seemed to understand but remained unimpressed.

"You, who are you?" Seldik asked, then tried to explain they were Aquarionite. *What was he?* But as he tried to press for answers, the man spat sideways in disgust. He finally kicked the skin away with his foot, bringing down a considerable wallop from one of the guard's batons. Kolkesh held his hand up in reserve, so the guard backed off. The man slumped over, knocked out cold.

After watching the conversation, the second prisoner looked up at Seldik and nodded toward the hide with his head. Seldik quickly pulled it his way and laid it flat in front of him.

"We Mentthhh. Mannato… Mannow." Seldik looked at him, shocked.

"Man, now?" Seldik asked, sounding it out. "You are Mannow?" The man nodded. Again, using his chin, he pointed at the hide.

"Draw." Seldik was shocked. It was his language that the enemy spoke out! Kolkesh stepped forward then.

"How do you know our language?" He asked, his eyes wide. The prisoner could only lift his head so high but murmured some words. "Met… Aquarion… south… sea."

"You met Aquarionites in the South Sea??" The prisoner nodded his head yes. Kolkesh pointed south with his extended hand.

Seldik quickly asked Kolkesh to unbind the prisoner's drawing arm, which he did, knotting the man's left arm behind his back with a lanyard leading to a guard just in case. Seldik pushed him the skin and char to draw, and the prisoner accepted. He pulled the southern sea at what appeared as the tip of Netherweir. Then a tiny island, some considerable distance away, shown to be many days' travel by the sun curves traced again and again from the ship to the island west, hundreds of Megarthy away. Seldik counted some twenty-five possible days or more as he used a multiplying sign "X" just like they did. The prisoner explained a similar Aquarian ship of thatch making, not wood, but the sail design and shape seemed to match. He then drew his recognized method of the sleek black vessel he was on as they met in the open sea. He showed an Aquarian ship sunk, and they took prisoners back to the westerly island. Then he set down the charred stick and looked at Seldik.

"Met, youth, south, sea," he said again. Seldik showed the onlookers the sinking ship drawing and shrugged his shoulders. "Why? Why attack, sink Aquarion?" Seldik asked, looking at Kolkesh for approval.

"Ours, south, sea. Ours," He stated, making clear they felt they controlled that area and the Aquarionites intruded.

"Did you ask us to leave?" Kolkesh asked, but the man just looked at him, unable to understand. Kolkesh looked back at Seldik and shrugged himself.

"Yours, South Sea, NOT ours," Seldik said, and the prisoner nodded his head yes. Seldik tried to figure out a way to better understand, so he drew more figures—the globe, the lands, and the island cities floating in the sea. He pointed to each.

"Aquarionites. Ours here, here, here," he said, now pointing to the island previously drawn. "Yours there?" The prisoner nodded yes, then reached over and tapped the hide hard right where Seldik had drawn the outer edge of Netherweir and said, "Ours!"

Seldik tried some more to explain that their race was peaceful. A claim to a land or sea was well honored by his civilization, and this type of contact is a misunderstanding that could be turned around with time. Still, the enemy seemed unable to fully process what Seldik spoke of.

Kolkesh had them re-watered and taken below again. This time, with orders not to beat them anymore. He still wouldn't feed them, but he felt relieved there was some clarity achieved.

At dinner with the other Souls, Kolkesh was happier than before. "You have again shown yourself useful, Seldik; you may be very special!" The others nodded in acceptance. Seldik blushed. The compliments from all whom he deified were too much, and he believed them to be nothing more than niceties—lies. Kolkesh began to speak again but was overshadowed by the other's enthusiasm for the day's catch of fresh fish.

"Kolkesh is a right, young one. You were able to interact with that man. You brought knowledge we never had. We did not know where they were from nor that they had a claim on this land." Nasok stated while raising a toasting glass of beer to Seldik. The others quickly followed the motion and drank.

"These enemies know the Nether and are prepared to act with war to protect it, yet we have found nothing of them inside the lands," Sylic stated, looking at Nasok for more discussion. Nasok only nodded in agreement. Edeldon stood to speak. Being the quietest of the bunch, everyone grew quiet to listen and turned their attention toward him, knowing what he had to say would be important.

"I had the vision long ago of our meeting with these unnamed barbarians of the sea." He said, pointing to the hide before continuing. "I know of the southerly islands. There are many, but only one matches what he claims as their lands." He pointed to the prisoner's drawn island, showing a swath where many are said to be.

"The vision was told to the Chief, and then we waited until now for the vision to come true." Seldik was now listening intently. His father had never mentioned these islands before.

"We were prepared because of that vision, but not entirely. I did not know how strong they were nor the level they achieved." Kolkesh spoke up.

"Now we do; you have saved us again, Nasok!" Kolkesh said, raising a toast, and the Souls followed the motion. Seldik awkwardly scrambled for his drink and lifted it in a delayed toast before gulping down its contents.

"And we know what they call themselves now; *Minoans,* they are!" Kolkesh laughed and snarked the while. Seldik decided not to correct his naming of them and stayed still.

"Thank you, but I believe we now know there will be more attacks; a vision is unnecessary for such a reality." Kolkesh nodded his head in agreement, abruptly sitting down without saying more.

"I will send word back to CED along with this hide so that they may learn more from what we experienced." And with that, the matter ended, and discussion of the journey ahead took precedence.

Seldik dreamt of the Mannow attack nightly, stirring regularly until he awoke groggy and disconnected from himself. His father knew of these heathens, yet nothing was said to alarm the city of imminent peril. *Why?* He thought. Even a Chief-Soul knows he must share information of that nature. *Maybe that was not a Chief Soul's way? Perhaps the information was treasure or brought power.* He felt his father stood for the protection of all and would do no such thing. But all kinds of new scenarios were arising, and Seldik did his best to maintain a spiral of truths.

Three days later, they had sailed further into the Nether within a giant ocean entrance that stretched in all directions. He could see sporadic islands, small and appeared mostly barren from afar. Called the "Straight" by the crew, this part they say is somewhat fair unless high winds hit, and then the Straight became a death trap. Seldik studied the sparse map as they traveled to their approximate location. The Nether encircled them on the western side, blocking the sea, and the eastern side stretched far into the great unknown. Except for partially drawn-in connecting lakes and rivers, nothing was charted to the east, but the north was the most interesting.

Kolkesh showed Seldik the proposed route and the stops they would make daily. When they did stop, they camped at anchor in the ship, but later, they would hit an outpost due north toward the narrowing part of the Straight in two days if all went well. If not, Kolkesh pointed to alternate beaching spots that, by the look on his face and reluctance to tell him, was not the best alternative plan.

Seldik remained on deck through the night, helping to mend sails. He loved gazing at the stars above, and on this night, he recalled his teachings of constellations and direct knowledge as he knew those skills were crucial for survival. Being more north than the equal region, or "equat'r" for slang, he could adjust the star's angle just from his hand's width and knew to await the rising of the big W that oblong circled the offset polar star. His teachers said the polar star would point true north in the night sky one day, tens of thousands of years in the future due to the Great Year's advancement. Seldik stared again at the polar star, dim and unimaginative compared to many others. Yet, historic observations covering a thousand years of their time and recorded charts from civilizations long before his have ample information as to the paths of these stars. Even the star's very patterns, they claim, will change.

Seldik sat on the bobbing wooden railing, careful to avoid splinters from the sea attack. He stared at the calculated rising of the extensive W star system and tried to imagine what the planet would be like in twenty, even thirty thousand years. It was impossible to fathom such a time gap. *Will there be the same creatures? Will my people still exist?* He couldn't imagine it otherwise; they were so strong. But after the encounter with the Mannow, Seldik felt certain there might come a time of significant loss. *Will man still exist in that time? What if the planet changes and things get wetter or even dryer? That would kill some animals and have others grow bigger in numbers. Will giant animals leave and then return, or will everything I know vanish in that time? Will my people live through changes to the lands or the sea?* He always pondered these thoughts, which is why he loved the stars; they were stationary high in the sky yet changed so that everything might change in time.

It is believed that a giant fireball fell from the sky, a dying star that pulled everything down with it. But nobody could find a missing star in all of their sightings. The story of that star is one of many historical recordings, and it is said to have wiped entire areas clean of life when it hit. It ended the last civilizations and was the rise of his own. It was a manifestation from the heavens of life and knowledge given to his people. It is told that the dying star hit the sea and leveled vast swaths of life in water, set fire to the land, and brought about a chill, freezing all that was left, or so it is written. The dying civilization knew they were at the end, resources gone, and ice covering the land. They began a vast creation effort by all to preserve their knowledge and understanding of the constructs they left behind.

Seldik read these histories but was always amazed to think of such a feat by a group of the living who had a choice: try to survive with every effort, knowing it was for not, or prepare vessels of knowledge within indelible constructs so that others may never suffer again. Seldik thought about this often and questioned the actions of these people. *Was it in the actions that one chose to preserve themselves forever by creating and putting effort into historical documents and crypts so that at least something survived of them? Or was it that they knew or had a vision that this was what they must do?* Seldik knew his response to such calamity; he would never give up. He would live and fight as best he could to survive, damned the future and what the Souls know of him. But deep down, it tugged at his being that he may be ready to do that same thing if there was a way to endure forever, like a rock upon the beach rolling back and forth but never fading from existence. *That is akin to godliness,* he thought, *to survive for all to see, forever, that you existed! Maybe that is precisely what I will do.*

"A shell for your thoughts, Seldik?" The incredible voice of Kolkesh came from behind, nearly making him jump overboard. "There, there, boy," Kolkesh said, grabbing Seldik and steadying him. "These feet are meant for stalking. Sorry." Kolkesh gave a little chuckle as Seldik collected himself.

"I was thinking of all of this and what it means for us," Seldik said, unable to grasp more while his heart was still racing.

Seldik looked even more noticeable in the dark sky at night. "It is a bunch, right?" Kolkesh said, pointing toward their course. "Out there lies the interior of the Nether, the most formidable foe ever to cross our path." Kolkesh sighed. "I've been here a few years, Seldik, and we have barely scratched the land's surface." He continued in deep thought. "We are here for many things: our advancement, our understanding, and frankly, our claim on the lands."

"Yes, you think since nobody is here, why worry about it." Kolkesh grasped the rail and leaned far to peer down at the water's edge. "Well, I can tell you there is much to gain if we stake our claim; others may hear of it. The land is no longer legend, and others are sure to tell someday," he finished, spitting out a big mouth full of tobacco in disgust.

"But there is something more pressing, and that is the vast resources we believe to be more inward. If there are resources all untapped, imagine what they could be." Seldik was shocked at the thought; it hadn't crossed his mind.

"Imagine what there could be beyond what we have already found." Kolkesh seemingly read his mind. "All the meat of land one could harvest, all the wood and unknown plants, above all, minerals." Kolkesh knew their empire's most extraordinary attachment to the land was supplies like the new metals, minerals, materials, and food not plentiful in the sea. "Have unknown animals been found out there, Kolkesh?" Seldik asked, now wholly enchanted with the thought of all these strange new wonders.

"Oh yes, boy! It seems many of the other land creatures, a little different, mind you, are all there, but there are also a bunch more we have never heard of." Not waiting for more questions, he continued. "And some we have not captured and killed yet, just seen." Kolkesh gestured all around him. "We have found them, beasts, birds, fish, and whales all around here on our exploration inward." By the sound of that, Seldik couldn't wait for more.

"What about the myth of the Skagg finding this land? Could they possibly still be alive?"

"We hope so, boy. We all believe it!" Kolkesh used the pause in conversation to walk off, leaving Seldik still sitting, pondering much more, so very much more.

Chapter Six

LEVIATHAN

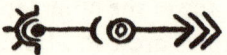

Seldik settled in a hammock tied between the rails on the bow and anticipated the morning that might bring them to the floating outpost at the entrance of the dreaded Nether. Thoughts of his home and the time he spent as a boy jumping from the swing ropes into the sea filled his mind. He swam, laughed, and played ball through the hoops; everything couldn't be more perfect. Visions came of him growing big enough to compete in great distance rowing competitions and the joy he would feel as he plowed his ore into the water all day and all night, reaching the ship far out at sea first. His life had been perfect, and opportunities were endless. He had been unbound to anything, able to do what he wanted, but it all faded slowly as Seldik fell into the deepest sleep he had in days.

Instantly, he was awakened as his body was tossed and flipped in mid-air in the still-dark night. He hit hard on the deck and swung clear to the railing, his back suffering a strong impact that took his breath away. Waves splashed over the bow, completely submerging him simultaneously with the cold weight of the gushing tide that pinned him against the railing. Seldik inhaled some water but was a man of the sea, having the instinct to hold his breath and grasp for survival. He found a railing hole where his hand latched instantly, holding his position until the wave passed. Though his ears were full of water, he could clearly hear loud cracks and booms all along the deck. Alarm quickly turned into confusion as he tried to catch his breath through fits of coughing and choking up seawater. He tried to catch his breath, but no air seemed to enter. The long-dreaded, breathless moments caused his diaphragm to cramp and his lungs burned, but he held on, trying to understand what was going on. The only thing he could imagine was that the ship took a grounding and hit a rock or some other large obstruction that protruded from the water.

More waves came crashing over the bow, but Seldik held his grip and, this time, only flung around backward. His entire body skidded on the wet deck until his knees slammed into the railing, bringing him to a painful stop. More water splashed high on his side but only rained on him, staying mercifully outside the ship. He heard the solid thump of something on the lower hull deep underwater, but it didn't sound so much like solid rock digging in as he initially thought. Instead, the muffled thump sent a ripple of shudders down the ship, causing it to rock toward the source so far it nearly laid sideways from below.

Seldik laid over the railing as the ship flipped so far to the side it seemed they would capsize. But the effect subsided, and the boat lurched back into a vertical position, swinging hard to the other side, leaving Seldik hanging parallel to the deck as the ship righted itself. Ropes and tools flew over the deck while large crashes and cracks became audible in all quarters as supplies toppled. The top of the masts snapped, swinging sails and ropes into the sea along with the railing opposite of Seldik as the ship rocked back and forth before settling into the upright position.

Seldik was still coughing up sea water as the rocking subsided but was well into catching his breath, thankful he managed to avoid being swept overboard. Though it was still pitch black out, he was able to make out vague images of what was before him in the distance. But as he strained his eyes, the only proof of what had just taken place was the local waves lapping and washing over themselves as they rippled out in all directions. *What just happened?* Seldik thought, pulling himself to his soggy knees while he finished coughing, still holding tight to the railing with both arms.

The terrible screams inside the ship's interior were unpalatable, causing him to quickly gather his legs and stand to assist where he could. Crewmates screamed as they breached the deck's level, while others yelled in unrecognizable slang from below. Those on deck ran to the edge only to discover no railing existed on the right side. Seldik, still unable to scream, sloshed carefully toward them, staying close to the rail, grasping it for safety when Kolkesh finally appeared and rushed to his side.

"What the blazes, boy? What did we hit?" Kolkesh's wide, white eyes were unavoidable in the pitch of black. "I don't know. Hit the rail. Winded," was all Seldik could muster while Kolkesh looked frantically over the side and then toward the bow.

"We're barely drifting! Nothing like a full-speed hit like that; it almost sank us!" Seldik furiously nodded his head in agreement.

"Sit, boy," Kolkesh said before he slammed him down to the deck with unbridled power he didn't realize he was using. He spun and started shouting orders for all to anchor themselves to the deck. Though he was yelling, there was a tinge of uncertainty in his voice. "Get to the bottom and check for leaks!" he commanded, and sent the forces who were still coming up the steps back down the stairs. "Start repairs and a bucket line if there are!" He bellowed.

Seldik got back on his feet after catching his breath. His adrenaline was now in full swing as he ran to Kolkesh's side, assessing the gone railing, and realized there was nothing left.

"It didn't sound like rocks, Kolkesh; it was like… something softer. But not sand at all." Seldik was piecing his thoughts together as he spoke. "Like it hit us!" Kolkesh said as he quickly spun and looked at him.

"You're right, boy. Onto something there." Kolkesh turned on his heel and ran down the stairs.

"Grab the harpoons! Everyone, get to the topside unless you're repairing. A Water-Beast be attacking us!" Seldik could not understand what Kolkesh was saying. *A Water-Beast?*

"What do you mean, Kolkesh?" Seldik asked, but Kolkesh continued his dire yelling.

"It's one of those seen but not caught monsters, boy, a real one, and they are big!" Kolkesh didn't wait to talk. As soon as the first harpoon was brought up, he grabbed it and took off to the bow, yelling for Seldik to follow. Seldik didn't hesitate and quickly fell in behind him, dodging the mass of hanging ropes dangling across the deck.

"Tie off on the rail with a line; it will get rough!" Kolkesh guided Seldik to a thinner line, which Seldik fastened quickly with a knot that would not slip at his waist.

"Turn ores! We need the hard right," Kolkesh belted. Soon, ores came out of the holes, missing every other one, likely due to crewmates who were injured or too busy making hasty repairs to follow the order. The ores started sloshing until they were within enough cadence to affect a turn. Due to the broken mast and lack of wind, nobody was at the sails, leaving the ores to be the only way to turn.

"Hold there," Kolkesh belted, ringing Seldik's ears from the loudness. "Steady there," he continued to spew as the ores went silent, raised above the waterline, and held there.

Kolkesh leaned far over the nose, peering into the black water, readying his long, sharp spear. "Here's where it went. That is where it will return from…." Kolkesh said in a whisper under a long, drawn-out breath.

"It's a whale?" Seldik managed to ask to clarify.

"Not just any whale. WAIT!" Kolkesh raised his empty hand in silence but then relaxed again and continued.

"It's some ancient sea creature with a hard beak full of teeth!" Kolkesh said, his eyes wide. Seldik understood it entirely now.

"It will holly hell eat you and this ship if we don't stop it. We moved into its prey zone; it preys on surface whales and lunges straight up at them from the deep to break their backs." Kolkesh moved his hand with fingers outreached to show the effect in the darkness.

Seldik felt a cold bead of sweat trickle down his spine. *The beast will return?* "And no ship's hard edge could likely hurt it either. It waits a few minutes, then moves in for the kill after the whale suffers. We witnessed it once from shore." Seldik spent the remaining moments in silence, peering as hard as he could out into the dark waters, looking for a wake or something to indicate the beast's return. While in his panicked trance, he hadn't noticed the others who had lined up beside them with spears in hand, tying themselves off to avoid falling overboard if the beast slammed into the ship again.

"There!" "There!" said a crewmate, but it was only a false wake. Not long after, another got it wrong as well. Everyone on deck was becoming jumpy from their raw nerves and survival instincts.

"Steady, boys," Kolkesh said, focused on the water more than anything. "You'll get your chance here soon enough!" Seldik could feel an icy chill wash over the deck as everyone fell silent and peered out over the black water.

Just then, in the light of the pale moon, Seldik saw a glimmer off in the distance of what looked like spines cutting through a wake, cutting the lazy surface like a row of knives. He pointed, unable to speak as fear gripped his throat, and Kolkesh nodded his head, motioning for the others to look toward the target.

Kolkesh watched with Seldik as the wake came closer, somewhat slow, not like the frantic first attack felt. Kolkesh held his hand up, solid, telling everyone to wait as he readied his weapon.

He let the beast come within feet of the ship's nose, then screamed, "NOW!" and everyone released their long, sharp instruments into the back of the giant. Seldik saw several go far past the visible spines, thinking they would miss. But all caught, and the thuds of the harpoon breaking through the beast's skin and the thin layer of water were heard again and again. Even the furthest flights of wobbling sticks were heard as the missile's smooth undulations reached the sea top. At once, the entire water surface in front of them blasted with motion as the mighty whale's body lurched out of the water with its tail flying higher than they stood at the bow in the night's air. Flooding water crashed onto the deck hands, and a thump was felt as a bubble pushed the ship's front up. The whale's mighty head flew up in the same arch as the tail, and all the men threw their heads back and stood, staring up at the giant's outreached head and lower jaw. It was so dark the only shine was from the moon's side, and in a surreal moment, everyone watched, mouths agape as the wet, smooth scales glistened under the water that flowed off its cheeks. The harpoon ropes also went up, creating an instant web from the trailing ends on the ship's deck as they uncoiled and shot outward.

The massive beast's head was long and thin, still more comprehensive than the ship's bow at its tip. Its enormous mouth was open, and the upper jaw reached even higher in the air, some sixty or eighty hands up. All along its visible moon side were rows of teeth clear as day. This beast was from one of the scariest tales of his youth he had ever heard. His fear was palpable and debilitating, and so was the crew's. Nobody moved as the never-ending image remained in front of them. A beast so big that no part of it could be taken in by one look, which did not matter as everyone focused entirely on the mighty tooth-lined mouth in front of them.

The beast spewed out a massive exhale with a sound only a demon could produce. The scream and rage were all-encompassing in the sound, and Seldik realized the harpoons did nothing but make it mad. It would beat them into twigs upon the water in minutes, and no force on the planet could stop it, he was sure. Its head began to fall as it screamed so loud everyone's instinct was to cover their ears and drop to the floor in hopes of not dying. Everyone crouched down, some falling flat with their ears covered. Kolkesh was the only one who bent over some in reaction but never lost his stance.

Seldik saw into its enormous gaping mouth as it lunged downward in growing haste as its lower teeth passed them by, and the upper rows careened downward in a chop that blew massive winds and filthy stink from the screaming depths of its throat. As it fell back toward the water, its head came down upon the tip of the bow, sheering it clean off without hurting the railing everyone was tied at. The winds blasted in everyone's faces with such force that Seldik and the others screamed.

The beast's long, thin head hit the water in another violent splash that sprung the ship's nose up high into the air, having all grasp for security along the railing as, once again, icy water showered them. Seldik noticed as he took a wave of water to his face that it wasn't seawater; it was fresh and murky or a mix, but not salty like he had expected.

Kolkesh was already yelling to secure the lines to anchor pins along the deck. The crew responded quickly and began wrapping and tying off the ropes as instructed. Kolkesh armed Seldik beside him as they avoided getting caught in the tightening lines from the backlash as the beast sank.

"Watch the line, boy; keep ahead of them," Kolkesh said as he grabbed the lines, checking for tightness. Seldik now focused entirely on the bars, knowing one could cut you in half if you got between it and the railing.

"All ores backward!" Kolkesh rang out as others yelled the relays down the stairs. Immediately, the ores fell into the water and began pulling back in cadence. The ship agreed in earnest and started cruising backward toward the stern. The zealous force was better prepared this time, and more ores made it out. Soon, they were moving back fast as the lines to the harpoons continued to lead out their ribbons in a fast whip-like fashion, much quicker than by the beast itself. The ropes zinged across the deck as they were pulled over the railings, and the braids contacted the edge of the wood in lightning-fast succession. The whizzing sound was rewarding in creation, but Seldik still wondered if they could hold such a monster.

"You see the size of it, boy? It was giant!" Kolkesh said while readying another lasso around him. "It's going to be tough dealing with this thing, but no choice!" Kolkesh pointed to the railing, telling Seldik to hold on.

"Coming up on the end of the rope! She's sinking, boys! We need to stop her," Kolkesh ordered.

Seldik could only see a few coils that remained on the dark, wet deck, knowing that if they were on one of the mat-built ships of his empire, they would all be dead by now. *How could a natural force overtake the mightiest vessel I have ever seen?* Seldik thought, beginning to doubt the strength of the ship.

The last coils were seen spiraling off the dark deck. The lines were sure to taunt or rip the ship apart. And then, one by one, they coiled out and sprung taunt against the railing, pulling the boat this way and that as they settled.

"Untie yourselves from the rails! They're going to go!" Kolkesh yelled after reevaluating the situation. Everyone made haste to undo the rail knots or cut them with their knives.

"She's diving, Soul," a crewmate yelled from the rail, giving rope length now. The lines smashed through the railings and hull walls leading up to them. Each ripped through the hard oak as quickly as cloth until the deck stopped the progression of cuts, and the entire ship felt like it was being pulled under from the nose. The hull waterline sank as it pulled down but stopped, leaving the deck only 12 hands above ocean level. Everyone yelled and cursed their fear aloud as the mighty ship pitched forward. Several reserve spears flew overboard, but a few crewmates grabbed what they could and tied them to themselves on the front deck after unfastening themselves from the mess. Loud groans echoed from the ship's depths, and ores fell slack as men inside scrambled to hold themselves on their benches.

"She's about to go under! Everyone to the top," Kolkesh yelled, but nobody could move from their secured positions. Just as they feared they would have to jump overboard, the ship slowly stopped sinking and began to rise, the bow levering upward as the heavier stern fell back to the water's top.

"Hold your ground! We're pulling her up some!" Kolkesh let out a gusty sigh of relief.

"Ores pull backward! Pull as your life hangs on it, boys!" Kolkesh screamed, now seeing a possible victory.

The orders were relayed down, and ores began clanking together as the Souls and crewmates below began to get back in position and row. The ship seemed to slip in place as the rows heaved hard into the water, beating and churning for power in a tug-of-war between an ancient beast and the most modern technology. The give and take was felt as ores dug into the water, and then the beast pulled in the opposite direction. Back and forth, the fight continued. No movement was seen, but now, the harpoon ropes were not straight down like before; they were angled forward. Kolkesh was trying to surface the beast, pulling on its back until it would have to come up or break free of its bindings. The sharp spears have multiple spikes meant to hold the whale's skin fast and remain stuck. With the giant's thick skin, they may work even better, Seldik thought.

"Stay clear of the front! Move to the rear to avoid the lines," Kolkesh ordered everyone as they transitioned.

"Ready the blocks to pull on the beast's nose," Kolkesh commanded as others ran a big block and tackle setups out and fastened the backs to long ropes anchored midship at the masts.

After some forty minutes of fighting ore to beast, the whale surfaced as long, sharp exhales of spent air were heard as it tried to intake more. Kolkesh unanchored the front ropes and ran them through the tackles as strings of men were running lines back and forth to get secured for the tug. Everyone stopped as the beast let out another giant open-mouthed scream, sending its foul breath rushing toward them, some 200 hands off the bow. It was a relief not to be directly under its thrashing jaws; few completely turned their backs on it to complete their jobs. The whale pitched sideways as it went back under the turbulent waters, and the wake of it hit the ship in a pitching fashion. The ores continued to pull on new orders, and the front harpoon ropes were soon leveraged as the crew pulled the lines with all their might. Kolkesh watched for the beast to resurface; back and forth, he encouraged them to draw with everything. This was a fight for their lives, and everyone knew it.

As sweat and raw, wet skin gave way to the relentless pull on the taut ropes through the tackle, the beast breached in high status, flying out of the water and into the air. Block and tackles snapped and instantly ripped a few men on the line from the deck and sent them into the sea in an instant. Others held, and two went limp, coming loose or breaking from the beast's attempts. Screams of agony rang across the deck as others ran and pulled men out of the way. Seldik and Kolkesh stood without injury; others reformed the remaining lines and held firm. Kolkesh ordered another line to be cut, as it had pinned two crewmates to the mast, who fell limp upon release from the strangling noose about their midsections. Blood and nerves remained for the top side, but little time was available to mourn what had happened. Everyone knew they must keep the beast held high, or it would attack again.

"Hold her up on the water, men! We can't let her go under deep, or she'll get us!" Kolkesh screamed now, rallying the troops to muster the unimaginable strength of their Souls to help in the fight.

The whale stayed just under the water, coming up to blow air more and more as it grew tired. The remaining front lines were held tight by a tackle to keep it from diving, and the continued reverse of ore power had its effect. Soon, the beast became still and glided with the tugging of the ores.

"We have slack, Soul!" yelled a crewmate on a dragline.

"Ores full forward! Get us to her as fast as possible!" Kolkesh screamed as his orders sent down were met with instant resistance to the backward pull. Seldik felt the surge forward in just a few swipes of the ores, and they were headed at the beast that was now almost a throw's distance from them.

"We must attach more spears to her side, or she will charge us hard!" Seldik had a new sinking feeling others seemed to share with their blank stares toward Kolkesh's words.

That thing will surely attack us again, Seldik thought, unsure if it would be from some dying act of defiance or an innate instinct to fight, but he knew it would be bad.

"Five hands of water are flooding the keel! We can't go faster, they say, Soul!" Yelled the officer of the order from the edge of the stairs.

"Keep it down there! We need all the weight we can carry if it attacks us," Kolkesh said, his worry now audible. *The distance is impossible to reach in time to do what is needed*, Seldik thought.

"Seldik, come," Kolkesh directed as Seldik sprung to his side. "What are your thoughts if we can't reach her in time? The boat is sluggish, and she will recover and hear us coming!" He said, with a slight waver in his voice. "If she does, she will hit us and sink us in one swipe. We have already taken on too much water." He said, looking at Seldik's dark stature.

"I... I don't know. It will attack because it must. Even if we get close, the ship can't take it thrashing against us either." Kolkesh looked perplexed at Seldik's words.

"Your right. It will tear us a new one. Either way, we can't run. What option do we have?" Kolkesh asked, beginning to lose hope.

"How about boarding her, trying to pierce her brain?" Kolkesh said but hesitated.

Seldik was deep in thought, formulating a plan.

"NO! It would thrash us off and kill any real attempt. It needs to breathe, to surface." Seldik said, still pondering the plan that was tickling his brain.

"We surface her! Take away her power to use the propulsion that gives her the strength to the attack," Kolkesh stated. "But that will do little if she gets the energy to hit us. We saw from the beach that it goes wild against its prey and just keeps attacking it!"

Seldik pondered the information. Then, just like that, it came to him. It was Kolkesh's plan but in reverse.

"We need to sink it!" he finally said to Kolkesh, who gave him a puzzled look.

"Take away its ability to breathe! Put it under the waves so it has to fight for breath, not us!" Kolkesh's eyebrows popped up in the thin twilight of what was becoming morning's light.

"You're onto something there. Yes!" Kolkesh said but became silent as he worked out the logistics. "How, though?" He finally asked. "We can only pull up!" He used his hands again to demonstrate to Seldik.

"We can use the anchor; They go down!" Seldik envisioned the process as his plan began to take better form in his mind. "Tie the lines to the ropes on its nose….." Before Seldik could finish voicing his plan, Kolkesh sprinted backward, yelling to the crew.

Quickly, they pulled open the ports that housed the remaining anchors— massive triangle-shaped stones carved from the hardest granite with a hole for threading a rope through. Only three were left, and one was still being moved up to position, now wedged against the hull side two levels down from the attack. All crewmates ran downstairs to help perch the stones at the hull's openings, ready to drop them when summoned. Ropes were lowered, and the anchor lines were cut and knotted to the unwound block and tackle lines going to the beast's head and frontal regions. The crew was working furiously when a loud cry was heard from the beast ahead as it thrashed to life and headed toward them with impressive speed.

"She's coming! Get it done now! NOW! NOW!" Kolkesh yelled over the side. Screams rang out from below as they, too, understood the haste they must make. Finally, from below, they heard "READY!" echo from the anchor ports.

"Wait!" Kolkesh said as he ran to the other side, where the men were finishing the knots on the right. After they signaled, Kolkesh gave the order as he watched the beast grow closer and faster in the beautiful pre-dawn twilight that now equaled the moon's dim glow. Out in front of them, the sheer mass of the creature could be measured. The wake from its gaping, toothy jaw to its tail was longer than the ship! It had four side fins that could paddle like ores, and it heaved side to side almost like a serpent as it also undulated up and down with haste to reap its revenge on them.

"Go! Lay anchor, men!" Kolkesh belched the order.

Seldik was fascinated with how fast they could push the giant anchors overboard. He watched down on his side when looking at the fast-approaching creature, now seeming to reach impossible speed in the water as it was almost upon them. He could feel his heart pounding in his chest, still hurting from losing air at the start of the attack. He and the others were now living off adrenaline and praying this plan worked. For if the beast broke the lines, it would hit the ship with far more force than before.

The beautiful sound of heavy splashes brought about relief after several long moments while the creature bore down upon them. The heavy ropes were whizzing out as the third anchor caught traction and was pulled overboard through the left port. The top ropes ripped from the men's grasping knots and snapped over the remaining railings, taking some more oak with them.

"Brace yourselves! She's going to ram!" Kolkesh gave one final order as he grasped for a rope and railing, which Seldik mimicked with quick pursuit. All above watched as the beast, now just a breath from the bow, came on like a tidal wave, ready to strike them in two and sink them all to the dark depths of the Nether's mouth. *The great Nether will claim me after all!* Seldik felt in an instant all his long-awaited fears were upon him in a wave; he would die this day without ever seeing his father again.

But the strike was not to be. Just as the beast sprung one last wiggle toward its foe who had hurt it so bad, the anchors sinking with gathered speed finally matched the length of the slack rope to the beast's head and back. Like a battering ram, the giant's long snout blasted underwater so fast that it made the back of the beast stand straight up out of the water in front of the helpless ship. Like a log sucked down to the depths, it was pulled under as fast as it lifted from the water; its massive, bulbous form ripped from the surface in a smooth grace, following its head into the deadly plunge. The crew looked out in amazement and terror at the long form so fluid and warped as it rose above the mast's broken tops.

Finally, the last of its form lurched up to reveal a mighty tail that was long and narrow, thrashing up and over with incredible speed as its body continued to vanish. Its tail overshot its body and came crashing down against the bow, throwing timber and lines toward everyone on deck. It pulled into the deep as quickly as it hit, leaving everyone thrown about like dust in the wind. Massive waves plunged over the broken bow and pitched the ship, washing everyone across the deck as it rocked. Little by little, the rocking and washing stopped, and silence filled the night air.

Kolkesh and Seldik were at the back of the ship's deck, washed backward with the remaining wooden railing they were lashed to. The beast's tail struck so hard it wrecked most of the upper portion of the deck, and large holes were now open in the front with no tip left on the bow. Half the deck crew had been thrown overboard by the blow, and others were desperately trying to pull them to safety, but some were already dead and drifting out into the sea. No sail was wrapped or strung, and the ship was poorly listing to the left. Ballast was flung toward the left from the heavy pitch as water helped sink it deeper each minute.

Kolkesh got the bucket lines to the anchor ports and torches lit to assess the damage. Over twelve were dead, including the prisoners. All supplies were soaked or washed away. Half the crew was hurt, and repairs were not going well. Oars were manned and were being paddled in reverse toward the shore to keep the bow from taking on more water. The rear motion slowed the movement as the crew hauled ballast rock backward from the bow to help angle the ship's nose upward as best they could. After the sun had come up, repairs of man and ship continued. Four more were dead or gone, and half the sails were damaged. A third of the oars were gone or broken, and little fresh water was left. Leaking oil drums were thrown out as they slimed the entire lower deck where water was attempting to be removed, making repairs and bucket lines even more challenging to engage. The ship might be saved if it could make it to land.

The day moved into night as the ship's bow was finally plugged enough to reverse direction and row forward, and repaired sails were hoisted on the lower part of the mast, improving their movement toward shore and the emergency landing option they were forced to resort to.

It's going to get worse, Seldik thought to himself—the Nether was coming faster than he had hoped.

Chapter Seven

DAWN ON A NEW WORLD

During the morning hours, they had made landfall. Beaching the bow on the shore, they ran sand anchors up the steep, rocky beach to moor the ship. Seldik slept on the first floor under the bridge, not waking for several hours, worn out from the night of terror. He came to during heavy hammering on the mast's tops. Those who had slept through the night were working feverishly. Kolkesh was groggy and on deck when Seldik came out, and they shared hot broths for breakfast, watching the fever pitch of repairs. The small boats attempted supply runs out to the Straight, but nothing was found, and, one by one, they returned empty. Now they were down to only foul water and dried goods, soggy and needed to be consumed. So meals were watery until they had time to go fishing.

"Two days if we make sail still, Kolkesh?" Seldik asked in desperation, like it might get them going faster.

"If we had not run into that sea beast, it would, but now we may not get that speed with a wrecked front end," Kolkesh said, leaving the topic as terrible as it was when Seldik brought it up.

"What out there is the worst?" Seldik asked, and Kolkesh pointed to the high mountain edge they were against. "See, we came over this way once…" Kolkesh trailed off with a sip from his cup.

"Are we in danger? What is out there?" Seldik asked uneasily. Glancing over his shoulder, he saw a large group garrisoning the beach edge.

"There be giant beasts up in those mountains, boy, and they kill on sight!" Seldik was wide-eyed as Kolkesh got up and motioned him back under the bridge. He followed without a word. Kolkesh fished out a trunk in a corner strapped to the wall. "My locker," was all he said as he opened it. He pulled out a small square fur and unfolded it for Seldik to see. It looked fantastic, striped with two colors, and was far thicker than it appeared. *It must have been a giant animal*, Seldik thought.

"A long tooth cat! Like the Moores in other lands, but much, much bigger!" Kolkesh raised his hand above his very tall head to show how big it was

47

as he continued. "This is only a piece. The rest I sold for good beer, and this is just the butt of the animal!" Seldik couldn't help but feel its prickly hairs. "One hundred stones or more of solid muscle, this one was." Seldik couldn't even picture something like a cat that size; even the Moores from Homegath were far smaller in size.

"So they hunt something even bigger?" Seldik asked, pondering his question of length to the man who could answer such. "Yes. One wears this." Kolkesh reached in and retrieved the only other massive object from the trunk. It was a giant horn cut into a drinking vessel.

"This is only a fifth of the full horn length. It weighed so much there was no transporting it when I evacuated with my life. I took the tip as proof." Seldik held the object. Though it was hollow, it still weighed at least ten stones. He had never seen such a horn, only heard of them.

"It was a wooly, all-black rhino and was the size of two of our anchors." Kolkesh let it sink in, his giant presence dramatically backlit by the massive afternoon sun peeking out from behind a cloud, enlightening his size in a shimmering outline, emphasizing the powerful man's words even more.

"You'd think this cat got us all, but it started with ten or so of those beasts coming out of the marsh right into our camp and smashing through it, trampling half our group to death." He continued. "They decimated our camp and our people. We had to flee to the hills to get away, those of us who made it…." Kolkesh packed the items back into the truck and kicked it to the corner.

"Every beast here is a killer. When we regrouped, there were six of our original twenty left. We tracked others who had succumbed to other animals while we were separated." Kolkesh pulled a map from his shirt and laid it on the table.

"My marks of the trip, as the only thing I had left, show how far we went inland—just one day of travel." Kolkesh pointed to the furthest spot. "It was here we set camp; over here they died."

"I made it, my other party did not, and it was all because that cat attacked us right on the shore at night." Kolkesh felt an icy chill wash over him, enough so that Seldik saw him shiver.

"It was as if it waited for us to settle for the night before it snuck up to attack." Seldik saw his despair but was too engrossed to stop him.

"We backed into the fire ring, but it jumped over, snatching a Soul right out from the ring of defenders at a speed nobody could catch." Kolkesh demonstrated the leap with his hands as he grabbed his fingers like the victim's skull had endured that night.

"We then dug our spears pointing out in a circle into the sand, the cat's second jump landed him right between us directly on the spearheads!"

Kolkesh crouched down and dropped his hand, as if it were the cat landing on the spearhead.

"But it didn't help in time; that beast had plenty of fight though it had a spear sticking out of it. It clawed off faces and arms and crushed skulls as it thrashed around having us all." Kolkesh rubbed his back.

"I got my guts almost torn out from its rear claws. I dove on top of it and drove a spear right into its ribs clean through to the heart before it fell dead." Kolkesh suddenly walked to the door and turned.

"But that was not the worse part; the worse part was having to kill off my friends with no faces or half-eaten bodies, then watch the rest die the next few days trying to make it to the skiff." As he walked out, he mumbled under his breath, "I was the only one out of there alive in the end."

Kolkesh left Seldik to his thoughts. He knew the burning reality was that nobody was safe, no matter the size of their force. They needed to get off this part of the land, and fast. Seldik did not sleep or rest until all the repairs that could be done were completed. The night made everyone jumpy, as what was left of the crew remained within the ship. An oversized watch with distant fires kept the site as safe as they could make it. They heard many terrifying noises echoing from within the tall jungle-like trees, keeping many up most of the night. Morning came as they pushed off and gave a run to find the ship mostly sailed straight. A slight shudder had developed from the broken keel somewhere in the depths that could not be mended until port. She was watertight, and chinking was heavily used. Three side hull planks cracked and bent from the water beast's attack. The bow was gone, but at the waterline, it was patched enough not to take on waves of at least ten hands high. The railing was replaced with temporary ropes and sails flowed well to the second set. The expected travel time was one and a half days at best.

A full day and night of sailing with a strong wind brought them within five hours of the outpost. Just as the morning sun began to break over the horizon, back-and-forth shouts of coded language quickly turned to cries of friendship as the damaged ship came to rest upon the soft mats of the outpost.

Seldik felt safer knowing so many of his kind were now present among them, and his spirit was more at peace, but his nerves were still shot. He offered Kolkesh a round of beers if he could point them to a pub, which is exactly how they ended the day, telling the local leaders about the journey from CED. Seldik realized he didn't care; the beer made him feel much better.

Morning came, and their temporary quarters were mostly cosmetic. Having not been filled in much with straws, they were drafty and freezing. Seldik had awoken with a dry throat from breathing cold air, feeling horrible. Ice had grown on the surfaces, finally allowing Seldik to consume fresh water before the sun rose to melt it away. As he left his quarters to find Kolkesh, he spent time checking out the floating fort. It was a single mat with many dwellings in the center, as well as bars and shops around the outer edge. He heard some three hundred people stayed on it, but many were ashore in huts just visible to the west of it. He could see a haze on the ground from that direction, suspecting it was the cause of the land-based fire.

Seldik made it through the traffic and greetings to find a large hut where Kolkesh could be heard. As he entered, he was again the star of the show—not what he wanted before breakfast.

"Here is the Soul of the Hour, Seldik, Hero of the Nether!" Kolkesh now only used his new title. A strange and unnerving man approached him. He was of obese proportions, very short, and had the long, dark red hair of Aquarionites.

"My name is B'Roll; I am the Lake Lord from the Straight clear until the lands to the north. I am in charge of the pathway," B'Roll said as he shook Seldik's arm. B'Roll had a very gentle grasp; it was apparent he did no work and instantly disgusted Seldik. "Hi, glad to greet you, B'Roll."

Seldik quickly joined Kolkesh at a table filled with food. He ate well as they discussed the specifics of the trip, details Seldik cared to forget. When done, B'Roll handed Kolkesh a new map.

"Here is your newest map, only slightly upgraded from the last, but certainly anything is better than nothing," B'roll said, like it was a gift of great worth even still. "I sent others to the northlands like you wanted, thinking I could conquer the passes and see what is beyond the mists. But they have never returned, so you're on your own." B'Roll got up slowly and went about is his regular activity.

"I must tell my folks the bad news and set new watches and route traveling to assure none of these barbarians get into the lakes uninvited and raid this outpost." B'Roll left uncaring of goodbyes, and Kolkesh made no gesture either. Seldik could tell the two didn't see eye to eye.

"I don't want you to follow that type of leadership, boy," Kolkesh said, leaving the words for what they were, his blatant hate for the guy evident. Everyone got up, left the hut, and headed for the opposite side of their peers.

"B'Roll will give us faster ships of a smaller size for the shallow waters ahead. We will be together but split into three separate vessels. They are being packed with necessary supplies, and we leave at once, with no time to hang around with him." Kolkesh walked ahead, leaving Seldik with the team to get him to the new boats.

By noon, they were setting sail north on three ships of a type he had never seen before. Supplies were stacked in the center, but the vessel still held high-water marks for the weight. Little ballast was in the lowest ribs, and two masts came out from almost nothing to stand tall for two sails each. The ships were sleek and long like the Manoans were, but were very wide in the center, with an exposed jib in the rear for maneuvering. The front swept up in the standard cultural shape of the reed boats, but they were made of wood and yielded a very slender form with a serpent head on the top, making it all appear like a sea monster.

The ship was fast. At full sail and even with the slight wind, they would be screaming through the water in minutes. *This ship is perfect*, Seldik thought as he watched it smooth out in an ideal wake, causing no splashes or curl-over from too much cut. The oars on board had long handles for navigating the shallows and thin blades for pulling in deep waters. Large wound piles of thick rope were carefully stacked at the front of the ship, and the hull was constructed with large thin planks with no visible chinking. Kolkesh could see that the fantastic combination of technologies was very impressive to Seldik, so he explained that the new type gave it much better flexibility. Seldik liked the new boats; he felt three gave backup. Twice, he mentioned to Kolkesh the sightings of giant whale heads traveling above the water looking their way. He wondered how these smaller boats would fare against another hit from one, but they left them alone.

Seldik's thoughts were of the shore. Seeing vast amounts of beasts was unusual for a sea-living person. Some herds had small and tall creatures combined, nobody knowing what they were. He witnessed two elephants with large foreheads and differing tusks fight each other along the water. It was such a spectacle that several nearby plant-eaters found it justified to watch like a match with fantastic odds. Seldik was awe-struck by the scenes unfolding before him but froze when he saw high up on a ledge, dozens of long tooth cats staring down upon them, raising the hair on everyone's neck, especially Kolkesh's.

"Let's not run into something like that ashore; our odds would be nothing," Kolkesh laughed, reserved as he spoke.

Seldik and Kolkesh set sail together, but just as they were leaving, someone approached the dock and jumped aboard the third ship. Kolkesh grunted when seeing him arrive, then returned to his chores, saying nothing of who he was. Seldik decided that was not the time to ask about him.

Two more days of sailing, combined with rowing shifts, made the travel mundane, despite Seldik's ever-growing worries about what was ahead. He kept the night shift, slept the early mornings, then repeated while fishing with a stick in between. Many freshwater species swam the inland waterway, and Seldik drew some on skins to remember their unique shapes and names. Early on, they watched two vessels from the outpost harpooning a smaller whale in the distance; they were unsure of the type. Shore was seen continuously on the east side. Large animal herds were everywhere in untold numbers, and the bird-infested fauna was thick with diversity. Bird migrations of unknown varieties flew high overhead in mass formations, crisscrossing the skies, but were never low enough to make out details. Long, stretching lines of dust pointed back to herds running from unseen predators or away from poor vegetation patches. Seldik had only learned of such beasts, but now, like a dream, he was witness to untold numbers. He imagined the lands had one beast per ship length; the thought was incalculable. Bad weather was brewing from the north right where they were headed and soon brought Seldik back to reality. The crews braced as the inland waters erupted in huge cross waves as they breached the storm's outer threshold.

"WE NEED TO FIND A COVE!" Kolkesh's mighty roar from the bow was heard over the whipping of tarps in the winds as he beckoned the steer full right. The other two ships were missing from view, so everyone was on their own now as the waves became more significant. They turned east to get to the beach, but the darkness mixed with high waves quickly made everything on the land disappear. They traveled on faith alone as they all shrugged down behind their capes, straining to see in front of them.

After a long time of ever-rising storm conditions, a spot opened as the waterway turned east. Finally, the ominous dark beach was before them. Kolkesh turned them forward with an angled sail staying parallel to the shore while he sought out a relief cove. He directed them in just as the second ship came in contact with the waterside. They floated into the opening with cross winds forcing sand bottoming on the downwind side whenever the gusts came upon them. But the well-engineered ships skidded on, never beaching as they held tack against the winds by rolling up the sails and using the ores to guide them into the darkness ahead.

The swells from the waterway slowed and forced the ships into the shallower trench as the constant bombardment of winds settled enough to see large mountains to the north blocking the gale. They rowed until they could light torches to see ahead as they dropped sounding stones overboard to see what they were up against, but the depth had not changes and remained at five fathoms. Kolkesh called a stop when he found a massive overhang of trees against the north bank they had paralleled for some time. Men waded ashore, fastened ropes to the trees, and dropped a rear anchor line to align the boats together at their sides.

Morning could not come soon enough. The violent storm howled all night into the morning, bringing cold moisture over them wave after wave. Seldik fell asleep from exhaustion when it subsided, then awoke in thick fog on a calm new day. Kolkesh had made onboard fires and cooked broth for all. He was famous for broth, which Seldik discovered the minute he put his lips on the cup!

"This guy who boarded as we left, Seldik, is named Efy." Kolkesh said, pointing to the other ship. Seldik peered over to see a strange-looking older man who was leaned against the rail, staring at them. He shuddered when he met his eyes. They were large and deep-set, accentuating his thin frame and lack of hair. The man nodded a wordless hello, but Kolkesh did not bother to look at him or rise. Finally, Efy got bored with staring at them and walked away. Again, Seldik knew not to bother asking about him.

"We might follow this cove just a bit to let the weather settle more before returning to open water," Kolkesh finally said.

"This little gem of a cove is not mapped. We haven't hit the sides this far up in a full survey. Look here," he said, showing Seldik the blank area on the hide.

They broke camp uneventfully, heading east along the canal-sized waterway as Kolkesh plotted. Eventually, the canal widened, and sailing became easier, moving them some ten Megarthy from the Straight. After a quick discussion with the other boat, they returned to the open water to look for the third ship. After a quick circle, they decided to continue north while maintaining the search, hoping they had found somewhere to take refuge further up.

They hugged the eastern edge of the map as they sailed into calmer waters. The storm, lasting only through the night, seemed to have no longevity, and the remaining day turned to a cold, star-lit night. With everyone tired, they pulled close to shore to lay anchor as Seldik stood guard. His visions of the Nether drastically increased as he sat staring into the dark hollowness of unshapen figures in the bush. He grasped his well-made obsidian more than once and pointed it toward shore, but he knew, deep down, that whatever he feared was only in his mind. Strange sounds again came from within the canopy of rock, where trees jutted out everywhere, followed by dead silence. Nothing here made sense to Seldik, not one thing. *I have come so close to the Edenic among the stars many times already, and we haven't even reached our destination*, Seldik thought.

Morning brought Seldik much relief. Being able to see what lurked in front finally gave him enough peace of mind to fall asleep. Several hours later, he awoke to find the missing ship had seen them and was coming in from the far west of the waterway. It had damage but was under full sail, and they had quite a story to tell. It seems, from their view, they had met what can only be described as a killer wave headed along a trough of waves as they attempted to break right and head to the beach when they had seen it. The craft's captain explained that a high tide about 120 hands tall rolled up on them due south. They turned into it and then rode it over before it broke, with the resultant drop in water height damaging the ship. They were so far out that no eastern shores were possible, so they trailed westerly until they hit the beach. Now with full force back together, the journey continued to the gates of the Nether.

The small, interconnected waters continued, weaving in and out of narrow canals and more expansive areas. A mapped waterway to the east and another to the northwest could now be seen, but where they led was not fully known as the entire path had not been sailed. So the party continued straight toward a few mountain ranges with more singular hills.

Unusual barren islands of small stature stuck out in spots, sometimes in chains, but none had been checked. *With their rocky appearances, who would?* Seldik thought. Kolkesh gave Seldik a night off to get some natural sleep, so he was up early the next day and helped prepare breakfast for the crew, who rose just as the morning nip became intolerable. Everyone was now bundled in heavy cloaks as they cast the sails and headed north toward a large mountain range. By night, they had arrived with a surprise tailwind, pushing them quickly into the mountain's breath.

"Keep to the west! It gets rocky ahead!" Kolkesh ordered the crew.

Sounding stones were tossed over the side just in case of a wrong calculation. If one hit, they would know trouble was ahead. Twice, the rocks touched some deep object and cries went out, warning the crews to swing their ships left or right, positioning them into a deeper part of the waterway.

Seldik watched as the mountains grew closer and closer as they sailed into a pinching so tight he wondered if they had reached their stop, but they continued through the narrows and emerged right back into more open water. Soon they entered a breakout where the mountains ran off in both directions, leaving a giant lake between them.

"You thought we would go into the Nether by land, not giant lakes like this, huh?" Kolkesh grimaced at Seldik.

"Well, yes. I thought the interior was land?" Seldik said, scratching his head.

"Nope! Far as we can tell, it's just endless bunches of lakes and canals spread out in all directions!" Kolkesh spouted as he opened his hand across the view before them.

"Our first stop will be just ahead on this lake. You have arrived!"

Seldik felt both exhilaration and fear swell up inside him.

Setting anchor at the entrance of the massive lake, they slept the night in the mouth of the Nether. There was no wind the next morning, forcing them to row their way across the lake or remain stuck. Seldik took turns in the seat, as did everyone, but it was not until night fell again that they saw the land they had been heading for.

Suddenly, a spotter shouted across the ships when he saw a blazing light high up on a hill. "The watch tower fire," he said, pointing in the direction as he yelled from a perch on the middle ship. Kolkesh brought his spyglass out, looking through it for long periods, intermittently scraping off ice that had formed on the lens. Finally, Kolkesh placed the scope back in its case, yelling that nobody was to make a fire spotlight to signal, and motioned the boats together for a talk.

"It looks wrong. I haven't been here for a while, but there are multiple fires over there. I don't like it." Kolkesh was dead serious now. Not even a usual, edgy word came from his mouth. His instincts were right, and everyone knew it, which may have been why all the ships fell quiet.

Sylic, Nasok, and Edeldon remained silent, but not old Efy. He immediately dropped his far-off gaze, stampeded over, and spoke up.

"I need to see what is going on over there, Kolkesh. This is my lake. Mine!" He asserted, looking back at the fire.

"I know, Efy; I didn't say we were not going to do that. I just need a minute." Kolkesh took a breath as he gathered his thoughts. "We will sail northwest of the harbor and then quietly launch a small boat to go take a look and be sure things are right, okay?" Kolkesh said, though he did not ask for a response.

Once they had sailed north and settled into a position far enough away to be unobserved even in daylight, they dispatched the boat packed with two rowers and Efy, who refused to stay behind. It was a pitch-black night with high clouds and no wind, so it didn't take long for the little boat to vanish toward the fire and into the darkness. Kolkesh relayed that only one fire should burn, and it should be brighter and higher up on the ridge than the two he spotted. Seldik asked if Manoans could be to blame, but Kolkesh knew they could not get here without being spotted. They could only wait and see. Within a few hours, the small boat returned, paddling fast and hard before it made contact, and Efy came aboard Seldik's boat directly.

"It's burning! The whole outpost on shore. My floating post is abandoned, and I see nobody around, Kolkesh!" *Efy looks even worse when he is frightened*, Seldik thought.

"I knew something was up. Did you see anyone or know how this happened?" Kolkesh asked, but Efy was already shaking his head.

"Then we go ashore, and we hit it with force. How many were there, Efy?"

Seldik saw the great man thinking strategically as he asked.

"About twenty in total, maybe five on the floating post. We were still building it...." Efy trailed off, falling deep into thought.

"There is twice that with us, so it is settled; we go now!" Kolkesh ordered anchors up, and they headed quietly to the post by ore power alone. It took an hour for the three ships to reach the floating post. As nothing more than a big circular pad with huts, it was not yet completed, being thin to water with little items onboard. They boarded it in mass to find nothing, then proceeded directly to shore a quarter Megarthy in. Kolkesh landed them on the beach, and anchors were dropped on dry ground for drags instead of in the water. Seldik held his spear firmly, worrying about what they would encounter. From a close distance, he could see every hut on the beach was either burnt, smoking, or otherwise destroyed. The fires higher up were coming from wood piles and storage sheds, but everything else was otherwise calm, giving the scene an eerie chill as the party stared, unsure of what to do next.

Just then, Kolkesh hushed orders out to both sides of the carnage as the troops were divided into three parts, Seldik joining him as they marched a group right up the middle. They crept along quietly in the sand, making no noise. Through the wreckage, they all worked, slowly inspecting what they could to decide what or who the raiders were, but nothing was found. Eventually, they all came together at the rims of the higher fires where it stunk of burnt skins, and lit pitch drained across the sands from the various stores housed within.

Kolkesh sent scouts to the ridge tops, then others to line a perimeter lookout as the leading group tore through the camp in search of survivors. Though the search was thorough, no clue or item of war was lying about, not even a spear. The ground was bloodstained, though, and scattered throughout were areas that indicated hand-to-hand combat had taken place. These sights were enough to gather that everyone here had died.

"We will set camp near the boats to await the morning." Kolkesh said as he settled the night. Double guards kept a perimeter outlook as others slept uncomfortably in bedrolls on the beach with their weapons ready. Morning brought a renewed search of the village that had grown on the frontier edge of the Nether. Nothing more was found, but tracks did lead off to the southeast into the rocks where they were lost. Drag marks and animal tracks of an unknown beast were seen plentifully, so it was decided a new violent contact with land dwellers had occurred, and those who perished were scavenged by the lurking beasts.

"What I think we witnessed here is the work of raiders from the Nether interior!" Kolkesh said, instigating quite a discussion.

"How can that be? We have seen nobody here." Nasok stated, disgusted by the idea.

"Yet here is the proof. There are tracks and blood; we were hit," Kolkesh said bluntly.

"They had fine food stores along with pelts ready to use, yet they were all left in place, proving they weren't raided for resources. Someone doesn't want us here. Someone *else*, I should say."

Kolkesh has the right idea. Anybody would have taken the pelts and food. Why would they not? Seldik thought as he listened.

"We must head north to the edge of the lake into the waterways to find a route to the next lake; that is where we end our boat ride." Kolkesh looked at Seldik, who was desperately attempting to process all of this information.

Seldik wasn't sure if he wanted to stay, and in this moment, returning to CED seemed like a great option.

"What of this post? Our backup for supplies and troops now lies days away." Seldik said, now realizing they were the only people of their empire this far in.

"We must send a ship back to tell the outpost to get a larger regiment up here!" Efy said, with Nasok agreeing sharply.

Kolkesh submitted to the plan and dispatched a crew to head back with one of the ships. Sending less was a bad idea, seeing how hard it was to get this far inland, but the ship pushed off right away, with a mission too direct B'Roll, by Kolkesh's orders, to send plenty back to get Efy's floating outpost operational and provide military strength protection to prevent whoever did this carnage from getting away with it again. Efy refused to go, instead trying to argue away ten more troops from Kolkesh's numbers to remain on the outpost and rebuild what they could. Kolkesh refused and then dragged Efy along as they pushed off to sail north. He promised Efy new and better spot to build an outpost, but he cried that this was the perfect spot to make a fortune as a major port since goods would flow in from three directions. Kolkesh, now growing frustrated, listened to his pitiful whining, then told him he could rule both sides of the gap instead, which Efy fell for, thinking that greed would succeed wherever he went. "You'd die here anyway, Efy," was all Kolkesh needed to say to bring Efy back to reality.

Chapter Eight

THE NETHERWEIR

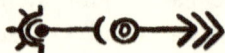

By midday, they paddled heavily as a constant current hit them head-on, but they managed to gain headway by staying out of the deeper delta-style flow along the edge as they headed toward the narrows flowing from the lake above. Kolkesh explained they had done this before, but it was not easy. They eventually landed against vertical black volcanic rocks and tied off the ships for a rest spell. Soon after, large ropes were put ashore, as the crew, except for one row team per ship, pulled the boats up the edge of the narrower river flow. The weight removed from the vessel let them sit very shallowly in the draft, clearing the high sandbanks and heavy reed growth.

By dark, they were halfway up the narrows, and guards were set heavy. Kolkesh chose a fortified cliff to make camp at, hoping its high sides would prevent an enemy strike. He stated they could embark and then drift down with the current extremely fast, so this is an impossible place to hit them with any success. Seldik felt good about this. He was learning much of the warrior way. *Am I a Warrior-Soul?* He pondered. They tied off and rested the night, continuing the arduous task in the morning.

By midday, they finally broke past the narrows, traveling fifteen Megs between lakes. Emerging out of the rocky terrain and into muddy sands too bad to walk upon, everyone switched from ropes on land back on the ships, moving via the ores used as push sticks in the mud. They worked them in waves along the sides until they cleared the scraping bottom of the shallows with thick growths and could continue rowing. Now entering an entirely different lake, Seldik was amazed at the giant mountains before him with peaks reaching clear past the clouds. They rose higher than anything Seldik had ever seen. The mountains they passed before were much smaller, especially on the lake's western rim.

"I never realized how giant mountains could be!" Seldik said to Sylic, who now rode with them since his boat was sent back.

"I never have seen them this large either," Sylic said, surprising Seldik. Sylic saw his quizzical look. "Well, not all land is the same." Seldik nodded his head, realizing this was a very truthful fact.

Seldik was amazed as he observed the rough terrain with impassible summits. High on the rims were giant snow regions, seemingly thick and ancient, with cracks forming strange shapes. Soon he realized both sides of him, even the shorter but still formidable mountains to his east, also had glaciers. Kolkesh reminded him of glaciers, or old ice, stating they would see much more of that soon.

"So, this is the last area anyone from my empire has traveled? The actual end of the globe, one could argue?" Seldik asked, and Sylic nodded that he was correct.

"But we went further that way, which is where it all fell apart, Seldik. We are lucky to be here." With a chest full of fear, Seldik looked in the direction he pointed.

"Kolkesh didn't say what happened up there?" Seldik asked, but Sylic just glanced at him from the corner of his eye and bent his lips, shaking his head as he walked to the rear to join Kolkesh.

Seldik felt incredibly uneasy. These were two of the most muscular men he knew, and neither wanted to discuss it. In that moment, Seldik feared he would not see life past that very same spot.

The dreaded time was upon them. Seldik felt it. Even Kolkesh was caught shuddering from the cold dampness in the air as they reached the very end of the lake. They carefully skirted a dangerous rock outcrop that could quickly sink a ship as they made their way to the cove. The port was the width of twenty ships and proved to be a natural alcove from the waves and wind. The water grew shallow but was deep enough not to jump over, so ramps to the edge of the rock were needed. Ropes secured the beautiful ships in a sunlit setting, with the gorgeous backdrop of giant mountains to frame the scene. Trees with thick fauna were everywhere, and water was equally abundant. They were along the edge of the lake that seemed to keep going, but Kolkesh said it got too shallow and had a sandy bottom, preventing them from going further. And since there was no port past this point to harbor the ships, they would leave them behind.

The rocks on shore had markings from Kolkesh's previous trips to the spot, with a few markings to commemorate the date of his most tragic journey. Seldik took time enjoying the weird sensations of walking on land. Having no wake and no flat horizon, it made him feel uneasy for some time. He had to stand with nowhere to sit as all options were made of hard, sharp rock, causing him to wonder why people desired to live on land rather than at sea.

"There are the marks of past failure," Nasok said. "We all about died last go around. I dread doing this again, but our empire calls." He looked toward Kolkesh, who said nothing.

Seldik changed the subject by asking where exactly they were to go from here. Instead of answering, Kolkesh earnestly ordered everyone to move out as the dreaded journey began.

"We will eat at the first camp, just before the mountain pass," Kolkesh said, and they hiked with heavy loads until dusk.

They set camp and lit fires along a great river that flowed to the lake and prepared a meal of dried meat and broth as they discussed their plan to summit the mountain the following day. "Morning will bring a hike over the mountains. If we are lucky, we will make it down the other side as well and not be forced to make camp within the woods," Kolkesh announced while they ate around the fire. Seldik listened but focused heavily on the sounds around him, growing more uneasy with each moment, then Nasok spoke up.

"Again…" he stated, letting Seldik know that must have been the place nobody would speak of.

"Again is right, Nasok," Kolkesh said before dropping his chin to his chest as he walked off, heading to his bedroll.

Everyone followed quickly, leaving Seldik with the warm, crackling flames taunting his thoughts. He thought it best to curl up in his roll near the fire edge this night.

Guards were on their assigned posts when strange and chilling sounds from the mountain pass started. From deep within the mountain forest came a deep howl, followed by a groan. The tone was so low the winds nearly canceled it out, leading the guards to hope they had dreamed it in their exhausted state. However, Seldik snapped awake only moments later as the same sounds came through again, much louder this time. Everyone jumped up from their bedrolls to listen and quickly rekindle the fire to grow light as fast as possible. Creeks and cracking sounds, like a bending ship in the air, came to their ears repeatedly. The cracks were sometimes quick, but loud enough to make everyone duck like the source rode the winds above their heads. Many got up to grab weapons, but stayed close to the fire with their comrades. One large, throaty moan increased steadily until it broke into a wretched scream, splitting the night's agony and causing everyone to hit their knees. All weapons were then pointed toward the black wall of terror before them at the foot of the mountain. Most shook with fear, but Kolkesh stood tall, readying his feet for anything as if he would leap up to strike it from the air. But nothing came. The sounds went just as fast as they arrived until all were wearily tucked back into their bedrolls, half leaning against each other or rocks by the fire.

"That must have been the mighty beasts in the mountain tops. Most likely, they were attacking each other." Sylic whispered to Seldik.

Sylic continues to tell him that they had not heard anything like that on the last trips. Knowing more than one trip had failed here, Seldik became even more uneasy.

Morning came, and they quickly packed up camp to head up the mountain as Kolkesh reminded them that it was vital they reach the summit and get out of the cursed mountains before nightfall. Seldik marched the tune as everyone did after the night's warnings were heard. Nobody wanted to be up there with whatever made that sound. Seldik wondered if the very mountains were angry. *Could inanimate objects be alive?* He thought, though nothing of this nature had been mentioned in his teachings. *Maybe the hills come alive at night and that's why they don't speak of it.* His mind wondered on this topic a little longer until Kolkesh came to hike beside him. He noticed then that he had fallen a sufficient distance behind the others.

"I know we have been sparse on the facts of our last treks here," Kolkesh began, checking to make sure he was out of earshot of the others. "I can assure you that these are all the facts you don't want to hear, but I'll tell you what happened." Seldik was all intent on the coming revelations.

"We once did this same hike, getting up there late. Mind you, on the first trip, we went more east, up toward another possible lake," he continued, pointing toward the tall eastern mountain range. "We took this pass, hoping to get over it, but you will see it is very long and steep. We made it to the summit and set camp, but then everything went bad. The guards were taken by a pack of long tooth cats on the rock rim, so we pulled everyone back to the fire." He continued without pause. "But that was not enough. Soon after, we heard footsteps rush in, and the intruders intentionally put out the fire!" Seldik looked at him in amazement, then shuddered at his words. *Someone?*

"It was not an animal, but a man like no other I had ever seen, a mountain man, I suggest." Seldik could not believe what he was hearing. *Another TYPE of man? One who lives here in the Nether, but nowhere else?*

"You think I am a loon, but in the fray of the fight that night, I caught a glimpse of one before the fire died. It was covered in hair and even larger than us!" Seldik stopped dead in his tracks, wide eyed in disbelief.

"Keep hiking. Your life depends on it, boy!" Kolkesh hollered back to him.

Seldik quickly marched back up to his side before Kolkesh continued. "They hit at night, put out our fire, but danced around like I swear they could see somehow." He paused for effect, then continued. "And they weren't alone, boy." Kolkesh leaned in closer now. "I think they controlled the cat beasts, so keep all your wits to you from here on. Use that head of yours to get the hell out if trouble happens. We won't hold such off long again." Kolkesh went back to hiking without saying anything for several minutes.

"That were fifteen souls lost up there, my friends. We had discovered all we know of this land so far together until that night."

Seldik looked eastward. "What about that route, then? What happened there to make us go this way?" He asked.

Kolkesh came to an abrupt halt, causing Seldik to freeze in shock.

"You wouldn't believe me, Sylic, or the other Souls, but what we got into over there was bad enough, too." Kolkesh raised his hands high. "I'll tell you now the craziest thing you may hear today. Over there, the rocks float!" Kolkesh turned to start his hike again, leaving Seldik perplexed.

"Come up here, and I'll tell you," Kolkesh said, seeing the confusion on the boy's face, then motioned for him to hurry up.

"My first group, some thirty strong, traveled upriver, only for us to get stuck within a giant gorge of fast waters from what must have been a lake above. We forced through the gap to find a natural dam upon dam of large, sharp boulders, some with obsidian."

"Once we got over them, we only made it halfway to the summit, as injuries mounted up from the climbing that tore into us, forcing us to set camp." Kolkesh's voice lowered. "It was a fatal mistake we made. The night came, and a storm high above the lake erupted. By early morning, the torrents grew louder, then waters rushed our camp."

Kolkesh stopped for a brief rest, the altitude beginning to wear on his lungs. Seldik gazed around, realizing these stories had taken place on the same mountains he stood within. Just as he was letting the chilling reality sink in, Kolkesh began again.

"The banks became a river, so we attempted to seek high ground along the cliffs where none was to be had, then all at once the crashing of the rocks came tumbling downriver and broke the dams." Kolkesh opened his arms as wide as he could, indicating the size of the boulders, then continued.

"But unlike a heavy boulder that needs volumes to get it moving, these blocks of rock were so light they could float with ease." Kolkesh slapped his arms back to his side.

"The force carried them down in the pitch of night and got us right in the open, the rocks ripping into the men and tearing them from the cliffs face one after the other." Kolkesh looked down, kicking a plant to uproot it. "Those who gained more cliff survived, but half the team was gone instantly."

"Morning showed a choked river with squared blocks of rock simply floating as they drifted down it. We quickly got out of there, never to find our mates again." Kolkesh turned, beginning hiking again, motioning Seldik along as well.

Seldik could not believe his ears. *Floating rocks? Unseen storms that brought immediate floods and death? What kind of evil was the Nether made of?* He thought, but said nothing. He was in no mood to go that way as he followed quickly behind.

As the day pressed on, the team wore down after covering nearly twenty Megs. But they were nearing the top of the pass, which was proving to be just as treacherous as Sylic had told him. The thick, massive trees were nearly 200 hands high and created a sun-choking canopy of darkness on the forest floor, worsening their ability to travel quickly. The terrain remained rock-covered with thin soil, but snow began to mix with a colossal amount of dead leaves and debris, choking their path at several points, causing them to change direction. Trying to keep a heading, they had their magnetic blocks around their necks that were at the ready as navigation was confirmed repeatedly. If they missed the pass, they would end up in a dead-end canyon, unable to get down the mountain's backside. Nobody knew if the range they were on was a lone mountain or if many more would be on the other side after they crested the top. All Kolkesh said was they had camped on top, a mistake Seldik wished not to repeat.

Seldik was amazed at how Sylic was so adept at climbing and hiking. Being more diminutive, he thought they would overpower his slighter steps to leave him behind, but it was the other way around. Sylic paced ahead and returned to them from the side repeatedly as he used caution to scout for the group, lagging him. He did not drink much, did not show sweat, and seemed not to rest—the life of a lander made you stronger, Seldik assumed.

Edeldon and Nasok stayed together, not looking like they were up for the climb, and Efy remained with the other troops, who generally kept to themselves but were packing the heavy goods on their backs. All had superior footwear, but Sylic's was the best, made with at least ten types of different leathers. Sylic was constantly asked about them, but he got them clear from the Homegath lands from a tribe who prided themselves in footwear. Seldik thought he must visit Homegath someday if he made it out of this hellish land alive.

The team finally broke the ridgeline with only a half hour left of the sun. Kolkesh pointed far off toward the vicinity of the old camp, repeating that they must move as fast as they could beyond the top and head down. Everyone kept a slight jog as they moved along the flatter ground of the low pass point. The sound of scurrying creatures made them uneasy. Everyone was sweating badly, attempting to heal their legs from the climb yet moving faster for the remainder. Another half hour passed, but they were still not across the pass's edge. Kolkesh stopped and ran back to the team for a huddle, then started shedding his pack.

"Take everything off, carry what good food you can stuff in your pouches, and leave all the packs, including the bedrolls!" Everyone hesitated as Kolkesh continued shedding his pack and realized this was a due-or-die scenario. To Hell with all the goods! Everyone began dumping their packs, then grabbed their weapons, a small cape, and what dry meat they could stuff in their pockets. They leaped to catch up to Kolkesh, who was already at a faster run. The same frantic thought was now setting into everyone's mind—*get off the mountain or die here!* Seldik was up with Sylic, pacing his long legs, and using his running acclamation to avoid losing the group's fastest guy. Sylic wove through trees gracefully, as Seldik slapped along beside him, highly aware that he did not possess Sylic's innate abilities.

They breached the summit's edge, and short glimpses of a forest far below gave them hope, as they now knew the mountain range was a single jut of land rising from the valley behind them. Sylic chose the best paths, so soon, everyone followed his lead. The older of the group, Edeldon and Nasok, were back some distance with Efy, so Kolkesh ordered all the guards around them, knowing they would be the slowest. Kolkesh kept right in the middle, looking around, which Seldik knew meant his war ears were on. His Soul was in complete form from the look of him, as if he was ready for anything.

The team remained relatively quiet, even in a run, due to the soft nature of the soil. But the occasional patch of rock was increasing, and their descent was gradually growing steeper, causing even Sylic to slow or risk falling or skidding from stone to stone. Seldik had not felt the patches of stone as he went down several times, but learned to watch for it. Even those who managed to stay on their feet were battered, collecting scrapes and cuts from the trees and underbrush as they moved along.

Seldik's breathing was intense now, the only noise he heard. The high altitude of the pass made him gasp more for air. *Is there less air here?* He thought? He cared little about the question, more concerned about getting better results from his body at that moment.

Soon the whole party was stopped and grasping at their sides. But after only a moment, they continued walking fast instead of jogging. Seldik's sides burned. *It must be the higher lands that cause this*, he thought as Kolkesh caught up to him and Sylic and hushed some advice.

"Rest a bit, but keep pushing the team down fast. It nears night!" he said, making the air intake steadily faster on Sylic and him. With a look at each other, they started a slow run down again, choosing a sideways angle to maintain their speed and avoid the straight-down approach that burned more energy while trying to quickly dodge the underbrush and stone patches. Sylic had better night vision, it appeared, as he chose paths Seldik never noticed as they tromped downward. Their leg muscles cramped, burning with their momentum constantly slowing. Seldik went down again on a dead branch, but Kolkesh swooped him up as he passed. Sylic kept ahead, not dropping the pace. Moans from the older members behind them were registering louder now; everyone knew the rate could not be maintained.

Efy was the first to drop off, stopping in a bent, cramped position as he leaned against a tree. Finally, all were stopped, just trying to catch their breath. Sylic returned up the trail but stopped short, uneager to climb the few feet to them all. Kolkesh sucked massive volumes of air, his larger form not meant to be a gazelle on land but more the heavy tortoise type.

Kolkesh waved them all to him except Sylic, who rested against a tree content to remain a few feet lower. Unable to talk or breathe, he pulled out his weapons instead. Everyone else followed.

"We go slower now. It is dark, so we must be quiet and prepared." Kolkesh slapped his weapons together.

"Keep them ready. I don't think we are low enough. Keep moving. If we get hit, all the Souls head for lower ground. Guards, you provide cover, then retreat as needed." The guards huddled around, shaking their heads. Only four remained in the dwindling group.

"Seldik, you will accompany the Souls. That is an order. Everyone in line!" Seldik had no chance to question Kolkesh's authority.

Though it made him feel better, being more protected, he started to feel it was wrong when they continued their journey down. *Why would Kolkesh ask me to do that?* He definitely did not want to find out right now, but with all his built-up fears, the doom was so real within him that he knew it most certainly would be this day. If he was to be a War-Soul, he must prove it here, where they all might perish. Or if he was some other Soul Type, then that must be confirmed in difficult times, not pleasant times. For it was withing a challenge that the Soul showed itself, not within peace.

The team traveled another twenty minutes, unmolested. All were now clenching their weapons as they scanned in every direction with wide, white eyes as they walked. *Were the demons who killed Kolkesh's party the last time he was here going to attack them now, or were they far enough down the mountain and out of the beast's domain?* Seldik was frantic now. His heart was pounding from adrenaline, and he could hear nothing but the ringing in his ears as he attempted controlled breathing. He realized he was not blinking. His dry eyes, frozen from the cold, turned to over-wet as they compensated, causing him to wipe his eyes on his arm. One at a time, he slowly lifted his arms, afraid to miss anything as he wiped them dry. Sylic was now crammed up against them, and the entire troop was almost on each other's heels. The quiet within the dark pockets of the wood was terrifying. Everyone investigated these pockets, imagining a beast springing forth any minute. Several times one stopped, frozen from a perceived noise or sight, then continued when nothing came of it. They carried on once the area was cleared until, again, someone would stop for a long wait that yielded nothing, then a few more steps were gained.

Finally, Kolkesh called a halt and ordered a fire to be built in a clear spot. They made haste, collecting wood and creating makeshift torches, before Kolkesh summoned them into a huddle. Sylic was put as a rear between the Soul's group and the guards as Kolkesh ordered them all to leave the burning fire as they headed downhill.

"That big fire may draw them in. If so, we will not be there. We must get to the valley," Kolkesh said as he pulled Sylic from behind and pushed him into action once more.

With little light, they moved along, still tripping but managing a pace. They endured another half hour without stopping, then suddenly, the same screaming from the night before rang out behind them. Everyone scattered beside trees for some protection they felt each trunk offered.

The screeches and cries came from higher up. Seldik immediately calculated they were atop the abandoned fire above. If so, Kolkesh was right; they tracked it and attacked the spot. He had no more time for thoughts and calculations as Kolkesh quietly pushed everyone ahead in a frantic attempt to get the herd moving. Nobody delayed, all now running for their lives as they desperately moved farther and farther away from the wretched sounds and farther into the Nether.

Chapter Nine

GIANT CONTACT

The team made another ten minutes in a dead run until Kolkesh fell over a stump, putting the team at a slower pace after guiding him to his feet. Everyone now kept at a slow gallop that created awful noises as they traversed the lower hill. Seldik knew this was not good, but despite his attempts to step lightly, his footfalls were anything but silent due to the agony in his foot bottoms from the many bruises they sustained from the rocky edges of the mountain pass. Though the ground near the bottom had softened a bit and was no longer solid rock, having been fractured by time and given way to a sandier, gravel-like texture, it caused the team to create a rough, scouring sound as they trotted across it. Eventually, Kolkesh stepped to the side with Edeldon and lit up torches. After passing them out, they were able to gain more speed and maintain a quieter path now that they had some light to better navigate the ground before them.

Suddenly, they heard a whoosh on their sides so loud everyone tore to a halt to form up back-to-back in a line of defense, a tactic all young Aquarionites learned during their military training. Kolkesh grabbed through to the center, pulling Seldik beside him. "Circle," he ordered as everyone slid into formation by dividing around him.

"Points out. They are here." Kolkesh aimed his over Nasok's shoulder since it was longer than the others and able to reach farther. Kolkesh ordered the circle to the edge of a rock, where they managed to sidestep along until they were atop its long, flattened dome shape. The rock outcrop was surprisingly hard with only a few loose stones, giving them excellent traction to maneuver. Kolkesh now left half the lineup at the rock's edge as he moved the guards into the frontal part of the circle to better defend the open ground.

"Pass the torches rear. Keep the light where we can see them," Kolkesh ordered.

Seldik looked around. No enemy was visible, but by the sounds emanating from the dark, it seemed some extremely fast beings were surrounding them. Seldik knew they were everywhere. Kolkesh had all bend down in defense form, so all blades were ready. Seldik realized the rock's rear cliff prevented an attack from that side but also cut off their escape. He could see they had a better chance in the open ground, then settled in for the unthinkable—a fight to the death.

"They will come to leap and claw us. Focus on their hearts and heads. They are big, so fight as one." Kolkesh had just gotten the order out of his mouth when a rock flung into the center of them from somewhere in the dark.

A guard took it upon the head, dropping dead with a loud thump as blood splattered into the faces of the rest. Seldik was mortified. *They throw giant rocks that kill on contact? How can sharp sticks defeat these beasts?* Seldik felt a rush of mortality spring up within him. His voice welled to cry out, but he had nothing to say to stop this night's outcome. The realization that this was the end rushed to his mind, knowing that nothing could remove it until death took him.

Seldik staggered, looking down as the torchlight flickered off the wet, fresh blood from the guard dripping off his tunic. The frozen vapor rolling off of everyone's lips appeared like a slow fog rolling past the torches' reflected light. Seldik felt slow to a crawl, like he was not even there, just a ghost watching others flinch and twist with weapons pointing out at nothing. His ears hardly registered the surrounding noises, and his shock was so entrancing that he was unable to breathe or think. He wished so badly to go home, to return to his stupid blinds in his hut, or play with his friends again. This nightmare had to end, but it seemed nothing would be able to delay his death for another day.

Seldik saw his handed weapon, the sharp black edge glimmering in the fire's glow. If he was to die, his Soul would be free to become what it would. *Can the Soul rise in that time and reveal its identity so I will die knowing my ultimate purpose upon the planet?* Seldik slowly looked up past the cowering crowd squeezed together on the rock that would become their tomb. Another large rock whizzed past on the left side, clipping a guard in the arm and bringing him to the ground, screaming. The sound came to Seldik's as a filtered muffle. The slow motion of the guard falling distracted all but Seldik as he stepped between the group on either side and out into the front. He heard Kolkesh finally realize his march forward, then screamed for him to get back, but Seldik was no longer in charge of himself, uncaring for what others commanded or wanted. He was at his climax of life in that moment, a moment in time that defined him purely by his purpose on the planet, and not the feelings he harbored, nor the many names given to him by his family or friends.

Seldik realized he was alone for a ride. He had lost all control of something deep within that guided this walk toward the unknown enemy. He felt at peace with it, ready to accept the fate that would come to reveal who he was at the end of his life. He knew he would likely die without a chance to defend himself or fight, but he now realized it was not a warrior within him. He was not a War-Soul, and he was not the hero Kolkesh made him out to be. He was an explorer. Like those within his empire, he craved the unimaginable, the unseen, and these beasts were both. They would either accept the kind heart of the explorer or kill him for his intrusion. Nobody but he would know how he vanished from the planet and why. His Soul would then journey beyond these mountains to continue exploring the whole of the Nether, for it was far more to him now—it was his resting place.

Seldik kept pacing forward, his mates yelling from behind, begging him to return to them and the safety of the fire. But Seldik blocked them out now, choosing to die alone by facing the enemy who he wanted to understand him. He then realized he had dropped his weapon several steps back, leaving it to dance on the ground from impact as he marched on. He did not mean his enemy harm. He just wanted to know who they were and for them to understand who he was. Though he was perplexed by the numb thoughts streaming by in his head, he knew his Soul had taken over his conscience, and every idea was now being dictated by his unknown type of Soul that was so bent on understanding that it was foregoing any act of preservation. But Seldik seemed okay with this, too, as he believed in his spiritual self. If this is what death feels like, he could deal with that. The fear was over now. He had taken on this journey just as his father had dreamed. He made it here, and that was enough.

Seldik felt his voice rise within his chest, beckoning to break free. He was shocked he had anything to say at all, but then came a rush of desire to be heard that well up until it broke free from his lips. Suddenly, his jaw open, and he called out to the darkness and the invisible beings within.

"SKAGG BRETHREN, I am of the sea!" Seldik could not believe his words. He yelled out to the "Skagg," his ancient descendants and the first of his kind, or so legend says.

Seldik realized he had called out in the old tongue of the empire, the first language and usually only expressed by the senior women of CED. Seldik knew this was all wrong. *Saying this to a Nether beast is useless*, he thought, then dropped to his knees in anguish, afraid his cowardness had doomed him to die alone for all to see. *My Soul is unimportant and useless. I've got nothing. I probably don't even have a Soul.* Seldik kneeled there, awaiting the end by an unseen rock to his head for what seemed like forever. *Why are they not striking me with stones while I'm so close? I'm right here...*

"Come on!" Seldik yelled in despair, bending over while placing his hands on the ground, not wanting to see his killers. *Why won't they kill me?* Seldik wept, but nothing happened. The silence in front of him remained unchanged. Seldik crawled forward slightly, but still nothing came.

"C... come on...." Seldik was now unable to force words from his lips, and his head hung low to allow the coming blow to be clean, ending his misery quickly. But still, nothing. No movement, no screams, not even a sound from the group he knew was perched behind him on the outcrop. Seldik gave a solemn moan of anguish as tears of regret streamed from his clenched eyes. He knelt in the cold dark with his heart screaming. His ears ringing were so high that sound no longer came through. He rocked back and forth and began to tremble violently, unable to control the doom filling his chest. *Why?* He thought, the question so desperate he did not know if he yelled it. *Why do they wait for my flesh when I am right before them?*

Seldik saw sudden movement right before him, and the unmistakable smell of a beast hit his nostrils as a massive hair-covered foot stepped within a hand of his bent head. It is now he who would pass to the great Edenic. But the moments passed, and the foot remained planted. Seldik, now shaking uncontrollably with pure adrenaline and raw nerves, began to lift his head. He could not help ending this standoff as he must have peace before his heart took him. He raised his head slowly, studying the dark hair of the beast's leg in front of him. He could not manage his arms to push him high enough, so he ended his gaze upward by tilting his head sideways to make eye contact with the beasts.

Dark and giant, the beast's head was far higher than Seldik's stance, some eighteen hands up from his cowering position. Seldik remained frozen due to his uncooperating arms. All he could maintain was the tilted position of his head as he awaited his execution. The beast remained still as a tree, and soon Seldik noticed others of its kind standing in the same fashion, slightly behind him. Through the flickering of the torch, barely reading this far away, Seldik could only make out outlines. The planet stood still then, with Seldik still unsure what would happen or why the delay in his death continued.

The beast then squatted, placing upon the ground in front of Seldik the stone it had in its hand. Seldik just stared at the big rock. *What is going on?* The beast gently turned its hand over, opened his palm upward, then extended its long fingers toward Seldik's lowered head. Seldik fell back on his legs, unable to even remain kneeling. He observed the hand and then glanced at the beast's face. Finally, the figure moved its hand closer to Seldik, making him flinch back as he imagined the beast snapping his head clean off his body like a twig.

But its hand remained, and soon Seldik realized he was faced with something far different from death. The mountain man appeared as if he wanted to make contact with him. Seldik tilted his head up more, finally getting the nerve to bend his torso slightly to see the beast's reaction. The giant remained quiet as the others behind him stood as tree trunks. Finally, Seldik managed to lift himself back on his feet in a kneeling position but remained staring at the hand. The beast again moved it slightly toward him in a gesture that broke Seldik's fascination.

He returned the creature's movement by slowly lifting his trembling hand and turning it with an open palm. The beast turned his over ever so gently, stopping as Seldik reeled back slightly with uncontrollable reluctance, but the beast kept moving his hand forward until it hovered above Seldik's. Seldik stared at their hands, not wanting to know what was behind the beast's eyes, for the killing machine was right in front of him. The beast slowly lowered his hand until he touched palms with Seldik, who again dropped his slightly in response. The beast again responded by reducing again until contact. Seldik finally held his own and completed the mountain man's greeting. He then offered the giant a hard-fought smile, but showed no teeth, as any wild beast would take that as aggression. But after producing a slight upward, close-mouthed grin, Seldik took a breath, as the giant seemed to understand and nodded its head down.

The beast then rose, making Seldik cower back, and walked a few steps to the others behind him. Seldik waited, still like a statue, and stared at them, then looked back at the scene of contact. He realized in that moment that he was living off of pure adrenaline. His body still shook to its very core, his heart was pounding harder than ever, and he was still unable to gain his feet after this ordeal. *How am I still alive? What just happened?* He realized his palm was still open as he gazed into it in the darkness.

Kolkesh finally pulled the rest of the team up behind him. Reluctant and weary, they reached him as Kolkesh placed his arm on his shoulder. "You alright, boy?" Kolkesh asked in his lowest, most sincere voice.

"I... I guess so?" he said, staring over his shoulder and at Kolkesh.

Kolkesh grabbed him under his armpit, yanking him up to assist his stance. Seldik valued the sharp pain of it as Kolkesh held him until the numbness left his legs and he was able to stand on his own. Seldik's brain screamed with thought, realizing how close he had come to death before it lead to his acceptance. In that moment, he was transformed. He had witnessed the bearing of his Soul as it took possession of him to bring forth an impossible beginning within this mythical land. If such a giant was intelligent, Seldik realized he knew nothing of the natural world; nobody did. He gazed around at the team. All but one was beside him, even now, and reached out to push down their weapons. He remained fixated on the charge his Soul had summoned itself for, but still didn't understand what it meant for his Soul Type. Seldik turned without speaking to interact with the beasts across from him, waiting patiently in silence.

He stepped away, pulling his arm slowly from Kolkesh's grip as he moved toward the being he regarded as the leader. He was again taken aback by the size of them. Now that he was standing, he realized they had to be at least twelve hands tall, towering over Seldik's nine-hand height. Their bodies were thin-limbed with thicker lower hair and lighter hair in all the highest places. Their arms were incredibly long, with giant hands three times the size of his. He knew from their hand contact that they were accepting peace and had spared them. Why Seldik had yelled out Skagg was unknown to him. *Does my Soul recognize these beings as my mythical forefathers?*

Seldik was full of questions and confusion, but he could not miss an opportunity to do more than touch a hand and then see them depart. His consciousness wanted answers. The curiosity was palpable now that his nerves ran on pure adrenaline. He made slow steps toward the first one and stopped at a distance from him, still scared enough of the giant to get too close. The giant maintained its gaze as it tracked his approach. Nobody in known history had ever presented themselves to the empire's people who were not fully human. Seldik was the first to make such unprecedented contact, submerged within the minute.

Seldik again raised his outstretched fingers with an open palm to show no harm, then watched as the others gave no reaction. He then reached into his tunic and carefully pulled out a piece of rolled up hide from under his arm that he had made notes on throughout their trip. He unrolled and grasped the char pencil that was snug inside it, then draped the hide upside down over his other hand. Steadying it, he drew a large circle. Once he finished, he gently held it out toward the leader. The giant took a single step forward, clearing over half the distance between them. Seldik's heart raced faster. He could feel it ready to burst. His lungs were burnt from the expelling of the engagement, but he held firm, unsure where his bravery was coming from. His terror from the sight of these giants planted his quivering form at the mercy of the event.

The giant reached out a finger and outlined upon the small hide a circular path directly within the larger one Seldik had drawn. The giant's finger went within again to the center of the circle and pushed around for another central process. Seldik was able to see the giant's finger in the dark just enough to witness the act's creation.

"Brooof," came a sound from the giant's lips, and Seldik's head shot up so that it startled them both into taking a step back. Long moments passed before Seldik finally uttered his thoughts.

"Do you speak?" he asked but got no response. "Speak?" he asked again but this time he used his hand, gesturing from his lips, out, opening his fingers to designate sound leaving his mouth. The giant repeated this sign, saying, "Broof!" Seldik was amazed, and his party behind him, which remained quiet during this encounter, let out several gasps. The giant looked up at them in response.

"Speak!" Seldik said while repeating the gesture, but the giant only copied without another sound. Seldik became more amazed than scared, having to follow up on this incredible discovery. For if the beasts spoke, it proved that it was more than just an animal, it was a civilized one. Seldik recalled the giant's mark movements upon the hide and quickly grabbed his char pencil to trace out the circles and put its motions into writing. The beast then pointed at the combined symbols several times, opening his arms while he gazed around him. Seldik nodded his head as the giant repeated.

He finally realized the similarity; the giant used a combined symbol to represent their environment!

Seldik looked up, pointing at the hide, "Autumn! You wrote the season symbol here?" he asked, tapping the hide. Again, the giant swung one arm around horizontally in response.

"Seldik," Kolkesh spoke now, "Are those words it speaks?" he asked, still positioned some ways back from him.

"They know of our written language, Kolkesh!" Seldik told his friend, then lifted the hide to show them the three circles. Seldik turned his head to the side to speak without yelling, unwilling to turn around.

"He completed my circle to form the symbol for autumn." More gasps sounded from within the huddled party, but Seldik did not pay them any attention.

He quickly wrote the month spiral on the hide before turning it for the giant to view. Seldik realized the giants had incredible night vision, far superior to theirs. The giant nodded his head in approval, and Seldik could not believe he was communicating with an unknown form of a man in his very own empire's language. *It must be that somewhere in the past, they were known*, Seldik thought, thinking back to his Soul calling out to them as Skagg. *Could it be?*

"Skagg," Seldik repeated to the giant in a curious voice, still fraught with tension, but the giant only looked at him.

Another in the rear from him moved a step toward its leader and made sounds that the other paid attention to but were unrecognizable to Seldik. It sounded like a continuous coo or whoop melody that reminisced a song. The prominent leader nodded when the rear member finished its harmony and looked back at Seldik.

"Sssaagg," came a confirmation from the giant. Everyone gasped, including Seldik, for he had just confirmed an impossible revelation. The Skagg were, in fact, the mythical ancestors of his people. *How can this be?* The giant made another attempt to say the word, but Seldik could tell through their interactions that these giants could not speak well, so he continued to confirm this by drawing several other vital symbols of the environment: dashes of rain, darkness, and the sliver moon now setting higher in the night. The giant quickly approved all, and Seldik drew the peace symbol of reverse arrowheads as the giant continued to nod. Seldik bowed formally to show gratitude as he asked the giant to wait with an up-reaching, flat, outstretched hand. The giant held still, so Seldik slowly turned and stepped back toward his shocked party, who was intently watching the giant's every move. Seldik showed them the hide symbols, and all were amazed, but Kolkesh remained on alert.

"You feel we can trust them, boy?" Kolkesh asked.

"I do!" Seldik responded immediately, and Kolkesh shrugged. The others were still too cowardly to ask a question of their own.

"According to them, they are Skagg!" Seldik most interestingly got out, watching all the frozen faces of shock in the torchlight. "If so, we have met our ancestors!"

Edeldon and Nasok stared back at the giants in disbelief.

Sylic was the only one still waiting with a weapon in hand, eyes locked on them like prey. Seldik finally convinced him to lower his point, but he remained beside the group, quietly watching them.

"You walked out from us and said, 'Skagg brethren,' boy!" Kolkesh repeated, getting nods from the rest of the pack. Seldik looked them all in the face in a long sweep before speaking.

"I believe my Soul did that. I did nothing." Seldik let it sink in for a time.

Nasok spoke up now. "If it was your true Soul, boy, you are like nothing else we know of!" He said bluntly, leaving the idea hanging in the air.

Thinking of Nasok's words, it dawned on Seldik that his behavior did not fit any Soul Type. No Soul knew to call upon a mental resource to attempt communication in a situation that would generally produce pure conflict and, in turn, result in a truce. Seldik felt he might be overthinking his act. *Maybe it was just some form of courage like a War-Soul usually responds with.* He thought, then pushed the idea to the back of his over-excited mind to ponder at a later time.

"Whatever it was, they were the first here, if our teachings are correct." Seldik said, relaying a fact that all had forgotten. Kolkesh grabbed his chin but continued staring at the silent giants before him.

"Either way, you spared us yet again, Seldik. We are all in debt to you now," Sylic said, as Seldik wondered what would happen next.

Chapter Ten

ALEELAH

Aleelah basked in the hot spring pond that flowed from the Mother, the steamy breath floating off the water and into the frigid air like a cooking pot, sending the plumes to roll and dance as they countered the wicked temperatures and disappeared. Such was the start of Aleelah's day, enjoying the natural fuming of hot waters caressing her naked skin as she soaked up the mighty sun's rays on her face. Geysers of boiling waters blew up into tall blast jets, blocking the sun's rays with the steam that rolled off them just down the ridge every twenty minutes in a perfectly timed event. Aleelah used their reliability to clock her time there.

Their band found this majestic place as they moved deeper into the lands from the frigid north. Generations before her sought passage southerly, but vast distances of pure ice were all they encountered, and none returned with any news of better lands. Hundreds of years before, Aleelah's great distant parents found an opening in the ice that eventually led a southward group of them away from the freezing homelands, told to be covered with ice and having such short days that it was black most of the time. Aleelah, and all she knew, had never returned to that mythical land to see if the other tribes were still alive. *Who would go to such a place willingly?* Aleelah thought to herself.

Sitting not far above the massive lake, Aleelah gazed and drifted into deep thought of the world and how amazing it was here. *Why is nobody on these lands?* As far as they were sure, they were the first, not counting the mighty giants of the mountains to the west, that was. Aleelah wondered if they were as big and robust as the exploration party stated. *If so, where did they come from, and were they thinking beasts like me?* She had so many questions, but she was pretty sure such ominous warnings were fabricated, probably to keep those who stray too far from going into bad areas. For, from that direction came the rumbling sounds of Mother, her breath so strong it blew the ground into the sky. More quakes from underfoot have been quickening in the last year, and rumblings and deep moans have come from that direction, threatening to unleash maybe more than had ever been seen before.

Aleelah's band had remained some twenty years within the region they now occupy, but talk was growing that their time here was ending, and they would move away from the great warning belches of Mother. Aleelah didn't want to leave. This was her home. The elders talked of more considerable forests northward where they came from that has more water but less sun, and Aleelah wanted nothing to do with that. Southward promised more sun and hotter days, which she was inclined to see, but that still didn't negate all the beauty and perfection that was here. Beyond the lands they could travel in a year were giant lakes teaming with life within them and around them, linked by a never-ending line of water running in every direction. But to Aleelah, this was paradise, cut by mighty mountain ranges stretching between the lakes like islands. One could walk along them between lakes or quickly take a boat and ore across the lakes to distant valleys. Giant Sloths roamed quietly along the beaches, and herds of camels and horses roamed along, keeping the giant cats busy hunting the weak. Keeping away from the land paths of the herds assured a safer life; any animal out here could be deadly.

Aleelah spent several hours walking about the familiar hot pools as she gathered water reeds and other foods she was supposed to pick here and tied them into bundles. She decided to return, but realized she had been alone for some time. Her interest peeked. She hiked over the rough-covered boulders, rounded with mineral waters pouring out of their tops, blocking her view. Once past the line of nature's water-birthing rocks, she was within the outer salt-crusted sands covered in scrub grasses. To the edge were flat plateaus of covered black flat-sided stone pillars that her band said were Mother's poles lifted to the heavens. Between them were ravines where all things traveled along winding down little creeks surrounded by trees that combined to make their hidden gardens in the otherwise semi-arid landscape of the plateaus.

Aleelah heard a commotion beyond the flat sand plateau she now stood on, coming from the depths of the ravine between. As she approached, the noises became more rustled and unsettling, and she almost turned back to run toward the springs but heard the sound of what seemed to be an animal in pain, and instead, ran to the edge and looked down at the scene. Her bad sense told her to seek a better view, so she quietly headed to the cliff's edge to see where it was coming from.

The sight was unsettling. In the scrubby trees near the edge of the creek stood a pair of hair-covered rhinos poised with heads down and horns angled forward toward something cornered under the taller trees along the next plateau wall. The animal was large but outnumbered and stomping in fear of the encounter, dust bellowing up in great quantity from under the canopy, completely blocking any sight of the cornered. Aleelah didn't hesitate. Dashing toward the edge of the cliff face she stood on, she hopped from rock post to rock post on her way down to the encounter. Her heart raced as she focused on speed and balance, wondering what she would do when she arrived.

Racing onto the sandy earth at the bottom of the ravine, Aleelah sprinted back toward the encounter, happening in much more commotion, seemingly a direct contact struggle between the prey and the victim. Aleelah saw a long, straight branch break off of a tree by the cliff wall to her left, and she darted over and grabbed it while still running. Picking the most pointed end, she flipped it around as she came into the clearing and yelled as loud as she could. The rhino nearest her caught her motion and wheeled around toward her defensively. She immediately recognized the pair as somewhat younger, so intimidation may be her only option. The furthest rhino was deeper into the dark inset under the canopy where the trapped was scampering and fighting against it, but there was no way to know who was winning. Aleelah didn't hesitate and headed straight for the closest beast, screaming at the top of her lungs, branch now held forward to strike at the eye or throat of the beast. The rhino leaned back, raising its front legs, and backed into the other, who was pushed down on its back feet in the sands as it lost footing from the sideways hit.

She knew the first was worried and decided to run or fight as it happened. Aleelah pushed the fake and kept running full speed, waving the branch high then low to give the rhino's weak eyes the illusion that something much larger was coming at it. Just feet before she reached the beast, a massive pair of legs came from high out of the dark under the trees, and the cornered beast appeared to be much more significant than Aleelah initially realized. The gigantic legs were light colored in the gloomy dust-filled pocket of rock and trees, but they towered above the other rhino, now trying to stand up on its back legs again. Too late was the rhino as the towering legs directly smashed down upon its head, instantly plunging it to the ground in a lump, and the other tore off as fast as it could across the creek until it was careening through the tree line and out of sight.

The sudden attack and size of the hidden beast and the bolting of the rhino made Aleelah fall backward to the ground as she watched the cornered beast that obliterated a rhino stroll out of the darkness toward her. She tried to get up, kicking back and leaning on the branch while keeping full watch of what she knew would now be her demise.

Stepping clear of the tree's high branches came the full-on form of a wooly mammoth, its massive trunk raised between tusks the width of two rhinos fully engulfing her sideways view. Its enormous trunk pointed up as it trumpeted a thunderous sound, warning all within earshot. Aleelah gasped as she dropped the branch and scurried back against a fallen tree that stopped her dead. The mighty elephant stepped forward, lowering its trunk where it now made eye contact with Aleelah's wide whites, scared she would be tromped on next like the dead rhino beside her. The mammoth rumbled the sands as it stomped, still furious and now incredibly deadly to anything in its path, and Aleelah was just feet away.

As the beast came forward from the bellowing dust, the form of the rider sitting on its back and the embellished headpiece across the mammoth's forehead came into view. The rider and Aleelah instantly locked eyes, and the rider screamed her name.

"Aleelah, are you okay? Rhinos attacked us! Did one hurt you?" The rider quickly jumped off her perch while the elephant still stood.

"Deneska, is that you?" Aleelah said quietly, still worried about getting squashed by the mighty mammoth just feet from her.

"Yes, Aleelah! Yes! Are you hurt, sister?" Deneska said in a panic.

"No, I don't think?" Aleelah was now looking about her fallen form, to be sure.

"I heard noises and thought it might have been you!" Aleelah now reached out as Deneska grasped her hand, helping her up.

"So, you took on two rhinos with this stick? Are you crazy?" Deneska screeched, realizing what her sister just did.

"It was all I could find on the way," Aleelah answered.

"You charged here with nothing? No weapon. Are you crazy?" Deneska repeated her question.

"You are the most incredible warrior I know, my beautiful sister!" Proclaimed Deneska. "Songs will be written about you someday, girl." Aleelah just stared at her, now back on her feet and brushing herself off.

"I doubt it. We will be in trouble. You and I were to be working here, not wandering around, getting attacked!" Aleelah reminded her.

"I was feeding young Blakely, my new hero besides you, Aleelah the mighty!" Giving Aleelah a smug bump on the arm.

"Is Blakley hurt from it?" Aleelah now worried about their friend.

"Nope, it never touched him; I was smart; I backed him right into that nook so both couldn't get to us, and Blakley could wait for the right time to show them who is the mightiest beast on the continent!" Deneska was revered for their teamwork.

"That was brilliant, sister. You did well. I was so worried you would be harmed. I had no choice but to attack," Aleelah said, now putting her hands on her legs as she bent, reeling in what had just happened.

"We had it under control. They were young, and Blakley didn't seem too worried," Deneska touted.

"And you know when he is worried?" Aleelah gave her a curious glance up.

"Yes. We have bonded, and I trust him," Deneska said matter-of-factly, and Aleelah just shrugged and walked over to pat Blakley's head and thank him for keeping her sister safe. Blakley seemed happy to see her and wrapped his trunk around her waist rather tightly, and they held each other for a time.

She finally patted him hard as she walked around, ensuring he was okay. Nothing was found, and they both mounted up quickly and high-tailed it to the geysers, where they snatched up the wrappings of vegetation and started the journey back to camp.

Chapter Eleven

A VOLCANO'S MIGHT

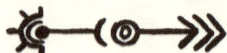

The parties of Skagg and Aquarionites finally managed to come together close enough to sit near the rock where the showdown occurred. The soldiers cleared the dead body from the perched area and began burial, the while the Skagg diverted their eyes. Seldik figured they felt little remorse for some intruder they knew nothing of at the time. After showing the Skagg their fire instruments, others gathered some wood that was sort and non-threatening, and they began a fire, which the Skagg sat at on their respective side. Seldik realized they used fire and were comfortable around it, another non-animal trait.

Several attempts for voice communications failed the same, except for grunts. They spoke poorly. Finally, several actions of hand motions and a blocking outstretched hand across the throat made it clear that they communicated less via vocalizations.

"They are mutes," Nasok finally gestured, using the empire's sign language. One of the Skaggs motioned yes from the leader's right side.

"This is why they probably communicate with written language," Nasok postulated. Much of the group engaged for hours, attempting a better sign language connection, and all had great success. Drawings on hides and ground were going around the fire. Names were becoming apparent, but before it was set who was who, they motioned to the leader in quick hand gestures that looked to Seldik as they had to leave easterly. The leader, now known as Mumot, motioned them on, and they got up and left abruptly, leaving him alone with them.

Mumot saw his new friends' puzzled looks and signed that something over on the east called their attention at a nightly event about the same time. They were with Mumot, and that was indeed plenty. Seldik was unsure of his interpretation, and the team members could not understand more, so the matter was dropped.

Mumot continued to sign but forwent food after the troops returned uphill and retrieved their dropped items. Hot foods were cooked and eaten, and wounds were tended while Mumot sat uncaring and occasionally tilted his head to the side like he could hear something they could not. Mumot went to urinate on a tree away from the fire's light and returned to the ground seat he had before. Seldik could not sleep, and Kolkesh ordered the others to get what they could. The Soul's remained up and highly focused on the continued interactions Seldik had with Mumot, and Nasok began dictating everything on his hides recovered from his dropped backpack. They were comfortable throughout the night, and some loud laughs were given that made no change to Mumot's disposition.

"The Skagg leader, it signed, was the third in leadership to be designated as the western border region's supreme leader and the last." Nasok wrote in his ledger, which he repeated to Seldik and Edeldon for confirmation.

Mumot, it appeared, controlled the entire western front, running several hundred Megarthy. He had related that he ruled hundreds of his kind, but now only a tiny handful were left. The rest traveled north decades ago to never return due to the climate heating up and warmth, not a place the Skagg do well in. Those few remaining were scattered on this mountain range, and one south had transferred the information that Seldik and his group were sailing up the entry lakes. Kolkesh was interested in the idea as it was his passion as a War-Soul to understand these things. Seldik had less of an interest in that and more in their origin.

Seldik relayed in hand sign language the Skagg's heritage. Mumot began a long, intense replay of their history in the Nether. They were friendly people, living in northern parts of the globe before coming to the Nether. The fact they were born "Small Ones" descendants was the knowledge passed down from their elders in ancient times. A discussion relaying how they, being old, were not compatible in the lands of the new children of Mother, and so they departed to find their own home far from everyone. This is how they found the Netherweir, which Skaggs call the Ahooniga, or Skagg's new home, a magic place left raw and ancient and a fitting home for them to continue their old ways of life anew. It had been that way for thousands of years. They were alone on the mountains and in the tremendous inner lakes, living in freezing and harsh conditions only the Nether seemed to project.

Along with the ancient animals who roamed, the vastness of the interior and the massive lifeforms swam the fresh waters of the lakes. Skaggs were not the tiny stature of smaller beings that seem to only come along now from Mother but of the last giant race from the distant past when something must have been different. Mumot relayed an unknown motion to this strange change and described their oldest stories were of even more massive giants the Skaggs themselves came from. He gave signs of names they were unable to understand of at least six different "tribes?" or "groups?" of these giants with whom the Skagg had wars and interactions with, not on the best terms.

Mumot motioned they had all been gone from the globe for time immortal, leaving Skagg as the dominant race. Seldik explained that this was all very close to his people's teachings.

Mumot surprised everyone in his next telling, catching even Kolkesh's attention. He began describing they were alone until some ten years back when another warring group of small ones came into their path on a lake-edge several days from where they are now. He signed that the small unknown group was startled by a two-person party of explorers hunting the draw, and spears were thrown at the Skagg, who defended themselves and killed several of their kind.

They were smaller than we were, Mumot signed, pointing at Sylic's thin stature to sign just short of even him. Sylic looked at Seldik to make sure that motion was not threatening but was relieved once Seldik shook his head no and went back to chewing jerk.

Nasok began a feverish communication to find out everything there was to know. Still, the fleeting situation only happened once. The separate parties left each other in haste to not make contact again. The small ones disappeared, as the Skagg were all warned what to expect if they re-encountered such folks.

It was one reason Mumot mounted the attack on their party, he described. He figured the two were the same if it was not for Seldik. Mumot signed the thoughtful action that stopped his group from destroying Seldik's.

Before bed, Mumot signaled that they all should heed the warning to remain vigilant for the Nether, its beasts, and this unknown new group of small people. Then they rolled up in their sleeping blankets to catch what sleep they could, trying to wind down from this incredible encounter. Thoughts of the Manoan's unseen faces coming in the pitch black to board Seldik's ship as the ships rammed together in great clapping sounds instantly struck fear into his mind.

A loud, thunderous clap jerked Seldik from within his warm ground blanket to the awakened state, and he sat up instantly. Almost black was the night, as the strangled embers of the dying fire at his side made him blink wildly, still shaking off reality from his dream state. He rubbed his eyes quickly to grasp what he was looking at. His mind settled on it being a dream that awoke him, but now, with eyes adjusting to blackness, he saw everyone dumping out of their bedrolls, grabbing armor and weapons in clanks only heard within the confines of the blackness of night. The air was chilled down Seldik's back, waking him faster. Realizing something was wrong, he stoked the fire with several logs to light up the area. Just as he grasped the blanket to join those already standing, a massive boom like the one he thought was in his dream sent everyone to the ground. The pitch was so deafening Seldik could only yell uncontrollably and clasp his hands over his ears as he buried his face in the dirt away from the noise. The loud boom relented just enough in mere moments to allow for the hearing of tens of quicker booming sounds echoing across the landscape on its tail.

Thunder was upon them, he thought, still screaming in shock but not even hearing his voice over the noises bent on consuming them all, his ears ringing with the effect. The dark images just out of the embers' light painted a terrible idea, as he could see everyone rolled around with covered ears as flat on the ground as he was, twisting and turning to escape the all-encompassing brutality that could only be from a beast above them as tall as the sky.

As quickly as the loud waves hit them, they settled into a pitching roar with thunderous sounds vibrating their hand-covered ears. But then the beast was upon them, Out of the North shot dirt, dust, and tree parts right into the group's camp area, instantly turning the black night into nothing but a wall of earth, impenetrable to the eyes and ripping out the fire embers, scattering all in camp to the winds. The winds were so strong they sent branches and sand flying, pelting the skin of everyone in camp, causing them to curl up in a ball as the only form of relief. Entire giant trees could be heard cracking dramatically at their bases as the soft crashing of falling trees echoed all around them. Winds howled to a pitch almost matching the low thunders of before and soon made the claps of noise seem background to the present shriek of gale force winds that threatened to pick Seldik up and sweep him away to the heavens.

Now, every part of his body struggled to cover his face and torso, trying to protect himself from a beast unable to be seen and so massive it must have decided to eat them right then and there. Dust was choking him and felt like blades across his exposed skin as it ripped by at unbelievable power and speed. All Seldik could do was hang on and wait for the end. Just as he knew all was lost, the ground slammed, hammered his body in jarring bursts, making dying in blackness so fearful that his body was shaking in terror. The same rock, so solid and ungiving, cracked and crumpled, and the buckling of it slid and threw his body about like it was the mountain itself that was coming alive and lifting heavenward to slide them off its back for good. Seldik now believed the beast's footsteps were so powerful that it needed only to put down its mighty paw once more and crush them all once and for all.

But the winds quickly waned, and dust was left overhead to angle down and begin covering them instead of blasting past. Now all was quieting down to slower thunderous booms and pulses of winds left from gasping origins, only flaring now to help compact the dust into ears and throats more. Seldik quickly yelled out for others, wondering who was left alive after the initial attack, only to hear nothing.

Seldik covered his head with his blanket and jumped up, wandering around, half crouching to bolt away or drop if the rumbling grew again or if the beast were to spot him. He passed through the camp slowly, feeling for anyone, anything left after the surprise but found nothing. He headed away from the sounds toward what he thought was the tree line and a rock outcrop that he remembered not far from the fire. It was pitch-black and dust rained down in all viewing directions. Seldik's eyes burned from the contact with the dry powder. He stumbled onto a giant log, and a standing tree fell on the ground. Skimming a foothold, he felt the softer blockage of movement that was, upon reaching down, someone's leg, which lay under the tree. Coughing out a call to its owner, there was no return communication, and he struggled to check its length to understand the position but found it very flat where the tree lay over it, realizing this person was now gone.

Stricken with the truth, he may be the only one left alive. He moved, feeling his way over branches along the tree to the thickest end, and heard moaning. He sought out the sound on all fours until he saw in a shallow depression the burly arm of the man he knew instantly as Kolkesh. He patted his face, yelling his name until, at last, Kolkesh mumbled a response. Seldik threw his blanket over him and dusted off his face, finally getting a grab on his wrist.

"Seldik, is that you?" Kolkesh's voice came clear.

"Yes! Yes!" He screamed back. "What attacked us so massively?" Seldik asked, still in hysterics, knowing the beast would soon finish them.

"That is no beast, boy!" Kolkesh grunted as he rolled and got to his knees, still coughing the dust violently from within him.

"That is Mother blasting from her mountains where I said we traveled on our first journey..." he continued coughing, "...where the floating rocks took our brothers!" Kolkesh finished.

"I heard those rumbles and felt the ground there. They were the same as now, but were much smaller."

"I saw Mother belching dust out of a large, pointed mountain in that same direction. It must be Mother now!" Kolkesh only snorted and blew out large volumes of snot onto the dry, dusty black beneath his feet.

Seldik was astonished at this but was relieved to know it wasn't a beast set on attacking them.

"Are you sure we are safe to look for the others?" Seldik asked, still frightful.

"No mighty beast is near?" Seldik offered as Kolkesh stood silent until the distant thunder was heard again, coming in a wave.

"Hear it's at a distance from us? It comes from that mountain string, I tell you" Kolkesh's reassuring voice made Seldik agree and begin the hunt for the others as soon as Kolkesh could stand.

"We must find everyone and then retreat from these falling clouds of dust. It is getting thicker on the ground. We will soon be covered and choke to death!" Kolkesh stated, pointing out a threat Seldik completely overlooked, a quickly rising layering already reaching past his ankles.

"This is soft and flat like snow!" Seldik noticed, grabbing some up to feel it in bulk. "It can easily choke us. We must cover our faces, then find shelter." Kolkesh said but was already moving away to find others. Seldik followed.

After much discomfort, they sloshed around, finding half-buried friends, wiping their faces clean one by one, then pulling them from the ash layer that partially buried them. One moan to another, the sounds of those recovering were followed in the blackness. Soon the second booming sound hit camp. Stumbling over branches lying everywhere from toppled trees, the rescuers climbed the crisscrossing jumble in the never-ending maze. Soon trudging toward them from the tree line were tall fire-tipped torches held by the remaining Skagg.

The torches soon lit up the gruesome scene, and nothing was as it once was when they had fallen asleep. Debris was everywhere, Cascades of floating ash made it surreal as a distant BOOM again came to their ears. Mumot led them all individually to the tree edge, where less dust settled until all were found and rounded up. All the Soul-Types were alive, but Seldik found one of their guards lying dead under a fallen tree. The survival rate of the group was remarkable, and many prayers were said while they sat together, tending to the various damages everyone received. Soon they trudged downward toward the south, following Mumot's command to take shelter at a nearby cave down-ridge an hour away.

The march was arduous; the path riddled with cracked and dying trees sprawled everywhere. They hurried over, then under them, as noises of more crashing trees could be heard echoing along the mountain face, succumbing to the weight of the ash.

The rest of the night was taken up in the march. Only a faint light of dawn crept through just as they reached the cave in a canyon far below. Everyone rubbed at their eyes, now dry and piercing from the ash scratching them and the burning in their lungs from the inadequate cloth they used for air filtering was overpowering.

The cave was a relief, as one Skagg was sent ahead to meet them with bloated skins of water, which were used to wash everyone's faces and drink their fill once seated. The cave was big enough to place them all with an angled floor unfit to sleep on, which is why, Seldik figured, Mumot did not bring them to it the previous night. No dust was falling within, and the combined torches gave the blackened ceiling an eerie shadow that cast along the bumpy surfaces. Seldik examined the ash, grey and without weight and texture.

Mumot explained this kind of event happened at times further north, reported by other sources of his kind. But never has it been this violent closer to the pointed mountains, he motioned. Mumot motioned they were hollow. Within them lived a fire bird of massive size, such that Seldik was sure his imagination envisioned was attacking them that very night!

They stayed there for the day as the ash continued to silently fall, but soon began slowing just as it reached knee level. Now no ground was visible. Mighty pines bowed heavily with the weight of ash that bore down on them, snapping along the otherwise quiet, spiny back of the mountain flank. The sun's light did not show through the very dark grey veil from high above.

Seldik began mixing some ash in a puddle of spent water used to wash someone's face and smeared it on the black walls. The grey finger markings upon the black rock were stylized images of the glorious event of the Netherweir. They depicted Seldik's interpretation of a bird in flight above them, showing a splendid view of the beast with a peaked mountain over it, blowing out dots of dust as their small camp was blown away by the winds as the ground shook.

Maybe fires burned fierce in the distance? Perhaps not, Seldik thought, but he drew the scene in detail from his imagination, giving him anxious relief from the event. He wondered the entire time what other things would happen to them in the forsaken lands of the Nether.

When completed, Seldik was delighted with his drawings. Others seemed impressed and mentioned that written form becomes a Soul of its own and gives the rock the power to be alive. All the witnesses were proud of the drawing, so eloquently combined in the scene—the native written work of their civilization. Seldik was pleased by the thought of displaying it, as he wanted this memory to endure the test of time for all who may stumble upon it long after he was no more on this forsaken land of peril. He had made the first record of his existence within the Nether. He could feel the power of the Soul forming into that story from his hands. He committed to writing down more indelible panels as his journey into the heartland of the ruthless Netherweir continued. *What if I never return to tell the tale myself?*

Chapter Twelve

MOTHER WARNS NO MORE

Aleelah and Deneska went back to the hot springs to relish the fight. They were soon laughing while reenacting each other's actions in the battle. After some hours, they finally began the long ride home to wind down from the crazy encounter with the rhinos. The hours-long trip lasted into the night, but eventually, they saw the outline of huts from the many campfires come into view when they crested the hill looking down into the low valley they called home. Blakely appeared uninterested as he continued along the well-worn path he knew led to fresh water and food.

"There is home!" Deneska spouted while raising her fists.

A deafening thunderclap erupted that made the elephant jump off the path and the girls scream as they covered their ears. They fought to stay mounted on the running beast as Blakley split off in an instant dash. The girls spun their heads around behind them off to their left to see the incredible sight of the entire mountain being blown off high into the dark sky, paralyzing them with no words. The event seemed to take place in slow motion, and as such, a volume of land raised so high in the air made them both gasp. Below the dark mass, brighter yellow, white-lit lava spewed upward, illuminating the mountain below. They quickly got the reins to halt the beast, but Blakley was pacing back and forth like he still wanted to sprint away.

"It is Mother. She warned us, but we are out of time!" Deneska yelled as the sweeping winds from the volcanic eruption came rushing in. Now constant noises in the air thundered past as rumbles were felt from below. The ground was trembling under them in wavelike bursts. The elephant decided to head to camp anyway, then took off, trotting briskly with the girls letting him do it.

"This is truly the end, sister," Aleelah said, now panicking.

"Let's get back to get what we can. We need to head away as fast as possible." Deneska shook her head as Aleelah spoke.

"Look, everyone is running from the village!" Deneska directed Aleelah's attention forward to the scene of the flight. They sped up Blakley as they tried to get home before all was gone. Time seemed to slow as they peered back at the now-encompassing plume of dust. Soon lightning was seen wrapping within the dark dust mushroom, which seemed to be halfway to them already. Some distance away, the lake in the foreground had become covered by white-water tops with high, violent waves slamming into each other as they peaked. The entire landscape was chaos. Birds flew in droves over their heads, and beasts of all types were herding in mass, coming toward them to race from the onslaught of death. Both riders forced their beast along hard to reach the village. People unrecognizable in the distance were only lit by the village fires as they were seen running alone or in pairs, heading away to the northeast, carrying nothing.

As the beast and riders crested the last hill toward the village, the hefty thumps of the impacts were heard from a distance. They both instantly looked toward the new threat, determining what it was. Over the valley across the lake on the closest side to the mountain, fiery boulders were streaming in, impacting the ground in violent bursts of fire. The raining down of boulders slowly crept toward the violent white caps of the lake as the winds again reached the girl's faces in a rush. They watched through dirt-covered eyes in horror now as burning rocks hit the churning water in a wavefront met with vapor instantly spewing upward. Each impact on land spewed columns of dust and trees into the air like tiny twigs caught up in whirligigs. But the girls knew they were fully grown trees, hundreds of hands tall, that were being whipped about like reeds.

The mammoth was now in a dead run without the rider's assistance, and they soon realized it was impossible to keep or slow him on the trail. They broke right to head down a shallow path leading away from the chaos. The girls quickly realized there was no going to the village now, as stones would bombard it in a short time. Aleelah grabbed her sister's hands and held them onto the reins tightly to know both would remain on the animal's back as it ran. The beast had surprising speed and grace, quickly outpacing all her village friends, and running in stride away to the east, far off in the distance into the darkness.

"Our Mother!" Deneska cried, but Aleelah held the reins firm. knowing it was what she would have wanted, for her to keep Deneska and herself safe.

They rode across the entire plains into the low hills beyond the valley, the mammoth finally slowing to a gallop but still far faster than humans could move on their own. Aleelah knew their friend could keep this up all night, so they hunkered down for the long ride, watching behind them as the rock grew smaller, pelting where they had crossed. The larger stones made it to the valley past the lake, plummeting the village region with aggravated pulses of whistling and explosions. They instantly knew it had killed anything or anyone left there, the many older villagers, the herd animals that were cor-ralled. Their fates were sealed already. They could not help anyone.

The dark plume in the sky covered the riders and their trusty mammoth, making it pitch black as ash fell like rain. The lightning soon ended behind them, making travel more dangerous. They walked for hours with Blakley to keep their journey onward. The ash poured down, covering all the ground, making finding their way difficult. Eventually, both dismounted to guide Blakley along to avoid pitfalls. Several times, they stopped to wash down the beast's trunk with water from the Boada bag on his side, knowing it was the last good water they would find for some time.

The girls wrapped their faces with materials to breathe through, but nothing could be done for the mammoth except to stop and give him drinks and wash his eyes. Soon darkness was total, making it so they could not move. Aleelah told her sister they would harm their friend if they tried to push on. Trees were scarce, but they soon came across a very tall grove where no underbrush existed, the trees seeming to block much of the falling ash. They led Blakley into the center and removed an enormous tarp from the pack strapped to his side, which they set up at an angle to shield them. It was enough to put Blakley's head under. They sat him down, then watered and fed him from the bundled vegetation Aleelah gathered what seemed like a lifetime ago, but it was just the last morning.

They lay listening to the rustling of branches releasing the ever-piling ash off their brows. Puffs fell, threatening to collapse the canopy several times, but both girls repeatedly beat the piled-up weight from the shelter. They fell asleep leaning against the side poles that would wake them when the canopy sagged too much. As it did, they awoke to clean it, then slept again.

The girls woke to the hellish, dull wasteland that stretched before them, so they packed up to set off in the snowing ash. Soon there was rain, which stuck ash to every part of their bodies, weighing down their forms as they marched. Guiding Blakley along was too dangerous for him in the deep ash layer, so they continued to kick through it.

They walked away from the mountain through the day, but it was getting darker again, so they found a better area in trees toppled against a cliff face in a big wash to camp. The mud on their mouth coverings choked off their air, so they had to succumb to breathing without them, which seemed okay as the rains kept the ash from entering their mouths. They again draped the tarp and then quickly fell asleep.

The rains increased through the night, but the tarp protected most of the party with the exception of Blakley's back, which was well covered in hair, so they weren't too concerned. The tarp shed glumps of sticky ash that slid off the covering, so they did not have to clear it like the night before. They slept, and by morning there was less ash and rain, but the ground was a solid mud pool. Nobody could travel easily without tripping or falling in unseen shallow depressions. Ash splashed up onto everyone's legs until it felt like it would set in place on them like mud cake.

The day's march was called off as they quickly returned to the tree-covered ledge to sit, uninterested in talking. They assumed that all who were there either got away or perished. They could not think of how many did either, but it saddened them. Not once had they run into any of their family or friends. They pondered if they were the only survivors, but neither would ask the question. Both knew their lives were over. They could never return to that land, as it would be covered in deadly ash for years.

Morning came a bit brighter, and though the ash plume went overhead to the horizon, ash was not falling on them directly. Only looking back toward the mountain was a wall of invisibility due to the ash suspended in the air. The team packed up and somberly trudged easterly in the soggy ash now packed down.

Ash rained several more times along the girl's journey, leading them to veer southward as the high plum seemed only to stream east. They figured southerly might get clearer skies if they traveled a few days. Their supplies were dwindling, marching daily, hoping their food would hold out until they were out of the ash. They ran out of food for Blakley the day prior. Water was down to just a day more, but they refused not to supply Blakley. They tried to set him free, but he just followed them, so they thought against it again.

A harsh, cold night on an open bluff was the best they could do that night, knowing they were done for if they didn't find ground without ash soon. The morning presented something better, a distant creek unmolested by the ash. They ran upon it, a fresh flowing stream with abundant foliage and fish, so they all broke away independently to scavenge what they could. It wasn't soon before Blakley was on the ground, stuffed with the water and the masses of food he'd consumed. The sisters were back together, building a fire, cooking fresh fish, and eating berries and grains they collected.

No wild animals were spotted since they saw them bolting away near the village, not even birds. Nothing made a sound. It was eerie with the ghostly silence. They decided to stay put, then continue south in a few days once they had their fill, deciding to await the hopeful occurrence of one of their villagers finding them, but none did.

Chapter Thirteen

A WATERY RETREAT

The next morning met the foreigners, a company of combined giants, ocean people, and a land dweller, in a gloomy grey-lit sunrise soaked in rains that commenced on the ashes heals. It remained down pouring since the night as the group moved down the now slippery slopes of the mountains to attempt to flee the sticky, soggy slosh of ash that embellished every inch of their clothing and footwear.

The descent was grueling, the pitiful complement belching complaints with every step. The rain was a mix of grey, muddy ash that clung to their forms until they were simply ghosts moving carefully along whatever pathway kept them from falling once more into the clotted soup they trudged through. No respite occurred. The relentless sentence of calamity was their only companion.

Finally, upon a cliff edge, lay a vertical ravine covered with mighty dead tree trunks, shielding the ground from the outside dampness. All were waved inside under the canopy with haste. After everyone piled in, a fire was attempted, but no branch would burn. The ash had been blown in under the trees. Seemingly, nothing could be set afire, so everyone scraped off what they could of the goopy clumps of ash from their tunics, rolling up to sleep where they were.

The morning was lighter than the previous day. Everyone stirred awake and fiddled for small food portions in their wrapped clothes' inner hiding holds. Mumot sat looking even more removed than usual, Seldik noticed. He wanted to ask more of the ash but knew Mumot probably didn't want communication, so he dropped the thought. He was underwhelmed. The ash and rain were grueling, and he was so tired that no sleep seemed to help. Soon Kolkesh and the other Souls were beyond the meager meals they found, and small talk commenced about their situation started.

"We can't go back. The mountain path is slick as snot on a porpoise's ass!" Sylic pointed out to them.

"Seems our only way is forward, away from this muck," Kolkesh said, disgusted. Edeldon, Nasok, Sylic, and Efy shook their weary heads in agreement. The remaining two guards kept to themselves, never participating in such discussions.

With seemingly uninterested intent, everyone stood to wipe away more semi-dry clumps from their outfits. Once Mumot exited the interior, everyone filed out into the awaiting dim day. The rain was just a mist, fanning out the surreal bands of unseen wind currents, drifting like a slow river surface past them like it was motioning them to follow, so they did. The muck was more condensed than the first day, not clinging, far reduced in thickness as the water tamped it down. Any rocks stepped on taught the travelers the combination was lethal, everyone taking a spill within the first minutes of walking. The path Mumot chose led them toward a dirt sidehill to avoid any rocks. The bruises gave the weary something to pout about on the slow, downward march throughout the day.

Almost everyone called lunch at once when a considerable mass of grasses lay piled up by smashed kindling. A fire was struck at once, with everyone chipping in labor until dried supplies were happily cooked upon the lapping flame tips. Everyone perched their outer garments upon sticks around the fire to dry, and a bit of excitement rose as hot foods were consumed quickly. The returning strength gave all hope as clothes were shaken off, cleaned, and everyone was again descending.

But the day was soon replaced with terror as a slow growl grew from the forest above them just minutes into the continuance. Mumot and Kolkesh responded with fists raised for all to freeze in silence to listen to the threat. All stood still, turning their heads uphill into the still-gloomy heights they had descended from. Creeping in agonizingly slow waves were creaks and snaps coming from left to right, high above them. Entwined in the breakage came gnawing and low rumbles that echoed past them in rhythms that made everyone cringe. Though seeming to come from far up the mountain, the pace was coherently quickening. Everyone quickly looked Kolkesh's way, and one by one, spelled out what all were thinking. "What is it?" or, "Do we dare take on something that massive?"

Mumot signed first. "It is the wet ash coming in a wave." Seldik understood as he stared at him in silence, wide-eyed.

Seldik snapped out of it with pure adrenaline. "It is the wet ash coming down the mountain!" he yelled to everyone as they broke into a downhill run, leaving Seldik stunned for a second before following.

It was a race that every man knew he could not win. Even as the fast-tumbling group scattered in all directions available, the high-above sounds grew more thunderous. Claps of boulder-on-boulder impacts could be felt as they shuddered the ground. The sounds grew closer so fast, Seldik knew it was flowing faster down the steeper decline, carrying with it rocks and trees with a wave of mud that would bury everyone before they could reach safety. The group spread, every man for himself. Some tumbled, left behind for a distance until the standing suffered the fate of falling as the recovered darted past them.

No screams or yelling were heard, and everyone focused on the headlong flight down the steep mountain finger they were on. After what seemed like minutes, the tree line broke into more sparse forest patches when the group found themselves in an open grass-filled pasture with less slope and better footing. The grasses were long, mixed with the ash dragged across from their running feet, and drug everyone down until the concession of slowing was forced into the minds of the fleeing.

As everyone rejoined closer together so as not to die alone, glances back made the observer's fears show more on their faces, pacing as fast as they could across the restraint of grass strands clinging to their legs. Behind them, whistles of air made Seldik finally look at his fate. Behind him, coming fast through the dense forest trees they just ran through, were splashes of ash waves that cracked against rock outcrops, sending whole trees flipping into the air, making a deathly whistle as they flew like small sticks thrown at rabbits as hunting weapons.

Rocks flew in violent bursts as they impacted other larger stones, the whole sight reminiscent of waves lapping upon a stormy beach. Still, these waves gurgled then sloshed unnatural and thick with froth causing carnage as they engulfed pine after pine. The forest behind was torn down in a thunderous procession, like mowing wheat with a sickle.

Seldik veered sideways as a giant tree was flung clear to where they were running, but landed further back than imagined. Seldik's eyes now snapped forward just in time to see Mumot, who was far outpacing everyone on the left side of the field, motion for everyone to follow him. Seldik found himself to the far right and had to run the furthest to catch up. At once, the group paced Mumot's way. Seldik felt even more fear come over him as he caught sight of the muddy wave breaking out of the tree line into the field he was now stomping sideways through as fast as he could.

Seldik could only trudge at the pace given by the grassroots gripping him while staring at the mighty wave. It was massive, tumbling down in a round frontal roll that looked like grey sand flowing. Trees stuck out and whipped the ground, tearing up the grasses as the wave consumed them underneath, showing the poor boy what it would do to him once it reached him. As the wave approached, Seldik almost turned away from the group. Only the kindred desire to be close to anyone in death made him stay the course as the wave showed its actual height, towering to the size of the pine forest itself. The noise was so close to his ears that he could smell the wet, ringing ash pungent in his nostrils.

Seldik had given up hope, but upon looking for the group he would die with, he realized they were nowhere in sight, as he was now where they were last seen. Frantic, Seldik charged with hands and feet, leaping forward with every bit of strength he had left, hoping for a miracle to happen that would save him, and it did.

Just as Seldik breached the edge of the curving grass-covered bluff, it sloped almost vertically, and at once down, Seldik rolled uncontrolled. The impacts blurred his vision, but he could see he was careening toward what looked like the edge of the world, and then he was falling.

Seldik felt the impact of the water, and all went black. When he came to, he saw the blurry vision of Mumot looking down at him. As he blinked to clear his eyes, he realized he was adrift in his arms and relaxed back into the blackness. After some time, Seldik finally realized he was lying on a shoreline with water lapping below him. He turned his head slowly, watching in close quarters as the lake water came to and from his form in peaceful precessions that relaxed him. Suddenly, his body felt terrible. A wave of sickness swept over him as he desperately turned onto his side and vomited copious amounts of water from his stomach. As Seldik coughed the burning waters remaining out of his lungs, he felt Kolkesh place a hand on his arm.

"Steady, boy. You're okay now!" Kolkesh said in visible distress.

Seldik tried to talk but coughed for some time as Kolkesh excused himself to help others. Once Seldik could sit up, he realized a massive wound was in his abdominal area. His left shoulder also screamed in pain when moved. He noticed a long stick protruding from his side clear through to his left. Luckily, he knew which way he rolled.

Though his shoulder screamed in pain when lying on it, he did not move until Kolkesh returned. At once, they had three people next to him, tending to his impalement as he carefully broke the stick at his back near his ribs. The slight vibration was enough to make him wrench with pain. Seldik grabbed the sap someone had made, then smeared it on both sides of the wound around the stick. Just as he felt numbness grip his side, Kolkesh pulled the stick out, holding the entry point tight. Seldik thought to scream, but it was stuck in his throat, along with his air from the intense burn of the effort. Then he blacked out.

When he came to later, he was on his back, covered by a blanket and feeling numb in the regions he had hurt. Looking around, he saw the bent heads around several rock stacks by the sand's end, realizing they had lost some friends in the event. He, too, said his blessings where he lay until they were walking to him.

"You see we lost some?" Kolkesh said softly. Seldik nodded.

"It was Efy and our last two guards. May they move onto their next life in peace!" Kolkesh raised his fist from his chest upward, and the rest followed his prayer.

"You still got me, I'm afraid, but just barely" Sylic came behind them and smiled fiercely at Seldik. "Well met, Sylic," Seldik smiled back, still coughing.

Chapter Fourteen

NEW FRONTIERS

Aleelah and Deneska traveled southward, Blakley in tow, awaiting days for anyone else to find them. But alas, they gave up hope, packing the new foods with all the fresh water they could carry on Blakley, then sadly continued in the only direction that promised life.

"Oh, you believe our family lives, don't you, wise sister?" Deneska said with the tear-lined eyes they both had many times since they were now forbidden from the lands they loved.

Aleelah shrugged her shoulders and held them high. She had answered this question this way several times now.

"Oh, sister, what have we done to deserve this? Mother destroyed us all!" Aleelah, seeing a complete breakdown, grabbed her up as they walked close together for a long time.

Aleelah pondered the thought. *What if we are the only ones left?* All her family, friends, and everything she knew were gone instantly. The idea was still unbearable, but it may be true, she decided. She thought northward may have been good, too. *Maybe some went that way before the rock.* Her thoughts quickly drifted in another direction, unaware of the horror of the flying rock pounding everything to bury it forever. They walked on, each thinking about the calamity and their future, being alone in a strange land.

The little group soon found camp, repeatedly traveling further from their now-destroyed homeland to unknown territory each day. They shared small talk, avoiding anything about their kin's outcome. Their mother, grandmother, and brother were all missing. Hundreds just vanished; they dare never think about it.

The gloom was behind them, still visible in the sky but no longer shadowing the sun from warming their skin or choking their breath. Soon their feet were on the natural ground with only skiffs of very fine ash. The group, even the elephant, had several red lesions where the skin was chaffed, ground in ash, and tormented for days. Salve was the necessary medicine, which they applied to everything. The elephant's eyes were the worst, but his breathing was harsher for some days, causing them to take breaks, knowing the beast needed more rest as its lungs cleared. He had not trumpeted since that day, so they knew he was terrible.

Days had passed, and they had not kept count, but assumed it had been nearly a week. Aleelah remained to look strong for her sister. She knew any sign of confusion or delay would trigger Deneska into a mental wreck. But soon, they were through the higher lands that resembled home, dropping into increasingly bigger and bigger valleys. Soon they breached a low saddle in tall mountains. What lay before them was breathtaking.

"Wow, look how big that lake is!" Deneska stated, taking the sight in. "There are no ends to it," she added as they both looked up, then down the valley. From horizon to horizon, the valley was filled with never-ending water.

"Well, at least it looks clean, so that is where we're headed," Aleelah stated, and they headed toward it.

"Look, there are herds of beasts there and there, with more mountains covered in snow on the other side of the lake," Aleelah said after spotting them with her keen eyes.

Deneska clapped her hands in happiness, touching Blakley's face and telling him what he would love about the valley.

"We may live here, Blakley. Our new home, right, sister?" Aleelah gave her a fake smile, trying to hide the knife's edge in her gut at the thought of home.

"We will see. There is a long way we should go to find the best spot," said Aleelah, realizing they must build a village alone. With no others, it will be a single hut for the two. A somber feeling came over her that she kept to herself.

They camped at the mountain's edge as they descended. They were building a big fire while talking of washing themselves in clear water finally. They rolled up, falling asleep quickly, their first solid sleep in a long time. In the morning, they were up with the sun warming them. Supplies were thrown into haphazard storage as they were just too excited to care, then set off immediately toward the lake. Birds chirped, others flocked by in groups so big it blackened the sky, and the giant rabbits, waist high, ran in all directions. A few smaller, striped dogs watched them from a ridge a long way away. The huge bison herds were everywhere, in dark dots to the horizon. The intruding girls slowed their pace, taking about all the fantastic new sights in. Other types of elephants were in big herds alone, but Blakley showed no interest.

They could see untold numbers of floating birds upon the waters stretching in all directions along the edge, in flight showing wings longer than their elephant was. Giant fish leapt into the air, catching birds mid-flight, dragging them into the depths. The girls noted to avoid those deeper waters.

Miniature horses ran as unrecognizable predators chased them into trees toward the mountain. High above, carnivorous birds soared with the size Aleelah knew could pack a person away. Single sloths, more giant than huts, roamed alone between them all, not allowing any friendly herding as usual.

They reached the water's edge by midday, stripping Blakley of his saddle and headgear. The girls stripped down, grabbed soaps, then dove in the frigid waters, with Blakley running in to shower them all. They yelled, screamed, and cheered for the first time. It was a new beginning for them. Soon the cold forced them out, leaving Blakley to his fun. They moved up the beach, founding great wood and cover, so they set camp with a roaring fire. Blakley returned to them. Soon, all were feasting on food, finding a small creek near-by that provided water. They ate the dried foods, deciding this might be the place to stay. By morning they were repeating the cycle, and by midday were both out fishing, catching giant sharp, toothy fish with pink meat.

"What about it, sister? This is it!" Deneska said happily, with no other care in the world.

"We should move down the valley a few days, just to see what we're missing; we can always come back; it looks mostly the same," Aleelah was uncaring if they found nothing; she felt moving made them feel better in the end.

"You're all about working, Aleelah. Take a break," Deneska snapped back. Aleelah glared at her. Starting a fight right now was not a great idea. Nerves were still raw from their losses.

"You will mind your tongue. I will not deal with you angered. If you don't like my thoughts, then ride Blakley. I'll walk us down there," Aleelah snapped back loudly.

Deneska got the hint and shut her mouth, wrapping into her bedding and grunting. Morning set neither's mood any better. Storm clouds had put in, and the constant movement of herds past them made them uneasy, since cats prayed on such. Aleelah tried to clarify that they should not be in the middle of herding lanes, but Deneska was set on not talking, so they packed everything up and followed Aleelah's plan, heading along the beach south-ward again.

They wandered out onto the shallow shoreline several times, seeing big groups of hunting cats. Knowing the cats hated water, they passed by with weapons in hand and Blakley at the ready, keeping an eye on them as they went. Several came too close to investigate, and Blakley smashed the water with his front feet, giving the cats a reason to beat it out of their immediate proximity.

"I told you. We are now in the middle of them. We can't camp anywhere here," Aleelah chastised her sister, who agreed.

"We walk on. Let's make fire sticks," Aleelah continued, stopping by a big pile of branches.

The girls set to breaking and gathering sticks. They wrapped the tops with grasses they had soaked with the fish drippings they cured and had them ready to light. Aleelah got their striking rocks out and put them in her clothes for instant use when they needed them. They affixed the sticks to Blakley for now. He was trained not to care about fire sticks lit on his back at night. They were ready to hike for a long time. They stayed resting until dusk there, knowing in daylight they were safe with all eyes watching for danger. It was the coming nights that would be the problem. The night inevitably came as they started the endurance hike through the dark.

Soon it was pitch black, as no moon hung, which meant little was out hunting, but something may still be. The girls armed themselves, then lit the sticks. Aleelah helped Deneska mount Blakley as she agreed to the offer. They burned three firesticks, saving the others for later in the night when these would fail them. The march was on and off, Aleelah stopping them often when she heard noises. One such time, they came right up on dark forms with glowing eyes right before them, and panic set in. The beasts took off every way, bolting, as Blakley reared and almost threw Deneska. In the skirmish, they realized it was a group of bison that got spooked off, then they continued. But Deneska quickly realized they had lost two of their remaining fire sticks into the lake during that event, but they were too far from them to go back. They continued until the sticks burned down, lighting the remaining two. They moved on, knowing only hours were left of them.

After hours of marching, Aleelah called it. They must head uphill away from the lake to find shelter and a defensive position. Deneska jumped down as they headed toward the grasses with trees dotting the landscape. The long shadows of the rocks in the brush played tricks on the girls in the dying flame. They found a dead tree, so they decided to set camp there. They built a brush pile with the big stump lit to burn high. Aleelah felt it was enough to ward off the hunters, but her hopes were soon crushed as it began to rain. The weak wood would only smolder and then stay lit by small areas of flame. Terrible smoke rolled out, which was good too, but not enough to last the night.

The girls put Blakley closest to the smoldering wood, sitting near him as he refused to lie down. They had two weapons, each now out at the ready, a spear and a small axe. The almost useless fire sticks propped out in the dirt helped little. If the fire went out, they would be helpless. Soon, it smoldered down, where virtually no visible light was emanating from the debris, as Aleelah stood up after hearing a relatively close scratch on a tree.

"We go now to the water. Mount Blakley. Now!" Aleelah said, not waiting for her sister's response. She grabbed the stump's most significant piece of fire left burning to hand up to her sister.

"Ride to the water, then get him in it. We will ride him all night to keep him warm." Aleelah jumped up on his back, and Deneska prodded the beast toward the water.

They were almost to the lake, with the light hardly helping, but it did what it needed to do. It lit up the glowing eyes of three giant dire wolves directly in the way of the lake. Blakley snorted loudly and stopped instantly. The wolves were growling loudly and began to surround them.

Chapter Fifteen

IMPOSSIBLE STROKE OF LUCK

Seldik recovered slowly as the remaining group camped at the shoreline, where they beached after the fall from the cliffs. Mumot was questioned about how he saved them by jumping off the cliff, and he signed that he had been along that ridge, knowing below it were deep, rushing waters that headed down to the lower lake they were on now. He had hoped the waters would wash them away before the ash buried them, then they would be swept into the lake's inlet in calmer waters a long way down the valley. He was unsure if anyone had seen him gesturing, but everyone promptly thanked him. All but Kolkesh, who had stayed extra time hunting for Seldik but not found him, finally jumped, leaving him to his fate.

"I saw everyone and Mumot," Seldik broke in, "but everyone was gone, and I didn't realize until I was tumbling down that it was a cliff," he said, and all fell quiet before he spoke again.

"The wave was so big, so loud. I didn't know if I would make it…." Seldik broke off, weeping softly, still trying to cope with how close the horror was to him.

"The one above, young Seldik, spared you. Your journey was to not end there. Even behind the rest, you were spared. Be at peace with the past," Kolkesh said with compelling words. Seldik sniffed up his running nose, then nodded his head in agreement, understanding that the only way he survived was by the grace of the great creator himself.

Sylic, Nasok, and the others told their tale of getting to the ledge and fighting for breath as they were flushed down the raging river. Seldik's mind wandered off, mixing reality with the past and letting the terrible weeks flow through him now. He shook at the daydreams that played in his mind as the others spoke their truths. Kolkesh finally noticed and sent him to bed after getting more salve on his wounds to deaden them.

Morning came on the week's end as the lake had turned to a putrid brown and grey. All the fish were washed up on shore, some forty hands long with giant gills fronted by barbed teeth protruding from enormous mouths as long as Seldik's body. They harvested them, and the meat soon dried in long rows of endless fires fed by the dead trees on shore. The entire surface of the lake was covered in logs. This led to talk about how they would get around it without a water passage. It was decided they would soon have to abandon camp to move southward and look for a way around the lake. The stench crept in the breeze by the third night. The smell became unbearable. They broke camp before the sun rose, as no sleep could be had with the smell. All were hiking by fire sticks along the dead, decaying beach. Along the way, giant animals of all types lay bloated, swept along by the same course the trees took. Not one living thing was in sight, and they soon realized that no good water would be available for a long time.

Chapter Sixteen

THREE AGAINST THREE

"AAAAYYYYAAAAAAHHHAAAA," yelled Deneska in a war cry that Blakley was trained for, reacting instantly to the threat. Aleelah was already sliding off his slick, rain-covered back, letting Deneska take the fight at them with the beast in full war mode. Immediately, as Aleelah hit the sands, Blakley charged the formation, scattering them every which way into the blackness of the night. Aleelah was quick on his heels, spear up. She was ready to fight any coming from behind. She knew how the wolves moved. They would attack from all directions, one being at the back. She was sacrificing herself for them to get into the water. Deneska shouted to sweep as the elephant started thrashing its massive tusks back and forth, catching one wolf too close and smashing it into the dirt. Blakley gave one big smack down on the neck of the creature, and it was broken into the sands instantly, seen in the piece of a flickering fire. But the delay had one on his back, coming right at Aleelah in the pitch of black, almost before she could point her spear with the waters rolling off her face. She rolled out to the left, thrusting her spear where she thought the head was as its teeth gaped wide open, attacking the hind end of Blakley in stealth. Aleelah caught it square in the ear as she followed the thrust through hard, cracking the stick in half as the beast fell dead to the ground. In the frenzy, Aleelah had impaled her leg with the spear's broken end and screamed as she went down. Deneska turned, not seeing her sister. She yelled a spin command, Blakley flailing his tusks as he stomped in a turn that brought him around to face the danger. Deneska waved the tiny fire-tipped wood forward to see her sister dropping to the ground beside the beasts.

"Stomp! Stomp!" Yelled Deneska in succession as Blakley started raising and stomping the dead beast's wet head into the sands like its kin. Deneska yelled for Aleelah, who motioned she was alive.

"Left! Right!" Deneska shouted as Blakley swung his tusks from one side to the other, prepared to head on the remaining wolf.

"A spear!" Aleelah yelled as Deneska threw hers down beside her sister.

Just as the spear hit the dirt, Aleelah saw the third wolf through the shimmering droplets from the failing flame's light, attacking Deneska on the other side. She screamed while pointing.

"Watch out!" Aleelah yelled frantically, seeing the beast lunge from Blakley's blind right side for his leg.

"RAISE" Deneska ordered, just as the enormous gaping jaws of the wolf were reaching out for the elephant's front leg. Blakley followed the order instantly, rearing up on his massive back legs, making the wolf miss and overshoot right under the raised legs of the elephant. Blakley didn't need the command to stomp, coming down instantly with all the tons of weight he could bring, hitting the back of the wolf, now entirely at the mercy of the mass above him. Immediately the crushing bones of the wolf were fracturing the night, and the enormous feet of Blakley flattened the wolf's chest. The dog gasped as the air from its lungs was forced out in a rush, then the beast's open mouth fell to the ground, still open, tongue lying out in the dirt. Aleelah was already on her feet, lunging the new spear into the eye of the beast just in case she didn't see all the damage.

"Right," Deneska screamed as she again turned Blakley to where the threat came from. They formed up, Blakley stomping and grunting, ready to kill more. They stood, Aleelah near the dead wolf's corpse, soaked from rain, with a spear at the ready, staring to the opposite side as the mounted pair faced northward. But no more motion was seen or heard as the fire flickered away. They quickly backed into the water, where Aleelah crawled up on Blakley, and her sister wrapped her injured leg.

The rains gave up an hour later, not growing in intensity. The mounted pair rode along, just enough to keep Blakley warm since he was in the water, but they all soon began to shiver. They walked another hour, quickening, then slowing him, but the shivering continued. From then on, they decided to walk him close to the water's edge, ready to dart into deeper water at a moment's notice to avoid him getting too cold. The shivering finally stopped, but they ran into debris, making obstacles unseen, so Aleelah called a halt. They came aground, sitting on both sides of Blakley, keeping what guard they could. No noises came, and the light finally showed on the horizon when they realized they were in a vast grassland that spanned several Megarthy, with no sight of animals anywhere nearby. They slept at the ready until the sun warmed them. Even Blakley lied down to nap until they stirred alive, then checked the elephant for any injuries. Blakley did get a scratch on his foot from the tooth, so they quickly cleaned and sealed the wound, but Aleelah's wound was tender, having some infection. They washed thoroughly then salve-coated it well, but no materials for a fire were nearby. They realized they were headed into a swamp area that filtered into the lake, which looked to be a long distance to go around, but they had no choice. So Aleelah mounted the giant this time for the hike.

"That was close. We should be dead," Deneska spoke. Aleelah couldn't agree more, three against Blakley and them—bad odds!

"We used our skills, and Blakley was magnificent." Aleelah patted Blakley, who quickly brought up his trunk to her, knowing she was injured.

"He is amazing. Without him, we would already be gone." Deneska realized they had the ultimate weapon in their group.

"We must find shelter, as the moon will be up soon. We can't do this with us tired and wounded." Aleelah spoke about what Deneska was already thinking.

The tiny group finally made it around the large part of the swamp, coming to a big, broad river. The ravine it was in had promise, as they crossed the river low, then followed it inland until they came across a gravel bar cliff with big rocks around it and dead wood falling all around from the top. The girl's setup covers using Blakley to lift a supporting trunk over two rocks. They covered it with more small sticks, which gave them a solid roof to put the tarp on. They built two massive fire stacks by the enclosure entrance, where they pushed sticks into the ground to seal off. They fished the river, catching some bottom suckers that provide great energy. They let Blakley forage in the high grasses, all settling in for a lovely night, feeling secure for once.

"Where are we going to go, Aleelah?" Deneska finally asked as they watched the fire after sundown.

"I don't know. Further south, I guess," Aleelah answered, knowing they could not stay here.

They fell asleep, taking turns keeping guard, and Blakley slept very soundly.

Chapter Seventeen

CLEAR WATERS

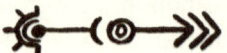

The days of traveling along the death stench of the shoreline were arduous. Nobody had fresh water anymore, and the putrid smell of rot and decay was becoming unbearable. The Nether had deemed them not worth of her lands and launched an unprecedented war upon them. They had lost over half their men, sent to join the countless Souls of the parties before them. Seldik's wounds were healing, but they needed to keep going, so he pressed on with pains he knew prevented them from healing fast. Kolkesh seemed to take it all in stride, along with Mumot, but the others seemed worse off than even Seldik.

Much debate about what they should do occurred each night, but their paths were committed southward around the lake. But the lake stretched forever, and only the thinning of debris and rotting fish led them to believe they were putting distance between them and the terrible conditions behind them. Looking back, the giant mountain with the ever-pluming ash ejecting from its throat was still the same distance it once was. By morning, they decided they would walk all night because they must find an end to this lake and its stench. All agreed, and Seldik hid his pains as best he could to look strong.

As night began to fall, they could see the lake's ending ahead of them. It was more choked up than the beginning of the lake, with logs stacked so high in all directions it looked to be an impassable area. They reached the sight by sundown, but it was too bad to move through at night, so they set camp grungily.

"You are holding up, kid?" Kolkesh asked, obviously worried. Seldik assured him he was.

"We might be at the end of this ugly lake now," he said, pointing out the timber piles to Seldik, who nodded.

The group made a fire to sleep again in the stench, and the breezes blew down from the north, bringing in the stench so thick, one could almost walk on it. But they survived the night to start moving through the mess of tangle at first light, without food and water, but the smell had everyone too sick to care. The trees bogged down the group, but they found a narrow area that looked good to cross with trees, making a bridge over it suitable to walk on. Soon they helped each other across and found themselves in much better conditions on the other side. The stacked trees kept the river below cleaner, but the waters weren't usable, so they moved down to find a tributary. Another day without water had them all ambling along with no talk until they set camp again. No fire was lit, however, only tired guards were posted. The night was pitch black, with no moon, and the deafening quietness made everyone uneasy and restless.

Morning couldn't come quick enough as they set off, yet the little hope of finding water seeming to fill their minds. They walked for a way, but Mumot soon sniffed the air, motioning for them to head more easterly. They realized he might be able to smell the water, and they followed with obediently. They were crossing dry, arid lands, and everyone wondered what they were doing. But as Mumot quickened his pace, the excitement grew as all tried to keep up. Soon there was a long rag-tag line of survivors trudging along, each kicking up dust clouds. Seldik and Sylic took the far rear as they lost ground. Nobody cared to check on the others, keeping their heads down to follow the foot tracks of the leaders in front and coughing dust from their scratchy, parched throats. It was a long, grueling hour before everyone in front of the rear guard vanished from view. Sylic clung closer to Seldik as they marched on. Once they, too, got to the peak of the high plain, they were greeted by a view so amazing they gasped. Below them, the warn trial of man and giant was leading downward to a plush, fertile field in a wide ravine that was teaming with life. The crook of a bow in a central river was seen dancing with reflected light between the thick trees shading its path along the floor. The two looked at each other with wide, cracked, split lipped smiles as they started their awkward march down.

Mumot had reached the water first, outpacing the others easily. But Kolkesh, with the beat-up team, soon joined him as they splashed and waded into the water, drinking large volumes before stripping to wash. There was no more a stench in the air or a piece of ash. They played, washed, and splashed until Seldik and Sylic finally emerged to join the party. Once everyone drank themselves full and washed their wounds clean before re-wrapping them, a fierce fire was built where the dry, unusable foods quickly became the central theme of happiness. They devoured almost everything, belching and laughing with still dry, haggardly voices injured from the desiccation. They formed an excellent camp, then fell asleep with large fires raging on every side of them. Mumot chose, as always, to stay outside the fire ring, as he blended into the environment so well nobody could see him, but his rather foul odor, even after washing, came through on a breeze now and again, showing he was close at hand.

In the morning, the entire group set out to hunt all worth eating. Finding hares and lizards the size of one's arm, they amassed a large volume of food others were quickly cleaning and dehydrating by the coals of the night's fires. Mumot carried in a massive deer with horns taller than Seldik stood. They butchered it to eat on the first night. The horns were broken into tools usable for weapon making. Metal tips of small knives were shown to Mumot, who was impressed with the firm, heavy substance, but he would not receive one as a gift, opting for nothing as a weapon or tool to carry. Everyone was happy, and Sylic even sang them a song from his homelands.

They all complained greatly of no alcohol, but the water was excellent. Even blood soup, which was new to several, including Seldik, tasted great. Pelts were scraped down, and bones were broken up for the marrow from within to be sucked out. Volumes of fat were blocked out, and soaps and face paints were made with charcoal drippings. Many adorned their faces as they danced around the nightly fires.

They remained in the camp for days, and for the first time, Seldik felt more like a man and less like a child. He was necessary, he now realized. Maybe, just maybe, his father was right about this adventure, he thought. Seldik thought of his father often, just short thoughts of if he was okay or if more war had come to CED. He was sure they were alright, though. He knew he must stay focused here if he ever wanted to return to the city. But Seldik had a slight reservation when he thought of returning now. *What will I do after this? Will I find my purpose, my Soul's destiny, and travel elsewhere? Is something deep down telling me something different? Do I belong here?*

However, the near-death incidents stood paramount against that, so he wasn't so sure. But he had survived it all so far. Still touching his tender side and shoulder, he somehow felt more connected. Seldik looked up, eying all his new friends, some odd, some far stronger than him, then Mumot, who broke the mold of what he knew existed in the world. But together, they had accomplished the impossible, something they would never have been able to do alone. *This means something,* he thought. *But will it last? Will we travel inland and find the resources Kolkesh told us we were there for?* He felt they just might, but with what had already happened, Seldik knew they would find much more than they expected.

Soon the party was over as they planned their next direction, knowing north was out of the question for some time. They decided to travel inland more, pointing out that before them was the long-off mountain range, white with snows so deep nothing else was seen on them, and so high no trees existed. They decided to reach the mountains at sunrise.

Chapter Eighteen

DEARLY DEPARTED

Aleelah and Deneska decided to break camp to head southward as the ominous, white-covered mountains to the east seemed insurmountable. They awoke and then packed up the mammoth, who showed no care about anything they ever did. The girls walked with the beast following them as usual, hiking back down to the lake before continuing southward with the marsh to their backs. Far from the edge, they could still see giant fish, more significant than their mammoth, jump into the sky to grab what must be birds.

"I don't want to go into that lake, sister!" Deneska stated in awe.

"Me either. What are those things? Giants?" Aleelah was at a loss for words.

"We have plenty of fire sticks this time with stronger weapons made. I'll take my chances on land." Deneska patted the side of the mammoth where a thick pack of spears was hung at the ready.

"I believe we need to go around this lake toward those mountains further south" Aleelah was deciding what direction was best, left to the big mountains or right toward other smaller rolling mountains that looked too close to the eruption chaos.

Deneska, glancing to the west, could see waters flowed down southerly the way they were going, agreeing it was probably ruined to the west.

"So, we follow the lake, get around it, then see if living conditions improve toward those mountains." Aleelah was relieved they had a good plan for the first time since becoming outcasts in this strange part of the land "And fewer predators too." Aleelah added, looking at Deneska, who was already nodding her head.

The two thin wisps of girls hiked steadily on, seen in the distance by hidden beasts observing them. They seemed just twigs shimmering in the scintillation of the sun's rays beating off the ground. No more delicious than a dry stick to the lurking creatures. Shortly behind them strolled the massive haunches of the woolly mammoth, oppositely seen by the tooth wielders as too big to take down quickly in any attack not dealt at night in stealth or concealment for an optimum surprise. Nothing gave them problems while they crossed the landscape and disappeared over the horizon.

For days, the tow hiked less worried about predators as the lake turned into a giant river flowing slowly with larger tree-covered banks that strayed up the hillsides where flood tides reached in lousy weather. Peaceful pools in large, rounded, grey rock swirled in and out of the primary current. The entire floor could be seen just feet deep. A gentle turn of the water meandered around solid, round stone boulders and the base, that had been eroded from the eons of water, was of the same solid rock.

The girls rested Blakley, then strolled out into the pools, finding a solid rock so slick and smooth you could slide over it on your feet. They crossed the waters, then called for Blakley from the opposite bank. He walked across, bathing as he went with his trunk filled to the brim with fresh water, lifting it high to spray his back with their supplies strapped to it. The girls laughed, then stripped down, and the elephant let them play in the pool with him. It felt like home, they both thought, the place they once called home so locked away in their minds that it was just a covering for the pain. But they would take it. The healing waters drowned out some of the bitterness of the significant loss of their family and friends. Blakley enjoyed it, repeatedly giving large trumpeting sounds while flapping his little ears. After their camp was set, fires were burning brightly. Nothing would get to them for once, so they slept high on the stone overlooking the great pools below.

In the morning, they decided to set atop the overlook a memorial to their tribe members who perished. Their hearts needed it, and it did them good to labor toward the effort. They piled stones high in pyramid stacks, placing colorful items around them to ordain the stones with paints from their supplies: dried clays and flower grindings. They built fires and then prayed to the great Mother, the natural spirit above, to care for the newly delivered souls, now forever wisps in the wind. The ceremony lasted hours, then they decided to leave the utopian pools to the dead and retreat toward the mountains early.

"That felt good, sister! I feel like we did well to mourn them as we did." Deneska gave some pain through her lips as she spoke of the ceremony.

"I feel the same, Deneska. We have lost everything we know. I am glad you were with me. I wouldn't know what to do, not knowing your fate." Aleelah avoided looking at her, knowing she would break down with everything still raw in her mourning. Deneska understood, came closer, brushed her arm against her sister, and paced quickly.

The group now hiked with renewed energy toward the mountains, climbing slowly from the lower valley. The ground grew steeper as they hiked, laboring them into more and more breaks as they went.

It took two more days and two more camp sites to reach the foothills, making it with no more predators in sight. The path remained open, and they walked high upon the fingers of hills sprouting out of the giant mountains like roots on a tree. Vegetation became taller, and soon, giant trees hundreds of hands tall became all they could see in front of them. The darkness between was daunting. The girls camped far away from its edge, keeping a steady eye on the piercing blackness until sleep overtook them.

In the night, long-away groans began. They were instantly up on their feet, throwing wood on the coals to make a big fire. More cries came from different directions toward their camp, like someone knew they were there. Both girls held weapons continuously now but sat after nothing developed for a long time. The groans soon became howls, and sharp sounds shot through the trees. Even Blakley stomped behind them in panic.

They packed up quickly, then stood at the ready, but again, nothing came as time passed. Moans so low and long, one would think a giant beast was dying, followed by sharp howls, set the hair on everyone's necks straight up. Then came rumbles that sounded like a herd would leap from the blackness to crush them where they stood. The sounds withered away to become distant several times, returning when all was relaxed to begin the fright anew.

After another hour, Aleelah decided some forest beasts were doing what mystical beasts do but staying within the forests, so they were both grateful they chose not to enter them. They finished the restless night by rising with the sun to hike half-rested. But that didn't stop them from hiking away fast to the south, being sure to stay out of the trees. Cresting the next finger ridge, they could see as far as the horizon. This continued path never ended, and nothing new awaited them for a long distance.

"I think we will have to go into the mountains, or we risk camping along them for weeks, maybe more," Aleelah stressed to her sister, focusing on the never-ending forest line.

They sat to talk of their predicament, deciding not to go west because the higher elevation now allowed them to see the carnage in the lakes below them. The north was dark as an ash plume rose in the sky like a snake suffocating the ground below it.

"It is south along those trees over the horizon or east into the mountains. Maybe there." Aleelah pointed down the mountain top heights southward, where a giant crack opened up the peaks.

"A low pass, maybe, without these giant trees with their fighting spirits?" Aleelah seemed to be convincing them both.

"That is only a day's hike southward. We might as well check it out. There is no climbing, even if we survive the forest monsters." Deneska pointed high above them to the solid white, barren peaks. Aleelah nodded in agreement as they began the next leg.

Upon daybreak, they awoke from the long march past sundown to find they were already in line with the possible pass through the range. They washed their faces and looked up at it, eating and talking.

"That looks far better than before. It is wide and far less tall than any-where else along the peaks." Deneska pointed out.

"Look at the rounded hills in the middle, smaller trees. There are fields up there?" Aleelah had not seen it before, but became more confident that this was the way.

"This finger takes us up, and there are no big trees that I can see. Let's head in," Aleelah said as she pointed.

"Those grasses are a good sign we will have food and water," Aleelah decided. "At worst, we won't make it, then decide what else to do." She left the thought open.

They packed camp, then started hiking up the shallow entrance. The heights of the mountains seemingly stood vertical to their tops. The thick, white snow became exposed above them as they moved deeper into the heart of the pass that made a broad sweeping turn. Soon they were on the snow layers and following the gently turning terrain as it wound through unimag-inably tall mountains on either side.

Within an hour, a breeze grew from the valley entrance, and eventually, high-gale winds ripped through the pass. The two quickly turned cold while heading for the cliff's edge, where they found shelter from it to rest. They dressed then pushed up further, but the winds became jets of force so great Blakley was buckling around in it. The twigs and cones on the trees were soon taken up in the gales, pounding the group's backside. They diverted into a cupula cove to the right side, where trees grew from solid rock. They tarped trunks on the windward side, shoving snow on the lower lip of the tarp until it was taut.

The gale grew in intensity, threatening to drive out the very trees from the ground and carry them away. Dark clouds blew into the draw as snow blew sideways, pelting everything until their sides were piled thick. They huddled close against the elephant, his long hair helping to keep them warm.

They had Blakley lay down against the tarp with them between his legs, calming him. Nobody was getting rest. They covered themselves as best they could, watching in horror at the display of Mother, attacking them on a level they had never seen before. It was not to give way, either. The winds increased for hours, now busting trees loose as they toppled against the rock, but only barely discernable from all the violent noises around them, and, eventually, the darkness grew to pitch blackness.

The tarp of fine pelts finally tore, busting loose and smacking Blakley in the back. At once, he was on his feet, but they could not direct him from the loud sounds, and he still had most of their supplies attached to his back.

Deneska handed Aleelah the bag she was lying on as Aleelah felt her attempting to climb Blakley's front to rein him in. Blakley stepped out into the direct winds as they desperately held his fur, trying to stop him.

Aleelah lost the feel of her sister's arm as she and the beast moved away, then bent down, grabbing her bag. She started toward where she thought they went, but felt nothing in the darkness. Yelling was useless, and the stinging winds blew her down countless times as she advanced out in it.

From Aleelah's close right, loud rock crashes tore through the winds. A chunk far larger than her shot past just inches above her. She knew the cliffs were crumbling down and instantly abandoned the tarp with only the bags left in her hands, hunting her missing sister. She bolted into the open ground as best she could, realizing the other side probably had falling rock, too. But she kept going, her back to the wind, and hunted for Deneska and Blakley. Though, in blackness, her only course was away from the shuddering rock-on-rock sounds that just missed her.

She worried now that the rock might have hit Deneska. She couldn't have been far from where she was. She tried going back some, but the winds made it impossible. Even the elephant would have to head uphill, keeping his back to the dagger-like edges of things blowing in the torrent. It wasn't long before close crashes came from Aleelah's left. She bolted right again, knowing she was probably too close to that side now. Onward she went, not going fast, as the snow had doubled in depth already. Her sister could be underfoot anytime now, Aleelah thought. She ran into a branch and broke it off, using it as a feeler in front of her. She soon worried about how far she could walk or even how far she had traveled in the dark. There was no knowing, as everything was now a blur.

She was panicked at the loss of her sister now. More crashes to her left kept her ranging right; there seemed no end to the weather. Aleelah finally stumbled upon a tall boulder sufficient to circle and crouch on the wayward side of the wind. She hunkered down, knowing she would have to stop if her sister lost Blakley. She worried they could have wandered too far by the cliff and falling rock if she had stayed with the elephant.

There was nothing she could do but wait it out now. She knew she did not have much in the bags she was carrying and took out some clothes to stuff in her jacket, using the bags now to block the snow. The snow built higher and higher until she was in a hollow with an open hole at the top, the brisk wind whistling as it streaked over the rock. Her sister was now lost to her, everything was lost to her.

Chapter Nineteen

UPON THE SNOW

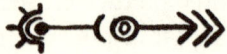

Seldik was healing well now, and the group was following the same river Mumot had smelled from a distance, saving them from their parched, stink hole lake where they had almost died. Edeldon and Nasok were begrudging the journey as if they had never walked before, and Sylic was bouncing around now as if he'd never need rest. Seldik assumed he was probably part hare to run around that much. Sylic seemed happy enough, but he did not completely open up to Seldik, and he assumed it was because their different cultures blocked such friendship. Seldik realized Sylic was older than him, but did not care much about that gap. Whereas Sylic was worldly, Seldik was fresh off the boat, you may say. *Oh well*, he thought, *better than being hated like Efy was*, the remembrance coming back to him of the loss.

Kolkesh was again far in the lead with Mumot, both looking like far-off beasts from the distance gained now. Several more camps were had beside the water as plenty of stores were eaten off the continuing food reserves running about the ground.

They all walked steadily on after resting for one brief half-hour wait. Once, Mumot was seen sprinting off the trail far ahead as everyone stopped to watch his incredible form move so fast. He darted out of view in only paces until not a minute later he came striding back to the formation carrying something long, narrow, and dead in his hand. Mumot carried it the rest of the day, only stripping the guts from what looked like a fox, but with a beaver face, at which point, while camping, Mumot ate it himself, never showing the others much of the poor dead thing. Seldik assumed it was tasty, but he greatly respected the giant's power after seeing him move so fast.

Camp was again called when they had finally crested the long grade, now standing in the wash looking up at fantastic trees so tall they reached the sun above. Within their deep, cracked bark trunks, it was pure blackness, even with the sun attempting to pierce into its heart. The team decided not to try that until morning, as strange things may wander that depth.

At camp, they discussed heading into the pass they had been heading toward since they left the dead lake, attempting to get well into it by the next night. The snow seemed lower, so it may be passable for them to push over fast. They knew there would be no more food inside the high elevations of the valley, so they checked that they had plenty of reserves to go the distance.

The crack seemed wide and inviting compared to the thick tall trees they would enter to get there. They decided to follow the river into the trees, hoping it would cut through the forest quickly to wind its way up the lower valley pass.

The group was up early, heading directly into the darkness, observing the vast pinecones on the ground twice the size of their heads. Occasional cracks of the falling cones in the depths unseen reminded them they better dodge any falling on them, or else. Mumot seemed tense in the darkness. A strange quiet ensued, and he darted looks in all directions as he went, making everyone uneasy. Twice, Kolkesh rounded the group up and huddled them close as they hiked, like an imminent threat brewed just around the unseen side of the mighty cracked bark trunks. But nothing came as they pushed on, the water gurgling beside them to lead the way up.

They never reached the valley entrance but were close, they assumed. They set camp on an island where water flowed around it on soft grasses, but they built fires high to encircle themselves, just in case. Mumot sat within this time, looking out in a slump that nobody could discern from a sleeping position or an alert stance. When all was quiet, the first eyes were shut for sleep. It seemed in no time, a growl came from a distance. Instantly, everyone was up with spears in hand, Mumot jumping over the firelight and into the creek right outside of it.

All remained silent as they looked around. The sounds seemed to come from various directions, all uphill from them. Again, they grew from soft, distant threats to close, increasing violence. Everyone was white-knuckled as each passed them by. For hours, the spirits played with them. The team soon found themselves sitting with their weapons lax, trying to rest for the coming attack that never came. Mumot even returned to the inner circle, sitting ready and peering into the darkness. As the sounds came and went, talk began on what the spirits were, deciding between winds blowing within the trees or beasts crawling along the ground hunting each other. The thoughts came again as the sounds left, only to return. Soon, only the small, irregular sound made all perk up with the possibility of battle.

For some hours, Seldik listened, pondering. He lay down, putting his ear to the bare earth to see if the very ground made sounds he could distinguish. But what he sensed was not sound, it was motion. Tiny vibrations came before the sounds howled, and he soon knew its source. He sat up quickly, surprised at his thoughts.

"I don't think it is any of that," he proclaimed aloud, and even Mumot turned to look at him.

"That is real, boy," Kolkesh stated, pointing to the constant noise.

"Yes, it is, but not from beasts, it is from Mother herself!" Seldik proclaimed in understanding, then didn't wait for the others to look less shocked.

"I listened to the ground, and small vibrations come right before each noise. I think the mountains are rumbling and amplifying the sounds down from the valley above," he said, then waited for others to accept his idea.

The others nodded, and several listened to the earth, repeating his findings as fact. Everyone relaxed after several more soundings. They all lay down, catching what sleep they could, but Kolkesh kept a guard awake in shifts to be sure.

Upon the rising sun, they awoke groggy but headed directly upward, breaking into the clearing. They ran up the right side of the valley against taller, growing cliffs as they went. The ground was grassy and the creek thinned, ultimately vanishing into a muddy, grassy pillow of land that was soggy to cross over. They continued higher as the valley became more immense compared to the surrounding mountains. It was one Megarthy across but narrowed higher up, appearing to break into a fork. They decided to choose a direction once they got to the fork. It was soon realized they would not make it to the Y by night, so that they would get as close as they could, then set camp.

The winds hit them instantly, coming up the valley they had just walked from in a torrent. Touching down from an unknown height it brought an instant chill to their skin. Everyone stopped to cloak up, knowing it might bring terrible conditions, plus it was getting dark fast. They were exposed entirely. Only higher up around the bend seemed to offer any shelter from the wind front. The clouds shot out over the high cliffs, plunging them into darkness. They stayed close but paced uphill as fast as they could, gaining much ground, hugging along the right side toward the bend, then darting to the left, hoping for better wind conditions.

They were down to a crawl, buttressing against each other to avoid losing the group. They gripped the backs of each other's tunics as they pushed on, helping each other not fall. No yells were understood, all realizing they must find shelter quickly. The winds were now blowing them over, and snow and sleet were blowing across their forms so fast everything became a blur.

Massive stone broke free high above in a silent fall and touched down upon the cliff rock below in a tremendous crack beside the stranded travelers. Its mass blew across them instantly, shards zipping over everyone's heads, where they each dove into the snow below them, hoping to avoid an unseen death. As Seldik looked up from his crouched position in the snow, Mumot rushed past, making Seldik freeze instantly as he watched, confused.

Why is he running down? Soon, two more unrecognized forms flashed by just in sight of Seldik, none even seeing he was stuck up to his knees in the snow beside them. Yells didn't help, as they were ripped from the lips as soon as he expelled them. Now frantic, he reached around, thinking Sylic was near, but nobody found no one. The snow careened by so fast now that his eyelids froze in chunks, unless covered by an arm.

Seldik started to head down, knowing now some were going that way, but the winds had increased so much that he could not bear to face it head-on, turning toward the opposite side, away from the falling rock threat. He tried tracing down backward, but another colossal explosion erupted by him. He instinctively bolted right to escape, but a piece hit his healing shoulder, throwing him into the snow.

Everything was numb, and he realized he couldn't stay out in the center of the pass. His head cover, stiff with ice, beat his face so hard he could feel it ripping skin. He kept his head low, crawling sideways to the right as he went, attempting to find anything he could for shelter. Just as he crossed, someone kicked him in the head, but the leg was already gone when he reached up. He groped around in a circle but found nothing in the blackness, deciding he must stay right.

As he moved on, the howling winds grew stronger, rolling him uphill even while crouched. He crawled uphill in the valley's center, hoping to find shelter in the pitch-blackness that engulfed him. He had lost his pack, he realized, quickening his pace, knowing now he would perish without something to hide under. Seldik was lost and in complete despair, knowing he would not make it through the night if he remained out in the open.

Off to his left, he heard and felt a high rumbling coming that was so loud it outpaced the winds, and he knew it was something other than rock. He realized what it was as it grew louder. A massive chunk of ice-hard snow pelted him in his face, bloodying his nose, and instantly froze his blood in the screaming winds. *SNOW!* He thought in horror. It flowed like a river down the valley. He instantly plowed his hands into the snow, heading right in a panic. His friends who were running downhill, he realized, will be caught in it.

Seldik squealed out a half-cry, knowing he could do nothing for them. He couldn't even make a connection with them running by. *Do they know of the eminent snow slide? Does Mumot understand what is coming?* He could not answer that question, but was hoping he was right. He plowed on as fast as he could, the snows twice taking him with it down as the edge caught him. He swam like he was on a stormy wave in the sea, somehow pulling off a slide each time to save himself. He was unsure how far down he had traveled, but he knew he must keep paddling and kicking uphill until he found shelter or died. The Nether, he realized, would have him soon.

Just as he was out of energy and about to stop crawling, he felt a hard rock under his hands, frozen from the contact of snow, but he could sense the firmness under him. He quickly crawled over it, hoping to get on the upward side, but his heart sank when it seemed flat as he squirmed over it. But all at once, his knees fell into a hole as he clung to the snow above. His feet dangled into nothingness, numbly realizing he was hanging over a chasm he would fall into if he let go. He kicked and screamed as he attempted to get a foothold, but none presented itself. He hung within a circular opening with no way to reach his feet to the walls. He was losing grip as the hole widened and swallowed him, slowly sinking as he clung with his hands into the snow, attempting to wedge anchors.

Seldik realized this was the end. He would be buried deep enough, never to be found, and doubted anyone in the group was left alive, even the mighty Mumot. His father would never know of his accomplishments, nor of his demise. He quickly prayed for saving, hoping that his Soul would not be discarded in this evil.

Seldik was slowly losing strength and his hold as the hole expanded. He calmed his Soul now, frozen from fear, but a peace swept into his core, showing him his destiny was this. He accepted it now, knowing he was destined to fall forever into the belly of the Netherweir as it swallowed him whole.

Suddenly, there came a terrifying hitting on his left ankle. Something was touching him and hitting against him. Fear gripping his core once again in unknown anguish that renewed the grip he no longer felt, he thrashed, kicking his feet, attempting not to be touched and eaten by whatever unseen beast was awaiting him in the pits below.

Gripped by fear, he could not think of anything other than the death that awaited him. Deep in the throat of the Nether, a beast was awaiting to devour him. His heart was now beating out of his chest. The harder he kicked, the more complex the grappling from below became, like a clamping jaw, until it finally grasped his pant with a firm hold, tugging hard at him until he lost his grip and plunged into the depths below. He screamed into the wind, so unforgiving that it devoured his last cry for help. He fell back against the rock wall as he slipped, knocking him out cold, and blackness overtook him.

Chapter Twenty

WORLDS COLLIDE

Aleelah was freezing, stuck within her tomb, getting covered by the snow more each hour. She would soon be out of breath from the top hole closing up. She could not climb the rounded frozen walls of the built-up snow to punch through. She lay weeping at the loss of her sister in the blackness, the quiet place insulating her from the brutality going on above where she knew her sister and their Blakley were getting covered in snow that would end them both. They had traveled so far, survived what devoured their tribe, to die in this mountain valley. How could it end like this? They were happy and safe weeks ago, living carefree in a utopia. Now they will die alone, probably frozen by morning.

She screamed quietly, out of energy and resolve, weeping with no tears, shaken by the solitude of the forsaken mountain that brings instant death to all who try climbing its back. How can a storm come so fast with no warning? There was little she could do about the pain or the cold except lay in the egg-shaped cavity against a rock face that would soon be her headstone.

Rumbling sounds began to echo in her chamber. The roaring pitched toward her until it was at her hiding place, then rushed past. The roar came in a long precession from all directions now. Aleelah knew it was the caving of the cliff rock above, now burying the valley in the snow where they dared enter. She hoped her sister did not suffer nor survive to endure this last attack on her. Aleelah prayed to the stars and spirits above where her kin now rested that they receive her sister's soul and take her far away from this horrible land.

Aleelah vowed she would soon be joining them, where they would be free to roam across the earth's skies together. Aleelah wept anew, realizing her death may be far more painful. She would not await such a fate. She would strip down and lay on the icy floor so death would take her fast, not waiting to starve or freeze slowly in the blackness. A death such as that would take days if she fought the inevitable. The lack of air would probably take her faster, she pondered. She would wait for the sounds to stop. She would mourn her lost sister first, then prepare enough spirit within her to do the unthinkable. Yes, that is what she will do. She closed her eyes, weeping herself to sleep.

Aleelah did not sleep long and awoke groggy. Surface snow had plunged onto her cloaked head as she lay on her bags. In her daze, she knocked the snow off, realizing the winds howled anew from the reopened portal above, thinking that there was probably a mountain of rock coming down upon her soon to smother her life. She should have laid on the icy ground earlier, and now she will pay the price with pain. But she heard something different above her.

In the pitch black, there was a motion above her. Something was dangling into the opening, making soft pats against the cave wall right over her head. Chunks of packed snow kicked loose from the walls. She worked hard to stand and get to the rock face to avoid it. *What is that?* She thought, confused. It was no rock. It sounded too soft. The repetitive swooshing and back-and-forth hits against the rounded walls began to widen the hole above. Aleelah knew then that whatever had invaded her tomb was alive. *Is it digging or kicking?* She thought, panicked. *What kind of beast braves a storm to hunt? Did it smell me? Does it even know I'm here? Maybe it's for the best.* Just then, she lifted her arm and began to swat at it, but instead of claws reaching back, flat fur brushed against her. *It's someone's foot!*

Aleelah kept an arm across her face, now carefully moving her hand toward the flailing bundle of fur, then WHAM, the foot smacked against her fingers, smashing them into the stone wall. *It's a human's foot!* She reached up again, more desperate this time, and tried to grab hold of the ankle as it swung and kicked every direction. Aleelah's mind whirled. Her sister had somehow found her. She yelled, her mind racing in the dark, realizing her scratchy voice would never be heard in the winds above, no matter how loud she tried to scream.

She leapt now, trying to grab Deneska's legs, reaching her cold hands out, desperately trying to grip anything that would get her attention, letting her know she was safe, but her feet flailed more frantically now. She knew Deneska didn't know it was her down here, so she jumped as hard as she could, taking blind kicks to her face, but her adrenaline prevented any pain from being felt. She needed to get her sister before she climbed out and was lost to her forever.

Finally, Aleelah caught hold of the pant bottom in front of the leg, holding on with everything she had against the shaking that now seemed incredibly strong as her sister fought with more power than Aleelah could imagine. She almost lost her grip but then reached out with both hands and wrapped them around the hair-insulated foot, pulling up her body weight as she felt Deneska finally slip down.

Aleelah attempted to catch her fall as snow and ice plummeted in, but the mass was more than she expected. The body landed upon her, slammed her head against the rock wall and pinned her against it. She fell in and out of consciousness as she lay by the crippled body of her sister. She felt the pressure on the side of her cheek that had cracked the rock face. She felt her ear bleeding, but they were alive and together, with air and protection from the deadly outside conditions. So she lay upon the warm fur of her sister's coat, reaching around to pull up the bag they were not already on to drape it over them just as she passed out for the last time that night.

The storm above raged on into the next day, whistling through the open hole. Snow continued to accumulate, and the hole became a tunnel several feet higher. Aleelah woke with a throbbing cheek and ear, but her head was no longer numb from cold but felt hot as she tried to touch it, wrenching her hand away as soon as she did in pure pain. She could barely open her eyes, realizing her right one was swollen from the pressure around it. It made her feel sick to her stomach.

Her face had been dragged down across the rough rock edge, ripping her skin away. Her head thumped with every heartbeat, but she was alive. She knew she had a concussion, if not a broken cheekbone. There was barely light above coming in, but she could now see outlines in the darkness surrounding them.

After a time, she realized her feet were frozen pretty severely, but she could wiggle her toes. She tucked them under the sack she was lying on, thankful she had put it down. She finally rolled onto her elbow, looking over her sister's form, pulling herself high enough to uncover the sleeping beauty's face to check if she had any injuries that needed treatment. Deneska was balled up in a fetal position, facing away from her. The giant cloak covered her face. But by her breathing, she was alive, though she must have endured much up in the snow before miraculously showing up.

In the darkness, Aleelah pulled the cloak back until she could see her face, but it was so dark she had to lean in, whispering her sister's name while she prayed to the spirit above, thankful for her sister's return. She was just inches away, squinting to see Deneska's face, but instead, the distorted image before her assured her that something was wrong with her sister. She struggled harder against her pain, placing her face over her sister's form so she could see the problem more clearly. Again, she peered closer, squinting, then moved her sister's face upward to get a front-on view.

Aleelah's eyes widened when she realized it was a stranger's face that she was holding. She jerked back, pulling herself entirely away, realizing it wasn't even a girl but a man! Her groggy mind reeled at the revelation, as she quickly grew frightful. *Where is my sister? Where did this man come from?*

We were alone on the mountain. The thoughts whirled insider her head, as there in front of her lay a stranger that fell upon her and knocked her out.

She sat in dead silence, watching the stranger. He was breathing, be it slowly, but he was alive. Aleelah realized he was not waking and wondered why. She thought of her safety and what she had to protect herself from him, and instantly pulled the rope from the bag's closure, found his hands, carefully pulled them together in front of him, and bound them tightly. Then she realized how enormous he was, well over three hands higher than her tall form. She carefully crawled behind him, felt along his chest and belt, and founding a small knife of a heavy dark smoothness she had never seen before. If he awoke, she would be armed, and he would be bound. If he was to become aggressive, she would kill him before he got a chance to untie himself.

She lay away from him after taking back her bag, moving it off of him to sit upon as she conducted herself and tended to her wounds, keeping one eye on him. Even with his hands tied, she was still scared, so she bound his feet together too. Since she was stuck with him in the cave, she wanted every advantage. She was impressed at how tall he was. No wonder she could not catch him, she thought. He was at least eighteen hands tall, towering over her. He was thin, not heavy, and his jacket appeared thick, but she remembered his legs as thinner.

Since he had not moved, she crawled carefully up into the growing light of noon to again look at his face. He was handsome with long, blond hair and sleek, tan skin that made her flush. His face was lean and beautiful, she thought. *Where did he come from? Did he come from the mountains themselves, maybe?* She carefully touched his hair, running it through her fingers. Never had she seen golden hair before. His complexion instantly warmed her with an excitement she had never felt before.

She felt behind his head, checking for damages that must be there, or he would not still be asleep. His head was warm, but not with fever. Then she felt the large lump on his head just above his neck and knew he probably cracked his head on the rock above when she pulled him downward. *This is my fault.* She cringed.

Aleelah returned to her position beyond his reach now, worried for her sister but still shocked at her new partner in the hole. She observed the strange knife in her hand, very strong and cold to the touch. The man was very strange to her, but he almost died up there too. Maybe he came from the other way, or perhaps he was a spirit reborn to the earth and happened upon her hole, she thought. She lay worrying about her kin as the sounds above showed no let-up. The day grew on until she dozed off from the growing mental and physical fatigue.

Something snapped Aleelah awake. Maybe a wind gust blew over wrong above or perhaps a rustle, but her mind came alive, less groggy as she realized she had fallen asleep. She brought the knife up instantly as she looked up toward her prisoner's form. There in the barely visible light lay the man, awake and looking at her with wide, bright blue eyes. Aleelah jerked her legs under her, ready to stand and fight if he turned aggressive, but he remained there, staring.

The man slowly moved his tied hands to his head. Aleelah raised the blade to show him she had his weapon. She figured he had been awake for a while, as he wasn't wrenching with his hands, maybe already realizing they were bound. But he put his hands behind his head and felt where she knew he had a lump and let out a soft moan, but she understood he had a harmful impact the night previous.

The man closed his eyes and blinked slowly as he wiped his face. He moved his feet, feeling they were bound, then sat still. He moved his hands down and once again looked toward Aleelah as she held the weapon forward, steady and able. He opened his hands slowly and spread his fingers apart, keeping them there for a long time before bringing them up to his chest still open, showing he was weaponless and maybe, she thought, showing he was not a threat, but she wasn't so quick to decide that for herself.

Aleelah lowered the weapon and motioned for him to drop his hands, which he understood and did very slowly. She appreciated that he was continuing to show no threat. He slowly looked at his bound hands, then leaned his head away from her and observed the room of snow and rock that bound them together. He could not turn back much, wrenching his head forward in pain. He closed his eyes several times for extended periods, and his form slumped. Aleelah motioned for him to sit up, which he did slowly but unsteadily.

Chapter Twenty-One

A SOUL'S MATE

Seldik was in a deep sleep, enduring the vivid nightmare of his friends dying under the snow. In a dense, white fog, he could not move to help them, forced to be a spectator in the terror unfolding before his eyes. It seemed it would never end. They were all trapped within a death spiral to be relived for eternally.

Then Seldik slowly opened his eyes, his body numb to anything. He was peering out with swollen eyes at his enclosure's white grave. All he could see was barely lit white snow and feared his dream had become reality, that he was buried and dead with his friends. Soon the throbbing of his head came through to remind him death came with feelings and he would not escape pain just because he was asleep. He looked around, blinking, focusing, and realized he was warm in places but still unable to move much. He raised his hands to see that they were bound, and he could not wiggle them loose. *How did this happen?*

Suddenly, his memory came flooding back to him. He remembered falling into the hole now, kicking at a beast grabbing him. *Did I hit my head or did something hit me?* He looked toward his feet to feel they, too, were bound, then saw the form of a girl lying asleep against the icy wall just past his feet. He squinted and blinked to focus until he could see the outline of her face. She was dressed in a thick fur outfit head to toe with fur boots like his. Her head cover had slipped off just enough to reveal the most beautiful face he had ever seen. She had dark, tan skin like his, but redder and more naturally dark. *Perfect*, Seldik thought.

He reeled with questions as he stared at her perfectly outlined face and noticed that her cheek was bruised and badly scraped. Her ear was blood covered too. *What had happened to her? Is she alive?* He thought, just as she stirred some, repositioning. Her lips were swollen and perfectly rounded below a thin cut nose that was dazzling in combination. Her unique look was so exotic compared to the women of CED that he was instantly enthralled by her. He just stared at her, trying to comprehend where or why they were there.

When she finally opened her eyes, she was in shock and instantly brought up his knife, pointing at him. Seldik didn't think about her being dangerous. *How could such an exquisite lady be hazardous*? He thought. But her stance and hold showed she was very capable of fighting. Seldik wondered if this beauty of the mountain snow would kill him where he lay. He opened his hands, showing he was unarmed and wanting to surrender. She checked him over, but her dark eyes maintained a burning stare right into his. Her dark hair with beads interwoven between the strands swept far down past her thin neck, making Seldik very warm indeed.

Seldik held his hands to his chest, said his name, and then pointed to her, but she would not respond. He did it again. She nodded in acknowledgment and did the same to her chest. "Aleelah," she clearly said. *Aleelah,* he thought as he repeated it. *What a gorgeous name.* There was a standoff for a bit, but then he thought of his friends and when he had last seen them. Looking around his dungeon, he realized he was in no better shape than dead as the storm raged on above. His grief overtook him, even with his new roommate. He slumped down more in the anguish of what had happened prior. Aleelah must have given up, too, as she let her guard down some, motioning him to sit up. It was daunting. His head pounded as he tried, but he was finally sitting, realizing he was far taller than her. His head pounded, so he bent it down, eyes closed, trying to shake the feeling, but he almost fell back over before catching himself.

Seldik motioned to her that he wanted to get a pouch from his inside jacket lining. Aleelah appeared to think it over, then warned with his knife to do it slowly. Seldik showed his hands again as empty, then slowly reached in, having trouble getting the pouch untied to get it out. He could tell Aleelah was getting worried about his actions, but he had no choice but to look down to undo it from within. He ever so slowly took it out for her to see, then just as slowly, he untied it slowly and let the top drape over, revealing the dried goods within. He cautiously handed it to her, making a show that he offered it to her without thinking of himself first. Aleelah was impressed, though still obviously wary of the offer, but then smelled the freshly smoked fish he had stored from the creek just days before. Aleelah pulled one piece out with her teeth, eyeing him the whole time, then returned the pouch. He felt this was a sign that she wasn't so bad because she could have kept it. Seldik took it slowly, pulled a piece out, and began chewing it so she could see it was good. Aleelah put hers to her beautiful lips and took a satisfying bite, just as her stomach let out a growl.

For the second time, he heard her angelic voice as she let out a small moan while she chewed, then quickly looked up at him. Seldik could not help but giggle, which had them both smiling largely. Her smile melted the ice he sat on, warming him instantly. *Who is this incredible woman?* He thought.

They sat eating and shooting shy glimpses at each other as they giggled. Finally, they both let out some laughs loud enough to break the tension. Once the meal was consumed and Aleelah refused any more from his offerings, he laid the pouch by the rock face behind him, an open offer for whenever she wanted food. She smiled, then nodded her head, yes, and his heart melted again. He knew hoarding it back into his beltline would show he denied it to her, and he wanted her to be able to eat whenever she wanted and to signal that he means no harm. Aleelah seemed to appreciate the offer as she laid back, taking her eyes off of him and looking up through the hole at the night sky.

Seldik saw it was growing dark and assumed she would worry about his actions at night. He motioned to her that he was going to rest again, pointing to his injury, and she nodded her head in relief, knowing he would fall asleep before her. He laid down, and after pondering it all, he quickly fell asleep, and the nightmares returned to taunt him.

Aleelah, watching her gorgeous visitor offer to lie down and sleep first upon seeing the light fail above them, was a relief. She felt much better about him, but still kept the knife at a distance from him. She laid back when she heard him snoring. His breaths were so deep and loud, she knew it wasn't a trick. She settled on the bag and found a position she could attack from, then quickly dozed off.

Morning had come, and the winds blew on, signaling no let-up to the storm. Aleelah had woken early, wrapping her head with a cloth from the bag, and waited for her companion to rise. When Seldik finally crept from his nightmares of sorrow, he was still in pain from the rock hit, but managed to rise with less nausea than the day before. The food helped them both as they repeated the delicate dance from the day before with the bag provided, but this time, with a sweet bamboo that Seldik convinced her to try. She fell in love with the taste.

He then offered toasted beans, which gave them an energy booster that kicked them into higher awareness and made them feel good. Seldik chewed a root and applied it to his lump. Upon Aleelah offering up another piece of cloth, he wrapped his head in it to hold the root in place. He offered such to Aleelah, but she refused. She knew it was likely a medicinal root but didn't want to take a chance. Seldik gave up on the offer and looked out the hole, offering some communication with the beautiful resident in his cage of ice.

He drew upon the bag with pieces of charred wood from his tunic. He sketched out his civilization's symbols, beginning with a double concentric circle with a dot in the center. He drew the month, a seven-spiral symbol, then the prominent "M" Cassiopeia star system symbol for the season, which

Aleelah recognized and nodded her head in understanding. She soon took the charred stick and drew the M as an E, an M, and a W and backward E to show it changed upon sundown depending on the season. Seldik agreed and drew in the other three seasons in association with the star's direction and then got it. He drew every one of the twelve-month symbols in procession around the figure eight of the sun's movement. Once she finally understood, they spent the day writing to each other. He realized her type had no written language, but she spoke, which gave him hope for their ability to communicate.

Aleelah recognized he was not only the most beautiful thing she had ever seen, but he was from a race with a written language that others could understand. Civilization was unheard of in her culture. And the scary stories of giants in the mountains that the elders told kids to get them to sleep were made real by his presence. He tried to draw the lands and lakes and rivers that lead to the ocean where he came from, but she could only recognize the volcano and the closest lakes. She plotted a point very close to the volcano north of where they traveled to show where she had lived. Seldik realized she was probably displaced by the eruption just as his team was chased away, yet somehow, they both had ended up here in this valley.

When questioned about places beyond the mountains, neither could answer and just shrugged. So at least, both knew neither had traveled that far before. Aleelah was shocked that his drawing showed him coming from far out past the land's end. She had never gone there, but stories and drawings by elders told of a distant spot where the lands ended. Until now, she had believed it was a cliff into nothingness. But now she imagined other lands out past the one they were on. She could see more and more lakes, surprised by their extent. The land was vast, and they only had a small look at it, two strangers lost together.

The day passed as they slept again, and morning came with winds that were not as brisk. Only the dark clouds remained stuffed into the valley. A reflection from the fog indicated a thick soup above when Aleelah finally unbound Seldik. He bowed to her as she laughed and showed him to remove his leg wrap, which he did, then handed it to her. She then surprised him and gave him his knife, but he quickly refused, handing her his sheath and pleading for her to take it. Shocked, she set the knife down, refusing completely, so Seldik lifted his front belt and jacket bottom, exposing another knife strapped sideways to his belly. Aleelah looked distressed and snapped up the abandoned blade, happy he never went for it but mad at herself for not checking, as she was right to think another may be hidden. She chastised herself, but soon was just grateful this wonderous man had remained docile. He smiled and again opened his hands in compliance.

Seldik, feeling better, was finally able to stand without being overcome with dizziness. Being very tall, he could reach up and touch the opening, which impressed Aleelah. She stood watching him as he tried opening it more, ripping snow down to expose more light. He smiled down at her, but she blushed and looked away. He then pointed up, but Aleelah knew she couldn't jump that high. Seldik began to motion something she didn't understand, but soon realized he was showing her that he would boost her out of the hole. *What is he thinking?* She thought quickly, realizing that he would be touching her, and she would literally be placing herself in his hands. She disagreed for some time, waving off his incessant attempts to make it so. She tried to ponder alternatives, but nothing came to her. The walls were too rounded to even use knives to dig out footholds. There was no other way out, and she was desperate to see if her sister had made it through the storm. So, finally, having no choice but to allow him to lift her, she agreed.

He showed her that she would stand on his shoulders, and with her height, she should be able to reach out and climb up. She agreed, strapped her bags around her neck, and bit down on the blade of her new weapon, holding it between her teeth, before surrendering herself to him, turning her back so he could grab and lift her. He did so instantly, and she flew into the air. Despite her discomfort, her mind slipped to how good it felt with his hands on her as she pressed herself to stay focused on her balance. She drew up her legs as he raised her straight above his head, then slowly lowered them until her feet were on his shoulders. Seldik stood up, both strangers balancing as they stood in the hole.

Aleelah carefully dug around the opening until her head was poking out of the hole and she was able to see the world for the first time since being trapped. She felt Seldik's strong arms holding her legs and didn't want to move. His touch was inviting and made her heart race, but she continued to claw upward, struggling to find a grip in the rigid, cemented snowbank. Her body quivered as she felt Seldik's hand push up against her backside as the other held firm around her leg. She shuddered at the feeling, growing uncomfortable when she realized she had lost control, and clawed her way out as he lifted her torso higher. Seldik recovered as quickly as he could, then reached down, placing both hands under her feet, and lifted her almost entirely out of the hole so she could step out. She composed herself, quieting the emotions flooding within her.

After a time, she dug from the top. Seldik dug from below and the hole was widened for his form. She dragged a nearby chunk of wood over and threw it down. Seldik stomped it into the snow, steadying to use as a step, then pulled himself out with her help. They laid on the snow, now looking around for any sign of movement.

When nothing came, they wandered around in the winds to hunt those they were missing. Nobody was found by either throughout the day, and eventually, the pair ended up back at the hole. They motioned to each other to head uphill after seeing the massive avalanche of snow that had completely choked the passage downward, indeed burying all the ones they knew. Both grew very depressed, realizing no scrap was left to understand what had happened.

The big rocks off the cliffs were piled high along the edge. They agreed that they must head up before nightfall, hoping others awaited them. Their combined hope was enough, so they begrudgingly headed off from their escape in a slow, steady climb.

Aleelah was slower but powerful, Seldik keeping back for her. She appreciated him more for it. She watched his massive form move, amazed at his sheer size, almost as tall as Blakley. The thought led her back as she pondered her sister's well-being as they went. Seldik was having the same issue thinking of his friend's fates, wondering if Aleelah had a man who she had lost here.

They carried on until dark, finding shelter at the split in the valley, so they set a camp under a log from the winds to get what rest they could. Aleelah watched Seldik in confusion as he walked around, striking rocks against his knife blade. He soon found one that threw fire, breaking it and bringing back both halves. He then gathered kindling, showing Aleelah how to strike fire with it. Aleelah was amazed as he guided her to keep the small rock for future fires whenever she wanted. They built a low one with enough warmth and they enjoyed it immensely. They warmed the dry meats, then consumed them happily, cracking smiles again before sleeping.

In the morning, they packed up, looking around where they were, finding no signs. The winds continued, the clouds never departing, leaving them in a thick fog from the frozen clouds they were in. Neither had ever seen such a sight, thinking it impossible, but it was not enjoyable as the bite of small ice particles clung to them. They reluctantly chose the better side, or so they thought. To the left, it was now devoid of snow since most of it fell down the valley. It had a large rock base to step on as they climbed. The other way was shallower but may have held the creek under the snowy flooring, and it ran into dark areas devoid of sun most of the day and felt gloomy all around for the little they could see of it.

The clouds continued to block the view not far ahead. Nothing could be gained by standing and pondering such paths. A way had to be chosen, so they struck out with the information they had. At worst, they could come back to head right if the conditions worsened ahead, which neither would want to do in the valley that took everything from them. They hiked quickly, enjoying each other's company, staying side by side, Seldik constantly slowing to allow Aleelah the steps to catch up. She saw it each time, smiling big at him, making him feel as though he had a raging killer whale inside his stomach, excited and blushing all at once.

He could feel the heat on his cheeks a few times as he smiled slyly. Aleelah picking up on the blushing, making her feel good. Her face was healing, and though it still hurt to smile, she couldn't help it. Seldik seemed to like her looks, even with a bruised-up face, and she fancied his inviting staring. Soon they were kicking snow at each other in play as they hiked, keeping them occupied as the incline grew steep.

Further and further, they traveled up a long, grueling grade, until they were forced to camp again. Seldik renewed the drawings he used to teach Aleelah his language. He eventually switched to sign language, showing her how easy each concept was as a sign. He believed she understood the written language enough to learn the signs quickly. Aleelah was a great learner, quickly picking up the concepts, finally adding tags and add-on symbols, and understanding that rudimentary combinations existed to describe more without a bunch of inline single-idea symbols to draw. He corrected himself. He realized she was becoming Aquarionite, the most beautiful he had known. Aleelah was enjoying his company as much as he thought. They rolled up in the thin bags, sleeping with a big fire keeping them warm.

In the morning, they ate the last dry foods Seldik had, primarily roots and stalks, but they were filling. They knew there was nothing to eat this high up, so they needed to get over the pass and down to find foods they hoped existed on the other side. They set out this time, knowing time was running out. The altitude was severe, and they huffed, puffed, and rested often. Seldik described he thought there was less air this high up, making breathing hard. He worried if they stayed this high too long, it might hurt them even without hiking, but he said nothing of the thought to his beautiful sidekick.

They suffered, taking what breaks they could. The winds slowed some, though being at their backs the whole time helped considerably. It was colder where they were, but when the clouds started to break, they could see sunlight on the ground ahead. This quickened their miserable paces, and soon, they broke out above the clouds. They were both in wonderment, turning to look at the unbelievable sight of the top of clouds, so dense it seemed you could walk out on them.

They sat, resting, absorbing the sun's rays on their backs as they took in the magical view. Never could either imagine such was possible. The mountains now held a profound feeling of wonderment once again. Nothing lived this high up, and a craggy peak dotted the line of the hills in both directions, high above them, down in the lower pass between. Now just a threatening breeze blew on them as off toward the volcano's high plume northward came more dark clouds even higher than they.

Snow of untold thickness rested upon the entire path. They walked on hard ice, not snow now. Waters flowed under them, and they could hear the torrent of it being under the ice some distance, they thought. It was a strange land on top of the world, floating on top of the clouds that seemingly cut the peaks off, moving them with the winds, it seemed. The winds remained, but the sun's warmth was inviting.

They moved on quickly, being in better spirits, pressing on over the ice as it began to angle less the higher they went. Soon they were in deep cracks. The ice went down tens of hands to the ground below where the waters flowed. They moved cautiously but realized they should be off the frost by night, so they pressed hard to move along. Seldik was able to spot a finger of land on their side. They went that way to end the ice hiking sooner.

By noon they were on big, rounded boulders of grey, heading across what looked like the crest of the pass several Megarthy ahead. On the crest of the pass, they paused for a rest. They had hiked the entire side of the mountains to reach the top of the pass, where their friends had not made it. Seldik quickly realized the natural pass contained giant unmoving boulders of a bright black surface. He cracked on one with a rock. The indent left a whiter inside, a perfect contrast to be seen by anyone crossing.

He took out his knife and started designing symbols on the face as Aleelah watched, realizing he was leaving a remembrance of the ones he lost and a marker of where they were crossing. She pulled out her knife, and he realized she wanted to help, so he lightly drew a few designs on a separate rock so she could then trace it with deeper penetration to leave her message. What it said, she was unsure, but it seemed it mentioned her, or her village, from the valley far to the northwest, two lakes away from the volcano behind it with dots in the sky. She quickly pecked out the lines, adding the outline of a mammoth, which surprised Seldik. When questioned, Aleelah showed that was their companion. Once they were pleased with the designs, they quickly headed down the other side.

Left behind were two panels, the highest in the land, depicting death and life and the groups' struggle as they met their demise in the valley far below the boulder. Resting under snow slides were a line of friends who were killed by the Netherweir. The second petroglyph panel spoke of death and of the two that survived. Seldik signed his insignia, "a†W," designating his family's crest on the floating city of CED.

Chapter Twenty-Two

UNITED FRONT

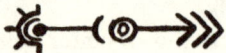

Deneska was pulled along as Blakley stepped away from their shelter into the black ear-piercing winds. She thought her sister held Blakley's rear leg, trying to yield the beast. Deneska tried not to get stepped on accidentally as she attempted to stop him. Blakely could not hear her screams to halt, and continued toward the valley center, where the winds pinned Deneska's small frame against his chest.

It took every effort to keep back and not get stepped on as he went onward into the blackness. He wandered with her clinging, sometimes dragging along. She knew if she let go, everyone would be lost to her. She stopped trying to move forward to his head but held on to two considerable ice-clumped fur lengths by his leg with her numbing hands. She knew she could not climb or stay on the mount, so she hoped he would stop long enough to turn him around.

Suddenly, a rock crashed in front of them in a loud echo only a few hands away and Blakley toppled toward her without warning. The large rock flew unseen across their heads in wisps louder than the winds bellow in her ear. She only got to step back slightly as he slowly fell toward her. His high back crashed upon her just at her chest level, plunging her into the snow. The weight of the beast's entire torso pushed her deeper. Her form was instantly compressed between Blakley and the form-fitting snow. Deneska gasped, moving her hands up to no avail. She was immediately immobilized from her neck down. Her head was just above snow level, and her arms had impacted the ground and were stuck toward her sides, with her hands just against the fur of the elephant. She knew she was in trouble, and so was Blakley. The rock must have hit him and shielded her from it. She knew he was probably dead. That meant she was trapped and would die where she was. Her sister may well be the same right beside her.

She tried to reach toward where she suspected her sister may be but could not move more than her wrists, so she tried hitting Blakley, but again, nothing. The winds were deafening and, soon, more rock was toppling, which she realized would quickly smother them. Deneska then realized she could not breathe very well, the crushing weight on her chest allowing only short breaths. Her face was flash-frozen from the wind that was now pelting them with snow. She felt warm against the beast, but the cold was beginning to creep up from the compacted snow, and she knew she may not live long, even if the rock failed its attack.

Each large crack of rocks splitting against each other made Deneska flinch hard, thinking this was the one, but each left only a dire warning that the next would get her. Blakley had not moved, and she now knew he was dead. She wept with frozen tears, making unheard whimpers to herself that were denied by the greedy wind's grab of each note she made.

Deneska wept and thought of her sister. She hoped she had gotten away. Hopefully in the morning, she prayed to the spirits above, she may find her sister. The land took all they knew and all they loved. She thought of home, her mind-numbing to the frost that crept steadily from her face. She would die before the rock even came, she now realized. The lack of oxygen entering her compressed chest would take her soon, her mind sharp enough still to realize her fate was sealed when her protector did his last saving act of taking the rock hit. She was slipping into darkness as the cold faded. She felt warm and peaceful. Even the sound of the screaming wind grew quiet, and she was dying, slipping away, letting the blackness take her.

Violent rumblings followed by vibrations increased, and her lower body became more compressed. Deneska came awake from a sudden rush of blood squeezed to her head. She felt the coming of the end, knowing the rock was now to cover them forever, but instead, blasts of snow pelted her face. She gasped for unavailable air due to Blakley being forced against her. She was seconds from a total blackout.

Then all at once, the compact snow stamp under her caved downward. She sucked in a large volume of air, now free to breathe. Her arms were free instantly, so she desperately tried to pull herself from under the elephant, but both started slipping downhill together. She could see nothing, but more snow shot over them, sometimes covering them, flowing away as they slid down with it. She could feel them go, like riding a wave. They flowed limply down the mountain as the snow ran like water.

She clawed to try to get from under the beast, but nothing worked. In the darkness, she could feel Blakley's head moving and held hope that he would move off her. She felt his head move back and forth several times, but the shaking was from something underneath them. As they slid over it, she realized she had lost all hope as her breath faded. But finally, Blakley's limp form slowly turned sideways, landing beside her. Then his legs sank under, and he began to flip over slowly.

Deneska was finally free to move, holding on tight to him as he rolled. She was riding on his chest as he lay with his legs pointing uphill, still unable to see anything in the screaming winds against her face coming from a black abyss. The winds ripping directly at her face forced her to shove her head deep into Blakley's hair, holding her cloak hood over her to avoid the onslaught. Down the valley they went, at a speed she knew was very fast, riding a torrent of snow blasting against the cliff's side over obstacles—a mighty wave Deneska could not comprehend. She remained as uphill as she could without losing her friend, knowing she may go under the snow if she lost him, but worried they would impact obstacles hard enough to kill her. Save me again, old friend, she thought to her poor Blakley.

The ride went on for what seemed like forever as they floated around in blackness, with only the thunderous icy wind scouring everything in its path to keep them company. Deneska prayed, thinking of her sister who was not with them, knowing she would join her soon, but then the ride slowed, coming to rest very near the edge of an alcove. Deneska climbed around her friend, realizing his limp body acted as a raised block against the wind. She kept herself at Blakley's side in case the snow pushed him against the ledge so as not to get pinned. Huddling down against him, searching, she found items still tied to his back to use as covers. She slept instantly, letting the wind's roar guide her to slumber.

A dull, almost untrustworthy light crept into the valley as the winds screamed on. Deneska opened her eyes slowly as she regained awareness of her dilemma. Nothing of the weather improved, but she was alive! She quickly composed herself, wrapping her coldest places tighter with what remained in the bags. She got her legs under her then crept up, not wanting to see what awaited her, but she needed to see Blakley's head. She could see enough to make it beside his eyes. There, her worse fear was realized as she saw a large gash behind his right ear high on his head. The blood was frozen solid, but the gash seemed deep, maybe even into the bone.

She touched his face, prayed, then realized her sister may be around, so she crawled around his entire form until she was convinced she was not there. She had lost her sister and feared that she hadn't survived. It was pure luck that Deneska had, so she wept anew. She lay now against Blakley's tusk, knowing she must leave this mountain of death to head back down. She would have to try surviving these wicked lands alone, as maybe the only one left anywhere.

Deneska found a blue rope in a bag and crawled back to her champion's tusk. She tied it on with a nice bow fluttering violently in the wind, his last gift from her before she moved on. To survive, she must head down into warmer weather now, so she prayed, then headed to his back to get what she could of the supplies. As she stepped, his trunk touched her ankle softly, and she realized it was moving toward her. Deneska spun around to find Blakley's eyes open, staring at her. She bellowed loudly into the winds as she dropped to her knees and hugged his giant head.

Deneska gave Blakley calming words as she spoke directly, placing her face to his ear. He seemed to know the effort as his trunk again reached her arm. She held its side with her hand. After a minute, Blakley lost consciousness again, and Deneska was frantic. Knowing the injury was terrible, she leaped into action. She scrambled in the winds back to the bags, finding a cactus needle, strong fiber threads, and some herbs she knew numbed things. She threw the leaves into her dry, frozen mouth and chewed with no saliva as she scrambled back to his head wound. He was still out, so she quickly added enough snow to mix with the herbs until they were mush. She cleaned the gash with snow, and some rock, then scrubbed more with snow, her fingers frozen. Once ready, she pulled the mush from her numb mouth, shoved it in the gash, then spread it out. She began weaving the needle through his tough skin. Pulling and tugging the tough little string, she crisscrossed, piercing herself with numb fingers, and pulled the opening closed. The feat would be more challenging if he was awake, so she kept it up until the job was done. There was nothing she could do now but wait. She would not leave her wounded friend now.

Chapter Twenty-Three

MUMOT THE SAVIOR

Mumot was in the lead again, overpowering the small ones he learned to like, who were steadying themselves along as the winds screamed higher. He looked back occasionally and watched them for a moment as he trudged up the mountains he was used to. Unlike them, he was well-equipped with thick fur and massive foot pads that easily kept him afloat on the snow's slippery surface. His muscles, well-tuned from a lifetime of running his homeland's high peaks, helped him keep a brisk pace through the land he had maintained dominance over for the last three hundred years. When he looked back again at the ambling group behind him, he recalled that his forefathers once spoke of their connection to his new friends Kolkesh, Seldik, Nasok, and Edeldon, but he was surprised to see a new land dweller in Sylic, especially since he was so small. He wondered on about the possibility of a new age rising, seeing now how much his ancestors have evolved, when suddenly, the wind reached its apex and his instincts kicked into high drive.

He quickly slowed his pace, packing his small band of friends tighter toward him. He could hear and see things they claimed they could not. Feeling the ground rumble, he sensed something ominous above. Having highly tuned senses in his feet, he froze, allowing his pads to rest directly on the snow as he listened intently to the ground below. Something wasn't right. He felt the first crack of rock above and knew immediately what was about to happen. He turned swiftly, grabbed those behind him and frantically pushed them back down the hill, one after the other, as they followed him into blackness. As they quickly plowed down the hill, he watched as the band separated, being pulled apart by the drift.

Mumot sprinted now, stopping just long enough to flip the travelers around and grab them up, sending them into headlong runs downhill with him until he let go to spin the next around. He knew they could no longer see him, as the snow-thick winds pelted his face. All he could do was try to save who he could as fast as possible. He hadn't run further than ten paces when the first rock crashed down, shattering beside him and knocking him onto all fours, but he continued to hunt down his friends. He knew he had grabbed Kolkesh, along with two others, but not Sylic nor Seldik. Frantically, he began searching through the snow for the smallest of the band when a new sound met his ears.

Mumot froze again to ensure his pads were in full contact with the snow. Through them, he felt the unmistakable quake of an avalanche headed straight toward them. Without hesitating, he sprinted uphill with all his might. The whipping winds faded in his ears as he focused on the coming thunder of the snow in front, now gaining speed.

He knew he must get his friends to the other side, if any were to survive now. And just as he made it up to where they were last separated, a small group came running down atop the snow wave trailed by trees and rocks that had been snatched up in the wake. Mumot jumped sideways, barely missing a tree, but the tide still swept him downward.

Instantly, Mumot found himself on top, paddling around, then clambering onto all fours using pure muscle. As he shot across the falling rock, he bumped into Kolkesh, who was holding onto someone. He instantly scooped them up. Turning back to the right, he dragged them, skimming them across the snow until he was nearer the edge of the thinner flow. He then chucked them toward it before turning again to head into the depths to find the others.

Using his keen eyesight, he spotted another, hoping it was the land dweller or young Seldik, but he couldn't tell until he bent down and yanked the body from the snow to reveal Edeldon, whose head had nearly been submerged in the drift. Mumot spun around and raced to the right with his new captive, who was given the same throw out to the edge. But this time, when he turned to race back up the hill, he struggled to gain elevation, as the snow was now moving too fast, and he was growing weak from the effort. He refused to give up, though, knowing the small ones were still out there, so he moved sideways and slowly made his way down, knowing that, by now, those who were left had surely been swept below him.

As he darted back and forth, he took several hits to his arm, making it hang limp from the damage. He was now skipping along on three appendages, breathing heavily from the exertion. Growing desperate and beginning to lose hope, he scanned over the tree line against the cliff's edge and saw a form clinging to a large limb. He stumbled over at once to grab him. He knew instantly it was Sylic and snatched him off the limbs so fast Sylic never had a chance to let go, taking the broken branch with him as Mumot raced left, holding on tight to his leg and dragging his tiny frame along behind him.

As he dragged his small friend along, the river of snow grew thicker, and his foot pads began to sink. Having one useless arm, and the other toting Sylic, he pushed on, now keenly aware that their situation had become dire. As the snow rumbled past them, it quickly shifted into an airborne quietness, and Mumot knew then that they were only seconds away from going over a giant cliff.

He tried to dart sideways, but nothing sped up his gains. The cliff's quiet lip was upon him, and he knew he could do nothing to get around it now. With every bit of strength left in his arm that clung to Sylic, he turned toward the cliff and flung the little one as hard as possible, hoping his toss was strong enough for him to clear the cliff's edge and survive. Mumot caught sight of the little land dweller one last time before falling over the cliff face and into the abyss below.

Chapter Twenty-Four

THE GLOOM OF THE SOULS

The morning was bleak as Kolkesh came awake, stuffed under a rock with branches wedging him against it. He came to, with barely any light, and howling winds still driving blinding snow past his cubby hole. He was contorted into a pinch that hurt his side, struggling to kick branches until he could pull himself around to sit. After checking frozen cuts all over him, he decided he was alive enough. He remembered his new friend, the giant, snatching him and Nasok up just as they went under for the final time, scooping them like children to carry them into the darkness to where he threw them to safety. Kolkesh sat astonished at the giant's power, quickly hefting the two of them with seeming ease, and how he felt tiny in Mumot's grasp. Kolkesh felt around, and sure as beans, there lay Nasok beside him in the same stuck hole. He patted Nasok's leg, and he began to stir at the commotion.

Kolkesh helped Nasok out of the wedge both were slammed into, realizing that if the snow kept sliding, they would both be feet under it. Nasok sat up, leaning back and groaning about his side, but Kolkesh checked his bones, and he seemed reasonably safe.

"I'm headed outside to see the others. No way we were the only ones our hero saved last night!" Kolkesh stated matter-of-factly. A slight shudder hung in his words, as he had hoped they were safe.

Kolkesh was the top of his Soul-Type, a master warrior who gave less grief with more of his skills and resourcefulness. Though he cared deeply for those he liked, this team was among them. He kept it locked away tight, as a Warrior-Soul would. Kolkesh hoped he stayed true to his vow to the Chief about keeping the boy safe. He pondered that his vow may have been broken this night as he searched around. Soon a moan came from behind a rock, and there, sat upright, was Edeldon.

"You okay, Soul?" Kolkesh knelt down beside him. Edeldon nodded his head yes, but wasn't ready to talk. "Stay put and rest a bit," Kolkesh said, getting up and heading to find others.

"Hey!" Kolkesh finally started yelling, but his voice was carried away in the wind's grasp. The patch was cleared of anyone, but still, he found no other, hiking back toward the survivors empty-handed. Where did they go? He looked over to the right above them, to the cliff wall not far across the valley that continued into the darkness beyond, seeing the snow had gone over it. He worried that may have been some of their fates, but he hoped not. Kolkesh believed in the higher Soul's destiny seen fulfilled in the world. Certainly, here sat three who were still alive and together.

The others in the remaining trio were finally up shaking off the pains of the avalanche just hours ago but soon huddled up with Kolkesh. It was still dark enough with the winds howling they could not safely travel along, so they spent the night in Kolkesh's hole, clearing it enough so they could all fit. They ate what they carried and slept what they could until the light returned anew.

The dawn blew heavy with wailing winds, but the light was enough to press on. They decided to strike uphill, reaching the edge of the great cliff face Kolkesh had seen. They found Sylic tucked under tree trunk stacks against the far-right cliff wall. He was awake and surprised to see them. Giving them hugs as they had shown themselves, he invited them inside, where a rather large covering protected them finally from the wind.

"I can't believe it. I hunted, but my knee is twisted badly," Sylic showed them as they all looked at the thick wrapping he had around his pant leg.

"It was some amazing thing. The snow river blew me downhill. I tried to swim but kept going under until, somehow, I was slid clear up on a giant tree hanging over by the left cliff." Sylic pointed across.

"Then, as I watched the snow rush by, I froze, not wanting to be back in it," He continued.

"But the tree was cracking and started falling, and then, out of nowhere, Mumot sprinted right up to me, snatched me off it by my leg!" Everyone belted in awe as he spoke.

"He drug me in pitch black across that snow like we were on the hard ground, I tell you!" he bounced his body around, mimicking the movements he made when Mumot pulled him to safety.

"But we didn't make it. Mumot started getting bogged down, so we were going downhill again, but then I felt him haul me up by my leg like a hare by the ears and throw me clear away from him. I didn't see where he went from there, though." He stared down at his leg and touched it.

"Darn, nearly ripped my leg off, he threw me so hard. I don't think I hit the snow again for some time." He made a long, rounded arc with his hand to show how he flew in the air.

"I hit, felt my knee burn, thinking my leg was almost pulled off, but I swam away from the loudest noise as fast as I could until I could get clear as the snow slowed down," he showed his enclosure.

"Found this in the dark. I was looking around for anywhere to hide when I found it, so I climbed in till it felt safe," Sylic said.

The stories were truly unique to each other. Sylic looked between them, now realizing something important, and they all quickly repeated their saving by their giant friend.

"What of Mumot and Seldik?" Sylic said, looking at them in succession.

Everyone bent their heads, shaking no. Sylic felt the pain of reality and fell silent after saying, "I fear they may have gone over the cliff's edge."

"Now, we don't know anything solid just yet. It looks bad, but we need to hold out hope. We all seen what Mumot was capable of, right?" Kolkesh said.

"I feel all is not lost to us. There is a reason for this we endure, and I feel in a world beyond the winds there is some life yet that we don't now see," Edeldon broke in, stating in his Soul seeking voice, giving everyone hope anew.

"I observe with much to think, and I focus on my thoughts to understand our world, Sylic." Edeldon continued. "You may not understand our Soul Religion of self, but it has merit and comes through in our darkest times as our singular self struggles in this world." He continued with resolve.

"I can't understand what I feel now, maybe from the night or my injuries or weak status, but through pain comes my power of Soul stronger, so I will say there is something out there for us; I dare say someone?" Everyone was looking at him intently.

"Like Seldik?" Sylic finally asked him.

"No, maybe not how you say it, I think..." Edeldon wandered off in thought a moment. "But I feel more. I sense another, Seldik maybe, but another... version, maybe?" Edeldon wasn't able to define his vision.

"You're saying he may have moved on to another life, then?" Kolkesh spoke more softly than he ever had.

"Unable to tell you what you wish me to say, old friend, unable indeed." Edeldon left it at that.

The group sat mulling the words over in their thoughts, mundanely checking their gear as they sat.

"I know you wish more; I will give you another vision to ponder, which I have not yet deciphered. You should all know it may be of Mumot," Edeldon said as they again stopped everything and faced him anew.

"A vision is a foggy event, mixed up, not in line with the normal time, and must be organized into something substantial in our reality to understand it," Edeldon spoke of the Vision-Soul way of life that he was a master in.

"I have pieced this unique vision together, just some, mind you, and it is intriguing." Edeldon turned to face them, continuing gracefully.

"I feel, no, sense. Yes. Sense," he paused like a spell had been cast upon him, "I sense another, a stranger, here in the valley!" Kolkesh gave a best-puzzled look as Edeldon raised his hand before the questions started.

"Let me explain because it is not Mumot in this vision. It is another, but of mixed, um, type?" Edeldon had lost everyone's understanding entirely now.

"Type?" Sylic now butted in, unable to stop himself.

"A beast, but yet a person. It cannot be explained as I said," Edeldon said, then abruptly dropped it.

"To add to this confusion, as I try focusing on Seldik, his transference includes a combination of humans, like he is split in two." Edeldon again shook his head in surrender to what he could give them.

"So these mountains may have a monster of man and beast that may be upon us at some point?" Kolkesh was thinking through his warrior plotting style out loud.

"And Seldik may be gone but back again as two people?" Nasok now joined the fray of questions that everyone was pondering.

Edeldon spoke little, deciding to bow out entirely at these talks. It was unnecessary to go beyond what he knew.

"Well, we must await the winds, but we will be out of food sometime within the week, as our big items are long lost. We have our stores left," he continued revealing the bad news.

"But we can't move downhill. The snow has packed trees in death stacks, and the piles cannot be climbed due to the threat of falling in these crevasses."

"It isn't looking great uphill, as far as I can see in this junk, but it has none of those traps. The snow is flatter so long as we don't hit more weather like yesterday." Kolkesh talked while sealing the entrance off more.

"I think we all agree. If Seldik and Mumot are near, they may get to us." Sylic seemed hopeful of his idea. The group agreed, set a low fire to help warm them, then settled in as it got darker.

The winds held on but reduced slightly. The light came brighter the next day, but barely. The group packed up what was left and exited the enclosure to start the arduous journey uphill, disheartened that none of their companions turned up during the night. Seldik and Mumot were still lost to them, and their sad moods showed. Nobody cared to hide it as they hiked on slowly. They kept together, worried about the man-beast Edeldon warned of, remaining focused on their steps as they hunted for their friends. Long hours passed before they broke for lunch, then continued for more hours.

The trail was more complex, with branches sticking up everywhere, slowing their steps to a crawl.

All soon decided to head onto the flow slide against the left bank, everyone aware that was the side where the most rocks fell. The snow had almost killed them, then concealed the truth of their missing, and they knew it was likely to cave again. But they had no choice, so they reluctantly crawled up on the higher snow to walk to the left cliffs, peering up at the heights in much distress of what came down the day before and now lies all along the sidewall. The anxiety they felt gave them renewed vigor as they punched their feet down faster, climbing to escape the devastation. Everyone hung closer together now. Sylic, having a hard time, dropped back many times from his knee injury until they all agreed to pace slower.

The day crept on uneventfully, all happy for the fact, but as they crested a considerable bluff with snow piled like a cliff wall some forty hands high, they halted, unsure of what to do. The likelihood that the snowy wall could come crashing down with one wrong step, forcing them to relive the trauma of the day prior punched them deep in the gut.

Kolkesh hung his head for a moment, and each stuffed down the dread they were all feeling before choosing to climb between the rock, packing snow and carefully building steps to climb up. It took some time, but they all managed the crest before resting from the effort before moving on. A single rock fell from above and cracked against the frozen ground below, small and harmless, but it made the team mount up to move on quickly. The path increased in complexity, with boulders mounding out of the snow in frozen blocks, sending cracks across the ground. They weaved this way and that around the boulders then over cracks, making only a short distance in an hour.

Winds rose, so they knew they could not sleep by that cliff, and decided to break right again before dark to find another hidden hole. They turned in single file line, heading quickly for the other side in defeat, knowing they would not yet leave this place of sorrow for another day. Kolkesh let the group around the bank, hopeful it would block the miserable wind for a minute. He was deep in thought, staring down at his feet as he paced, and stepped squarely between the massive swept tusks of a Woolley Mammoth. Kolkesh halted in shock and looked up with wide eyes as others behind him hit against his back, just as withdrawn in their own thoughts. Kolkesh realized he was now face to face with a giant mammoth head sitting in the snow. The mighty beast raised its trunk over Kolkesh in a panic, letting out a trumpeting so loud he threw himself backward, careening into his stacked friends, knocking them into the snow behind.

Kolkesh toppled over then rolled off to the side while the others were belting shocked remarks as the beast trumpeted again. Kolkesh scurried backward to create distance between himself and the beast. The others frantically shoveled their arms into the snow, trying to pull themselves backward before hitting a dead end against the rock behind them. They could not keep their eyes off the beast. Whether it be the warning from Edeldon or knowing such a beast could easily kill them, they were all prepared to flee from it without a fight.

Those who had a full view of the beast were frozen in place as a girl jumped up right behind the elephant's head with terror in her eyes. She quickly shook her head and blinked, staring at them lying in the snow. Kolkesh, being the closest, lied on his back, arms behind him, staring back with his mouth wide open. The group looked at each other, equally shocked, then those who had managed to hide, ducked further away, watching the others gawk at whatever they saw as silence fell over them. The girl finally broke the stalemate by jumping clear over the elephant, raising a spear and pointing it toward them. She yelled something that the winds buffered, but they got the gist that it was a warning she would attack them. The elephant remained facing them and was not turning to attack her, which everyone, still widemouthed, noticed, and they continued to watch the incredible sight before them.

Finally, the others behind the rocks struck their heads around carefully to see what was happening. The girl became aggravated when she realized there were more of them and screamed more unrecognized sounds muffled by the wind. Sylic was the one who peaked. He still had his mouth wide open but threw his arms up in surrender as soon as she threatened them. The girl looked puzzled by his motion, sticking her spear toward Kolkesh, who was now slowly raising his hands, too, not wanting to fight this impossible girl or the elephant.

Eventually, the rest of the group raised their hands in surrender, showing they were not attacking, and hoped she noticed that they were just as confused as she was. Kolkesh then motioned his men down onto their knees, which they did, to show they meant no harm to the duo, but the girl held steady. Though she was small, far smaller than they were, they realized she knew how to use that weapon. Sylic was probably the closest to her size, so Kolkesh was the first to conclude they were both from the land. He tried to sit up more, but she instantly became more aggressive, so he raised his hands higher. Her eyes remained locked on him. Kolkesh studied her stance for a moment, noticing she wasn't in a position to throw the spear or launch an attack, and prepared to take the lead. He was dead wrong when he did. However, as he leaned forward against her threats and reached down to remove his knives, she instantly turned sideways, then, with one quick action, rolled her hand around, throwing the spear so fast that Kolkesh barely had a second to react, catching the spear just before it hit his chest. The girl stepped back in shock as Kolkesh looked down at how close he had just come to death.

But the girl didn't hesitate long, reaching to the beast's side where a bag was strapped and grabbed two more spears. She stood back a bit further now, realizing the giant man could catch the spears, and set up for her next move. Kolkesh, seeing her reset, reached down with one other hand and pulled out his knives one at a time, and tossed them forward in surrender. He motioned the others to do the same with theirs, but they were reluctant, unable to do what he just did as a War-Soul. The girl stood unmoving, now hesitating from the offer. So, one by one, they gained enough courage to dislodge their weapons and ever so carefully toss them out into the same pile ahead. After a moment, the girl seemed to relax as she looked at the pile of surrendered weapons. After a long pause with no movement, the elephant calmed down, and with that, the girl lowered her spear.

She then motioned to them, pointing up and down her body then pointing at them. Confused by her gesture, everyone wished desperately for Seldik's presence. He would know what to do, they all thought. She continued the motions with great effort, using her voice as the meaning failed them. Kolkesh tried to calm her with open palms pushing down to say relax, steady, but she would have nothing of it and finally banged her hands to her sides and stopped motioning. Kolkesh didn't, though. He pointed up and down her body, just as she did. He pointed to his eyes, then swept his arm into the valley below. She seemed to agree with his interpretation, and with a hopeful gaze, she nodded broadly in approval. Kolkesh looked at the others while raising his shoulders. Then Sylic had an idea.

"I think she is asking us something about her out there!" Sylic said, shouting to overcome the winds. Kolkesh pointed to him and looked back toward her.

"She hunts another like her, maybe?" he pondered, looking down, now sad to give her the news if she truly desired. He shook his head from side to side very clearly, then looked at her. Her head fell, so he knew she hunted another lost to her. Kolkesh felt horrible. She finally walked sideways and laid softly against the elephant's head and wept.

It was getting darker, so finally, Kolkesh motioned toward her then pointed to his group, showing they wished to go past to the other side. He then pressed his palms together against his head to show they needed to sleep somewhere. She paused but then motioned them past, pointing to keep their distance by making a large arc around her as they went by. They slowly stood to walk around her like she insisted, Kolkesh waving them off from the weapon stack. They surrendered them, and he wanted to make sure she knew that before motioning that they would get them later, seeming to prove to her they meant no harm, even in the dark. Kolkesh, with the others, gave a short bow to the two as they passed, but the girl seemed off at their size compared to hers, keeping a healthy attack-ready look to her as they went on. Kolkesh waved them on, turned to her, then pointed in the direction they were going, and said "We will be that way and stay that way," then they traveled on out of sight.

Chapter Twenty-Five

BETTER WITH TWO

Deneska stared as the band of strangers passed around her, single file, each bowing their head as they passed at a distance safe to her. She couldn't believe the enormous size of these men and feared they were the giants from her village's scary stories. But they did not attack her, and even gave up some weapons. She glanced back at the pile they left behind and again stared at them, crossing over the snow away from her. They did not even take the weapons or try to retrieve them. The biggest one easily caught her spear, which she threw as fast as she could, yet he still didn't attack. She wondered if it was Blakely they feared. He was lying on his stomach, watching them walk out of view in the dark gray evening. They motioned for sleep, obviously needing to find a place to hunker down. Even among giants, warmth was important, she thought, recalling their garments thick with fur.

Deneska sat listening, but little could be heard with the winds, then she looked up into the valley above, knowing her scouting below proved they could not leave this place downhill. Up was the only way. Her friend was hurt, and the giants had not seen her sister. She sat weeping, the excitement renewing the gut-wrenching pain of losing her sister and reminding her of her perilous situation. If Blakley could not stand for long, she would be forced to decide whether to stay with him or abandon the only friend she had left in her life. She could not bear to think of it, so she let her mind wonder back to the giants, realizing that joining them may be her only chance at survival. But what if they refused her or her friend? If they denied her, she would be lost. She should have stopped them right then and offered to surrender. They certainly could have killed her, despite Blakley. She was not a shy girl or timid. If that is what she must face, so be it. She decided that in the morning, she would go to their camp before they left, surrender, and elicit their help.

The next morning, Deneska woke to the sound of Blakley standing up. Excited, she jumped up and rushed to his side to check him over. He had no other injuries, besides the one behind his ear, she concluded. He seemed stable. She reached into a bag to find food for him, but only dry reed was left, which he happily ate. The rest has been lost in the snow. She pulled him around carefully and saw he could walk fine. His eyes were open, appearing happy while he wrapped his trunk around her waist. She gave his cheek a quick pat, then, with a big smile, headed him around to walk toward the giant's camp, hoping to catch them. She came to a stop along the ridge they had vanished over, and the group stood staring in her direction, again showing open hands.

They just stood there. Deneska knew it was now or never. She held her palm against Blakley's forehead and ordered him to stay as she slowly walked toward them. She grabbed her spear out of the snow and used it to steady her as she walked toward the group. When she got halfway, she stopped. Looking at them, she dropped her spear on the ground, slowly opening her hands to them in surrender. She waited as they talked, then the biggest reached over and sent their smallest man toward her, but he hesitated until a firm push had him approaching cautiously with hands held low but wide open.

When Sylic got close enough to make eye contact, he held his hand to his chest and proclaimed, "Sylic," then pointed to her. He bowed slightly and cracked a smile, which Deneska found charming. She couldn't help but turn away as she broke a half grin, which made Sylic chuckle.

"Deneska." She gave her name on her tongue, but he repeated it exotically. "Deenezka," he said clearly as she nodded her head. He then turned back to the others, shouting, "Deenezka!" They all nodded in approval.

He turned back to face her and stepped forward. With his hands slightly open, he pointed to her spear in the snow. Deneska stepped back as she looked at it, now taking in his closer features. He had a narrow, tan face with tiny, bright eyes that pierced all they looked at. She watched him tuck a long, stringy piece of hair back into the pile under his furry cloak hood and noticed his hands were just as thin as hers. Deneska saw him slowly reach for the spear, then stop to stare at her. She remained unmoving, knowing she was going with them either way or she would die here. Sylic reached down to grab the spear, but instead of picking it up, he bent down on both knees, slowly turning it sideways, then picked it up and handed it to her. Deneska felt a warmth come over her from the offering of peace, especially since it came from the stunningly handsome man she felt like the world had handed her.

She snapped out of it when Blakley trumpeted, pacing back and forth from the act he witnessed. Deneska turned to him and reached her palm high up, pushing it at him as he calmed down. She turned back to Sylic, then reached out quickly to grab the shaft. She surprised herself when she did not yank it away from his open hands, but remained with her hands on his as they made eye contact. She removed it gently from his hands, bowing slightly with a full smile. Sylic smiled broadly and gave her a timid giggle, which she responded to in relief as she exhaled with enough force it was audible despite the windy noise. Chuckling, he raised opened arms toward their pile of weapons some distance away. Deneska blinked her eyes, then waved him on in approval. Sylic turned to motion for the others to come over before he proceeded, waiting beside her as they approached. They, too, stopped short, with Sylic naming each, starting with the biggest.

"Kolkesh. Kolkesh," he said slowly, then moved to the others. "Edeldon. Edeldon." He said each name twice as she repeated it with her tongue in cheek. "Nasok. Nasok," he finished, then went to him again, smiling, "Sylic." He bowed for her again. The others followed his gesture and bent forward politely. Sylic again repeated to his fellows, "Deenezka," and they all nodded and shared a smile with the girl.

Sylic continued over to the pile of weapons himself. Kolkesh offered Deneska to sit with them for a minute, and she complied. She sat staring as Kolkesh repeated Seldik's prior motions on the ground, but she did not recognize anything. Kolkesh instead moved to draw the valley they were in and pointed to the cliffs, which Deneska did recognize. Sylic returned and walked around to her side, dropping weapons nearby instead of bringing them closer. Deneska appreciated the act. He then approached, sitting closest to her. She did not move nor look toward him, but smiled. Kolkesh drew the lower valley with obstacles across it, pointed downhill, shaking his head no to her, which she acknowledged. Hence, he drew the upper valley, pointed it up, showing a big circle, then walked up the drawing with his fingers, pointing up to the summit. Deneska nodded her head, agreeing with their plan, and the meeting was broken up.

As Deneska went to Blakley to pack up, Sylic offered to join her. The elephant didn't seem to mind him, but Kolkesh made Blakley uneasy, and would not turn away from them. Deneska and Sylic sensed it. Sylic showed her it was okay, that he would inform them to keep their distance to avoid any problems. She showed him the beast could walk easy then showed him the wound, which made Sylic flinch after seeing its severity. Deneska indicated that she felt the same, then pet the elephant's head forward of his ear.

Sylic returned to the group, picked up their weapons, then waited for the duo at a distance. He informed them of the animal's reaction to the bigger ones, and informed them to keep their distance and remain only in front of the animal, to which they agreed.

"He'll warm up to us eventually," Kolkesh chuckled. "Can you believe a girl from the Nether rides upon the biggest beast in the land?" Everyone was impressed. They had shared much discussion the previous night about her and where she might have come from. They confirmed Edeldon's vision of a half-beast, half-human up here, and hoped that meant Seldik's journey wasn't over yet.

Deneska and Blakley were now headed up, and Sylic joined her in the rear as the giants went on ahead to keep their distance. Deneska patted her friend and told Sylic, "Blakley," and Sylic smiled broadly.

"Blakley, well me, big sir," he said to him and politely bowed to her elephant. Deneska laughed, as did he. They headed toward the unknown above happier, but a few glances back into the dismal, dreary view behind them showed that they were all leaving something very dear behind as they went.

Blakley seemed to be back to normal, moving along with powerful strides. He climbed, outpacing Deneska and Sylic, who always lagged together. The elephant wouldn't quite reach the heights of the giants without stopping and waiting for them to catch up before continuing, preferring to stay closer to Deneska. The two young, small ones found themselves unable to keep eyes off each other. They often caught glances, and the chuckles were infectious to both. Deneska fumbled her footing often, and Sylic always reached out to assist her up over things he danced over. She was impressed with his hiking, knowing she could match it but didn't want to, instead keeping up the ruse of not being as able. Sometimes they crossed solid piles of rock as Sylic kept hold of her hand for the entire time. Deneska grateful the stone came. The giants looked back, commenting unheard whispers in the winds about the two. Even Blakley looked back occasionally to find them lagging for unknown reasons. Once on open ground, Sylic looked down, realizing their hand holding was not needed, and reluctantly released hers. Deneska only smiled at him and then kept close to him.

Lunch was called, and Deneska showed she had no food, but pulled a tuft of grass out to feed Blakley. Immediately, all hands were out, offering her something to eat. She felt warm from the offers, taking a piece from Sylic. The giants made an unknown gesture and handed him a couple of scraps, which he, in turn, handed to her. She bowed to them as they gestured her effort off with smiles, patting Sylic on the back. He looked embarrassed as Deneska went to tend to Blakley. Upon her return to the huddle, Sylic was telling them something of Blakley and said his name. He pointed to her and drew the volcano in the snow, pointing toward its top, indicating the eruption in the valley. Then, he motioned that they came here because of it, too. Deneska sadly hung her head. She earnestly looked into each of their faces to show the sadness she carried for her sister. She motioned toward the lower valley, raising four fingers to ask if they had a count of four with them. Kolkesh slowly raised six fingers, then covered two of them. She sadly realized they were missing two. They all bowed their heads low, knowing they had all lost someone. She split tears as Sylic raised six fingers and dropped two slowly again, the rest staying still with grief.

Sylic pointed to her and Blakley and raised two fingers, but they were now in grief as she slowly raised three fingers and began to shake violently.

Sylic reached over and cupped her outstretched hand with his own. Deneska wept openly in a burst of tears. Sylic crawled over close to hold her. She pressed her face deep into his inviting arms and stayed there for a long time. The group sat quietly, each thinking of their losses until the girl recovered to give all fake smiles as she tended to her fantastic beast Blakley.

"Poor girl been through it, hasn't she?" Kolkesh said with remorse as he sat back. "She has her only friend there, probably been with her since she was a child. I guess him some thirty years old."

"She is strong for what she has endured. She even stitched him up. He's got a wound that should have killed him." Sylic pointed to the long laceration behind Blakley's ear.

"She was wicked fast with that spear. Almost got me even though I'm a catcher, mind you." Kolkesh let the ordeal sink in.

"You think she lost a father, mother, or sibling?" Kolkesh wondered out loud. "Or all of them, maybe. She's young, must have had many more around before Mother blew," Kolkesh ended.

"She looks to be from the plains, maybe far up by the volcano, closer, then had to head south. It was someone very close to her, whoever it was, but we saw nobody," Nasok stated.

"Well, we may have lost the best of us, you all. Let's get back to it." Kolkesh stood and started up again.

As they approached the fork in the valley, they realized the elephant would fare better by going right with less angle and snow, but the darkness ahead looked a bit more ominous. Deneska also pointed right after thinking on it as they marched on with Blakley, walking uncaring behind them. At once, Sylic saw something at a distance and then wheeled left, yelling ahead to stop, but the group was buffered by the winds and continued. Deneska paused, deciding what to do, and finally capitulating toward where Sylic observed something in the snow. As she approached, she saw what he was looking at: tracks! Human tracks!

Sylic looked at her with surprise, then darted toward the group, stopping them ahead to turn them to look. Deneska excitedly went to hold Blakley, then returned to the group surrounding the imprints. Deneska put her foot near one. The small size came close, while the other was a giant's track. They all studied them, patting Sylic on the back as they did. But as they searched for more headed up or down, nothing remained, the winds ripping away everything but a bruised snow mark with very little depth on the frozen ground.

"Not Mumot's print. His is rounder," Kolkesh yelled across to the others.

"Seldik then?" Said Nasok as everyone perked up.

"She fits the other print. Is it from who she seeks?" Sylic suggested. "Maybe another girl?" Kolkesh came over to observe her foot.

"Could be. We need to go this way, everyone," Kolkesh yelled as they grouped up.

Deneska was sitting, staring up at the long, rugged trail of snow, then looked at Blakley. Sylic realized this was impossible for the elephant, or at least not recommended, and told the others about the issue.

"We must split up then," Kolkesh stated. "We must reach where they reached, maybe not far up?" Kolkesh continued. "We could turn them around or cross over to the lower split to regroup up past the pass." He stood, taking in both ways now.

Sylic spent time trying to explain a plan in the snow to Deneska. They would not let her go alone. They would split up, find the ones ahead, then cut over to meet the group going up the easier route, maybe past the pass above. Deneska showed much gratitude for doing such as they ensured another would be with her and Blakley. Sylic immediately pointed to him with her as Kolkesh laughed.

"Yeah, you're going to go with her and the Blakley beast, Sylic, of course," Kolkesh chuckled. Deneska looked at both, wondering what was spoken about her.

"Honestly, either way, it isn't great. Whether we split or stay together, it won't help our survival, but it helps our speed, and we need that," Kolkesh stated as he tapped his food pouch.

"We have a day's rations at best each. The elephant maybe does not get food after today," Kolkesh said blankly.

"So, we split. You two little ones head to the right, and the three of us will go left to follow the tracks. If we catch them early, we still go over the summit to try and break right toward you in the lower saddle. If it remains lower, that is," Kolkesh said.

"Listen, find them or not, don't wait. We must continue off the mountain heights to find food and warmth, so keep going as you can. We won't be far behind," Kolkesh was talking directly to Sylic.

"Keep going to water and food, then wait, build good smoke. We will find you then. Have no doubt," Kolkesh said, though he seemed concerned.

"We don't know what is over these mountains, but we can't be here, so make the best of it," he continued. "At worst, head north our way some. Maybe the mountains end." Kolkesh reached out a hand to Sylic, grabbed his arm, then shook it. Nasok and Edeldon shook him, too. Then, hesitantly, they each lightly shook Deneska's tiny hands with theirs.

"I see a future for us all. Travel in peace," Edeldon said prominently.

"You two are alone, but you have the beast, and we have ours!" Nasok pointed to Kolkesh as they all laughed.

Deneska hesitated long at her friends' side as they watched the three depart up the steeper grade. She prayed to the spirits above that her sister was the one who travels with another. If so, by taking the easier route, she felt she was abandoning the search for her, but she knew she must take Blakley to better ground and walked on to the right, following Sylic.

Chapter Twenty-Six

ONE HIGH LAKE

Seldik enjoyed Aleelah as they walked steadily along. The downhill slope was much better, and they maintained a faster pace in the high mountain air. Fewer winds bucked against their chaffed legs, so it was warmer but shadier as they went. They stayed far to the side, trying to catch the finishing rays as the sun fell. Finding a solid tree group, they crawled into it to make a raging fire. Staring across the firelight at each other had them grinning, thinking secrets as they watched a full moon trying to cut through clouds that mostly resisted. They had no food, but Seldik found some giant cones, and after toying with the nuts inside, found they contained a woody and smokey flesh. They gathered them in bundles to roast over some coals. They found the food delicious, picking and eating morsels until satisfied, then gathering more to roast and tuck away in their bags for later eating.

Seldik saw pitch drip, igniting fire from the cones, and soon, he was covered in it as he tried to ball some in with ash. He broke off the cone bottoms, then finished them concave with his knife. Aleelah gazed at him and his unusual construct as he worked. He smeared the black pitch on the cone's rounded form, then threw it in the snow. When he retrieved it, he showed her the melted snow within. Her face lit up at the sight of water, so he handed her a full one. She admired its creation, drank, then refilled it with snow, warming it near the fire again. He added nuts, and the low steam off the water made a broth. They sipped from the same cup, both impressed with the taste. She seemed impressed with Seldik, which he noted, realizing he liked the attention. After that, they positioned nearer the fire and fell asleep on a noiseless mountain.

In the morning, they got up late, packed up the new bowls, then headed down again, walking for hours as their strides increased, though Seldik still had to reserve himself for her. Eventually, they walked straight out on a snow-covered patch of the cliff overlooking the beyond. The clouds below them still blocked everything but ridges on both sides, so they sat a while, picking open nuts to eat. Occasionally, they chucked the hulls at each other, growing more playful as the days passed, neither of them no longer in a hurry. When they finished, they readied to hike back to the valley, but a significant gap in the clouds crept by under them, revealing what was on the other side.

They both stood in awe at the sight, sliver by sliver unfolding as the window unveiled the pieces in succession. It was a giant, beautiful lake surrounded by trees and snow as far as the eye could see. It was as blue as Seldik's eyes. They glanced back at each other, not wanting to miss anything about it. It was a massive lake but still far up in the mountains, a high-elevation wonderland. It wasn't a broad, open valley like the one they had come from, but a cascade of rolling hills filled with pine and snow deep to the shoreline. The gap in the clouds closed before the lake's ending was revealed, but it was enough to tell the newcomers this was their destiny. Cheerfully, they moved steadily down toward the valley.

By night, they realized this was no small lake. The trees were again giant, and they knew that their size must have created an illusion, making them think they were much closer than they actually were. It would be another day or more before they reached it, but their good fortune remained when they found a campsite with a tiny spring running off a rock in a flat area full of soft pine needles to sleep on.

Again, they built a raging fire, and once they were settled, Seldik stepped away to pull a large, rounded chunk of bark from a dead tree and propped it up to the mouth of the spring, allowing the water to flow off behind a bush, creating a make-shift shower.

Seldik offered it to Aleelah, who appreciated it immensely. Grabbing a washing root from her bag, she stepped behind the bush to strip down. He could see her head slathered with white foam, and wondered what the root was. As she rinsed the foam from her long hair, she caught him staring, then turned around, smiling. She cleansed her clothes with the same root, then stepped out and over to the fire, wearing only a thin piece of leather around her chest and another longer piece around her lean waist. Seldik could not keep his eyes off of her. She ginned back at him, tossing him the slimy root, then showed him to roll it between his hands in the water. Seldik nodded in understanding, then stepped behind the bush as she hung her clothes on sticks to dry by the fire.

The water was freezing, and, being much taller than Aleelah, he was mostly exposed over the small bush. After experimenting with the root, he produced a thick lather that smelled like cold, wet earth. As he scrubbed, he caught Aleelah looking his way. He smiled, but bashfully turned away, just as she had. He continued on, scrubbing the inside of his fur clothes, then felt embarrassed, realizing he had nothing else to wear except his waist wrap. He knew he could not put on his furs, seeing how wet they now were, so he held them in front of him and wandered back to the fire.

Aleelah was watching him from the corner of her eye as he hung his clothes to dry, then sat down across from her. They hid behind the tall lick of the flames until their clothes dried and they were able to dress. Once they did, they foraged for more nuts, then sat close together, elbows almost brushing as they roasted them. When they tired, Aleelah laid down her bag close to Seldik, who leaned back against the dead log, unmoving as they slept.

In the morning, clouds broke just as they stepped into the valley proper, seeing the lake in its entirety for the first time. They were coming into the upper end, where large rivers flowed toward the far shore that vanished on the other side, just out of view. Mountains bracketed the valley like a picture all the way around. They headed straight for the river, following it downhill toward the water's edge. Soon they were walking the primarily flat ground within tall pines, seeing large deer and other fast beasts darting around as they walked. Large birds shrieked high above, unseen as squirrels the size of a fawn with different colored tails ran up trees to disappear. The raging river was impressive as it rushed by, and they picked up their pace, eager to reach the open beach. Before they knew it, they were sprinting, Seldik letting her outpace him, but the race wasn't as easy as he let on. She could run very fast. Watching her form move ahead of him sent him into a daze, causing him to trip, falling hard against the ground. Aleelah heard the thump and ran back to fall down beside him, laughing. She realized long before that his land skills were not as tuned as hers were, but knew he probably fell from watching her. She bumped against his arm as he examined his knee. It was the first contact she made with him, and he smiled.

They reached the shore, looked at each other, and deciding to get in. Aleelah reached down to touch the water and then jumped back in shock. He tried it, and found it was beyond ice cold, so they chickened out, and instead, decided to walk along the beach to find a shelter then try fishing. They walked for hours, taking in their beautiful surroundings. The beach came and went, and they climbed around tall cliffs, revealing new beaches, each their own dreamscape.

They climbed over a long-swept cliff, heading toward a tucked-away cove with an island in the center. The beauty was unbelievable. They clawed up, finally having to stop, realizing they must climb the cliff hump to get into the paradise. When they finally reached the top to stand on solid rock, the magnificent views beckoned them to stay awhile, the massive trees now appearing tiny on the other side. They took it in as Seldik looked far northward against the lake's inlet. There, he saw the slightest motion in the tree line, too dark to make out. He tapped Aleelah's arm, pointing to it. They stared together, trying to make out any familiar shape as the sun's setting rays highlighted it. Eventually, the motion began to rise above the trees in a slow back-and-forth path. When it finally peaked above the treetops, they instantly realized it was dense smoke, likely from several fires.

Aleelah jumped up, Seldik right behind her as they squinted toward the smoke. When they were able to make out three fire lights, Aleelah reached out her hand in excitement and grabbed his arm. He looked back toward the paradise they were headed down and took another long look, then motioned her back down the way they came, headed toward the fires. They reached the bottom, then walked miles toward the fires. When it got dark, they made a pitch torch, lit it, and continued along the beach through the beginning of the night, the bright moon helping to light their path. The night was placid, and they could clock along fast, gazing all the time into the lapping waters of the majestic lake as the moon's reflection rippled over it. Both wondered who they would find once they arrived, but Seldik proposed it couldn't be anyone he traveled with, soon realizing it may be some of her kind. He pointed to her then at the fires as she raised her arms, saying she was unsure, but she then broke out in a little dance before grabbing his arm anew, hopeful that it might be.

Seldik wished they could talk easily. He wondered if their relationship would change if it were her folks, but he was happy she was happy. They shared simple words as they went, picking up a few of each other's terms like rock, stick, snow, cliff, and sun, but nothing that resembled real conversation. It wasn't until after midnight that they realized they were still far away. The giant lake was playing games of the distance again, so they turned up into the trees and slept the other half of the night away.

When they woke up, they quickly set out again, eating roasted nuts along the way. They walked for hours, sharing more small words, and taking breaks on the beach until the last hour of sun began to gleam through the trees. Eager to discover the source of the fire before nightfall, they pushed on across a frigid stream, cutting around the edge of the lake.

Finally, they smelled smoke and saw an ashy, grey cloud creep over the canopy high above. Stepping into high gear, they made it into a clearing that held several huts with thatch roofs, all rounded, and tended by people doing various chores along its perimeter. Someone spotted them and announced their entrance at once, everyone dropping what they were doing to stare at them in shock. Aleelah and Seldik stood still, taking in the new group when just then, a scream rang out from within a hut, and an older woman with a bad foot burst out, running toward them with arms wide open. Aleelah dropped everything and yelled, "Miaaa!" then ran to her, where they met with an embrace. They held each other tightly, then dropped down, crying and yelling as others began to run their way. The entire village was upon the two reunited women, and hugs were given all around. The small village was roaring with commotion, everyone speaking her tongue as Aleelah dragged the old lady toward Seldik. The woman was reluctant, but Aleelah convinced her to come. Seldik put down his stuff and stood up straight. When he realized he towered over them, he looked out at their gazes and tried to make himself appear more meek.

Aleelah turned to the lady in tow and told her his name, before yelling out "Seldik," for all to hear.

"Ah!" said the crowd of onlookers as the old lady came closer, carefully looking up at his tall form. "Sel… Seldik?" she said, then looked at Aleelah, who nodded her head, and the woman reached out to shake his hand. He bowed as they all came closer, looking him up and down, curious about his height. Aleelah stepped beside him, grabbed his arm, then started toward the fire after saying, "Mia." He assumed that was her word for mother and was instantly happy for her. She had found survivors! And as it turned out, her mother lived! Seldik was impressed they escaped the deadly ash to make it here, knowing what they went through.

They made it to the fire, where much food was brought to them, along with warm clothes. Everyone huddled around to discuss the loss of Aleelah's sister and what they went through. Her mother cried, then they cried together, leaving Seldik feeling helpless, as he could do nothing to ease their pain. He knew she had looked for her since they explained each other's lost ones in detail. Aleelah had broken down several times on the journey, and Seldik just sat by her and waited, but Aleelah was tough, never falling in his arms, so Seldik respected her time before they moved on. This reunion was a big help to her. So Seldik let them talk and excused himself to walk the beach line, wrapped in his new, warm blanket and look out at the water reflecting the moon's soft glow.

Aleelah eventually came to find him and sat by his side. She pointed to the blanket draped over him, which he offered half to her. She cuddled up against him underneath it as he looked at her with wide eyes. She had found her village, her mother, but had come to check on him. She smiled at him in the dark and pushed hard against his arm. They sat looking toward the water for a long time. A party was being had behind them, and everyone was dancing, singing, and passing around some spirits by the fires that now burned so bright, that the two left their retreat by the water to join them. The newcomers danced, Aleelah spun, and the awful-tasting spirits made Seldik feel great. When they finally tired, they collapsed in sweat and exhaustion on the sands as the party wound down, Aleelah scooting over until her head rested on Seldik's arm. They laughed loudly until they could no longer, and when they fell silent, Aleelah reached up and kissed him hard, which he returned eagerly. They stopped to laugh again, but she pulled him to her as they walked, holding hands along the beach until settling into huts her mother pointed out, dividing them for the night for the first time since they met. They snickered but complied to avoid offending the mother.

In the morning, Seldik rose with a mission in his heart. He left his hut, then headed to a long, smooth rock face covering the ground above the village. Here he settled in for a long day as he carved away symbols on the front to commemorate all that had happened, letting his grief pour out with each strike against the stone. He found himself again in the act, realizing he was also the happiest he had ever been in finding Aleelah. As his emotions toiled within him, he chipped away the vivid visions that came to him. By midday, Aleelah had found him. As she offered him food, she wandered around the rock floor, seeing all the images. Soon, she was helping Seldik as he outlined his panels for her to follow, carving them deeper with more meaning, giving thick to thin lines, fully covered bodies for blood spilling. In the end, the pair stood back for a time, studying their creation before holding hands again to head back to the village.

Chapter Twenty-Seven

A PASS TWICE TAKEN

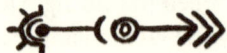

Kolkesh, Edeldon, and Nasok hiked uphill in great stride, no longer waiting for the small ones to catch up, since their giant lungs could take in better air at this height. Each day, they powered up the snow and rocks, not resting until they could no longer see in the dark. They found shelters of sorts, huddling up hungry and cold each night, after conserving what dried reserves they had. In the early dawn, the winds howled, but they pushed through the thick clouds, many times, turning the wrong way within the valley and having to slow, moving side to side until they could climb up and carry on, resting only when entirely out of breath.

As they neared the top, they broke out of the fog. The clouds now settling below them. "Well, the tops look like the bottoms. Now we know," Kolkesh chuckled and headed on, the rest following.

They pounded on, but in the sunlight now. The winds were still sailing strong, flapping untied strings into the eyes of the unprepared. They hunkered down, deciding to push over the top and down the backside, chasing the footprints threatening to blow away in the gusts to leave bare rocks in their place. They powered on, lungs burning as sweat pouring from a grueling pace. Finally, they were at the top of the world, looking north to south at a long peak line high above them into the looming clouds, threatening to break toward them.

Kolkesh looked over the top, then back down, and was about to motion onward, but spotted a flapping string near a boulder to the south. They hiked over to it, and were in awe as they observed the fine, detailed carvings that depicted a great journey. They relived the experience in its detail, then looked at each other, knowing at once that it was the work of Seldik. They roared and cheered, throwing up their arms in success, knowing he was alive and well. Beside it was another rock with a similar language. It held other unusual images, one being of a mammoth and a village. At once, they realized the girl Deneska hunted was with Seldik and was okay! They happily slapped each other, Kolkesh taking way too hard a whale on the others as they yelled anew, just in case Sylic and Deneska could hear them far off down somewhere east.

They stared at the images for a while as a wave of grief hit them, knowing their friend, the yet-to-be-understood Soul, thought they were all dead, the mountain claiming them. They each read the rock, its terrifying images surreal, as Kolkesh looked at the other two and then yanked out his knife. They stared at him as he went to the rock to put some crosses over a few perils that were not the truth. Below were written the three Souls' identifying marks as survivors. They also wrote Sylic's mark beside them, then went to draw out the images of Deneska and Blakley. Kolkesh added a small smile under the grouping to ensure those who see in the future will better understand what happened. Kolkesh added a prominent figure for Mumot, marking him sideways, not upside down, because they were unsure of his demise. They scribed count marks under it. Happy with the now finished depiction, he put his knife away, and they resumed their hike with a renewed bounce to their step.

The rescuers camped, then hiked again at dawn until they saw tracks to a tall cliff they, too, headed for. In front of them, far down, they saw a massive, magical lake entirely entrapped within the mountains, and beautiful clouds that puffed around the shore. They knew then where those two would be, so they headed down. They made the valley in the dark with the help of the moon and their big eyes. Though not as seeing as Mumot's were, they were impressive, as they seemed to double their distance from the day before. Finally, they camped when they found the makeshift shower Seldik had made, plus the small drawing carved in a tree of an attractive naked woman, and they chuckled. They made a fire over Seldik's leftover coals, discovered his secret of the nuts, gathered more, then roasted to devour until they were full.

The three happily told stories, sang, ate, then bathed in the waters as the prior residents must have. They fell asleep soon after to take off hiking as soon as they awoke, finding the big river to follow as Seldik and Aleelah did. They followed the partial snow and pine needle foot tracks heading downhill until they breached the shoreline, admiring the water. They studied the tracks, seeing them come back over themselves into the lake. They followed, freezing waters flooding their feet, but they held their boots high and went barefoot. They dried on the other side and quickly hunted along the beach for the tracks to continue the hunt.

At once, they broke out into the opening before them and saw huts with fires still smoldering from the long night's party before. Nobody was around, and all was quiet. Kolkesh wondered where everyone had gone.

"Hello," Kolkesh said, his loud voice bellowing through the valley. They awaited anything, but nothing came. He said it again, finally letting out a whistle that could skin a rabbit. Suddenly, there was a clammer inside the huts. At once, doors popped open as small ones of darker skin and dark hair like Deneska popped their heads out, looking toward them in shock. One yelled, then ran toward a hut on the end where the door opened slowly, but the giants saw only darkness. Then, the fantastic, familiar form of Seldik jumped out, still putting on a shirt.

"Seldik!" yelled Kolkesh as the other two shouted praises to the heavens. Seldik gave up the shirt and ran toward them, yelling out their names in happiness. He slammed into Kolkesh, first to step forward, but the effort didn't even rock the giant's frame. He wrapped Seldik up, yelling and smiling widely as the others waited to hug him. By then, everyone was outside watching. Soon, a beautiful young girl stepped forward, holding an older woman's hand. The giants stared at them all, some twenty packed together in silence in front of them. Seldik ran back, grabbing Aleelah's hands, then pulled her with him as she smiled, but trembled with worry. She followed him toward them, half dragged along until they were standing in front. The small woman looking up at the towering giants, Kolkesh being the most apparent infliction in her wide eyes staring at him, and he burst out laughing.

"This is Aleelah," Seldik said, showing her off. Then, one by one, he bolted out the names of his once lost companions in tremendous excitement. Aleelah nodded to them, slowly trying their names again, but getting them wrong, then Seldik introduced them to everyone in Aleelah's tribe, again repeating their names.

"How?" Seldik finally asked them, then realizing something.

"Where are the others?" Seldik said as he now noticed the small number standing before him. The others shook their heads slightly, but Kolkesh took the lead.

"Are we not enough, young one?" Kolkesh joked dramatically, but then raised a somber hand for silence and gave Seldik a grim smile.

"Yes, Sylic lives, young one. He went southward. I will explain later." Then Kolkesh set his bag down and knelt before Aleelah as she took a step back. Kolkesh was as tall as her, though he was kneeling.

"You, young lady," he said, pointing to her, "you probably know someone we know. You remember DENESKA?" He said her name loud enough for the entire village to hear him, and gasps rang out all around, the shock making Aleelah instantly fall to her knees as she trembled and shook. Kolkesh broke into a smile larger than Seldik had ever seen. Aleelah burst into tears and wept in her hands.

"And do you know a big guy, Aleelah? His name is BLAKLEY," again, saying the name loudly, and Aleelah cried harder. Seldik jumped to hold her now as she wept, sweeping her head to his chest.

Kolkesh reached out slowly, bringing her head out of Seldik's chest to look at him. He smiled as she did, nodding his head up and down in large sweeps. So dramatic was the effect that Aleelah cried out in happiness and her mother came running to her from behind, wrapping her daughter in a strong embrace. They held each other for a long time, crying.

"She lives, Kolkesh? Her sister lives?" Seldik asked gleefully as Kolkesh nodded, as were the other survivors.

"You could say we ran into them." Edeldon and Nasok laughed. "And you could say she damned near took out Kolkesh," Nasok ended dramatically.

"They are fine. We hiked up to the divide, but the big one couldn't climb it. Sylic saw your tracks, so we had split up, them going to the right and us tracking you two," Kolkesh said, proud of their feat.

"Sylic is well!" Seldik was so happy that Sylic lived and was now protecting Aleelah's sister that he could only shake his head in disbelief. Their mountain-top prayers were answered from beyond the grave to again rejoin the group to its former glory upon this beautiful lakeside beach.

"We just arrived two days ago. You came fast," Seldik said, surprised.

"Well, we didn't have little ones slowing us down, boy," Edeldon stated.

"What of Mumot, Kolkesh" Seldik asked, realizing the real giant was not present, but the bowing of heads told him all he needed to hear.

Soon the villagers warded them over to the relit bonfires, where they were fed and warmed with blankets as they all sat around in a big reunion catching up.

Chapter Twenty-Eight

JOURNEY SOUTH

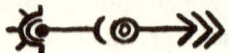

Aleelah was up early, packing supplies and weapons. Seldik heard the commotion and, given the alcohol consumed the night before, wasn't feeling the day yet. Whatever hooch they concocted was fast and tasted horrible, but it did the job as they celebrated the impossible reunion of friends.

"We go to your sister?" Seldik said, catching Aleelah's eye, then signed the question as she somberly nodded her head yes.

Seldik rose in the morning to begin packing when Kolkesh appeared at the thatched door.

"You would try to leave without us, boy?" Kolkesh gave him his much-missed large smile.

"We will not leave each other's side again, War-Soul!" Seldik swore with much more resolve than he initially decided upon as the words left his mouth.

"The Souls are ready as ever. You two better hurry. Clouds above threaten again." Kolkesh pointed skyward. Seldik wasted no time hurrying up their packing.

The agglomerated group gathered in the village center as others packed away food and blankets in their already full backpacks. Aleelah, with her mother, made their goodbye ritual as she promised to bring young Deneska home again as soon as possible. The men of giant stature stood in the center of the crowd like trees as they awaited the commotion to finalize. With Aleelah joining them, the five departed on their mission into unknown territory.

The group spent the day hiking south toward the ridgeline until they discovered a pass low enough to attempt in the deep snow, so they headed for it. The snow was like a rock, frozen stiff and ungiving, so the expedition walked very fast along it. Snow started falling in large flakes as Aleelah took the rear. Seldik held back as the group pulled away again. They passed the top, extending to another vast lake system below them. Only the snow clouds blocked distant views as they charged downhill. The mountain fingers edged southerly, so the group had to stride along them as they descended. By nightfall, they were off the mountain and near the lake edge, where snow turned to heavy rain, so a halt was called.

In a pleasant white-bark tree grove, they found shelter from the water coming down and built a fire. The party was tired from the hiking and the remaining bad alcohol from their systems and quickly rolled up in their covers to sleep. The morning continued the downpour as all quickly packed, hiking at first light. Aleelah could not see as well as the sea-fairing giants in darkness, so the pace was slow until more light shone through the clouds.

Soon, the heavy rain became apparent as water flowed down from every draw and cliff from the mountains, filled with temporary rivers as they flooded. The group was increasingly forced toward the lake to cross each obstacle until they were pinned against it. Seldik suggested a boat construction after he explained the task to Aleelah. The rest started gathering wood at the beach, where Kolkesh was hard at work lashing it together. A simple raft of flat timbers was fashioned to fit the five. Only Aleelah seemed much impressed with the construct as the others kicked at it, worried if it would even hold together. Aleelah saw their true power as the others quickly heaved it up, easily pulling the large raft into the lake. Once Kolkesh boarded it and jumped his massive weight around, he gave it the thumbs up, and everyone boarded. Long poles were set on the sides as Seldik, Nasok, and Edeldon lifted them, then, in combined rhythm, pushed the boat along, digging the poles into the sands below to move them. Kolkesh remained center rear with another pole, guiding them along and keeping his weight off one side, or his weight would have pitched the raft sideways. Aleelah stood in the middle, impressed with the creation and use of such a construct. She enjoyed the calm of the water, as no winds blew, but disliked the drenching rains that remained.

Aleelah wanted to talk to the others, but their lack of understanding of the other's language was frustrating, but they were polite enough. Then Seldik had reaffirmed to her that another of their team was with her sister, a capable person of her size, he mentioned, from a far-off land. She was unsure if that was what was relayed, as much of his language was still unknown to her. Aleelah was so happy they would all go so far as to keep both of them safe. Aleelah would not have survived if not for her mighty savior, who she was now very fond of. She had told her mother of his help and how much she liked him.

As they floated along the lake, Aleelah could not see her future without Seldik. She realized for the first time there was no going back to her past. He was her future now. Discovering her village had not completely perished, she felt her life might return to some normality someday, at least as much as expected with Seldik in it.

The group floated past the obstacle of raging waters on land using Seldik's barge, making it to the end of the lake by dark, where a mighty river flowed down from another southerly lake. The barge was drug up into the trees to be used as a cover as fires were set again. Food was cooked, and the party was happy to be out of the constant rains soaking them through. Once coats were set to dry on sticks, they rolled up again and went to sleep. Aleelah and Seldik remained awake a bit longer, cuddling as they watched the rain pour onto the lake below until it was pitch black, and they drifted to sleep.

Chapter Twenty-Nine

FROM ICE TO MUD

Deneska and Sylic were getting to know each other, and Blakley trusted the tan, thin stranger with much ease. *If he likes Sylic*, Deneska thought, *so do I!* After leaving the leading group of giants, Deneska was thrilled that Aleelah was alive and well enough to travel with the company the others trusted. With three more bearing down on them, Deneska hoped she would be safe until they met again. The weeks had almost killed them so many times, she thought; then, to get separated where their fates were unknown to one another was nearly the end of her. This new hope was all she needed to go on with the handsome man beside her.

They appreciated that lesser winds were now within the confines of the canyon, but still, some blew at their backs. Mixed with the dark patches, the cold was still unbearable as they pressed on. Sylic felt full of energy but was still nursing his bad knee. Otherwise, he was fit, darting around looking for weak areas in the snow that would not hold them, walking on it to steer the elephant around it. Sylic thought of Mumot and what must have become of him, as nothing would have stopped him from rejoining the group. Sylic owed his life to him, but knew the thanks would never be given.

Deneska was the most beautiful creature Sylic had ever seen. His feelings for her were very overpowering, almost euphoric at times. His fascination with her ability to harness a giant mammoth was surely only one of her many strengths, he thought. Her ability to throw a spear was another, almost costing him their leader. Deneska liked his forward nature, as Sylic could not get enough of being near her. Blakley was a character, too, he thought, recalling occasions when the elephant would playfully throw snow at him. What a combination—a young girl and a massive beast, surviving here together in a hostile landscape.

The two decided to make camp early as Blakley wasn't moving fast, and Sylic continued to stop to rub his knee and re-wrap his bandage. Deneska wasn't up for the low oxygen at these heights, suffering from an inability to catch her breath mixed with bouts of vertigo. They were not to any apparent pass, just more long winding canyon with water heard rushing under thick snow. There was no getting out of the shaded zone, so a spot was chosen with the hope that the morning sun would wake them.

Deneska tended to Blakley as Sylic foraged firewood and copious pine needles to provide some warmth. When night came, Blakley laid down beside them, his wound doing better but still significant and full of frozen blood. Little dried food was left, so they heated it on the fire then consumed what they could. The camp grew warmer as Sylic and Deneska enjoyed each other's company, watching the flames dance off each other's faces. Sylic stacked burrows of needles close to the fire, then they mounted their spears outward and laid down to sleep, Sylic keeping the first watch.

Early morning some snow came down but very leisurely, the winds occasionally buffeting the brush they lay beside as Sylic ran close to being out of wood to feed the fire. As he was dozing in and out, something caught his ear during a moment of silence between the winds as he spun to his spear, bringing it up to the ready. Deneska woke instantly, fumbling up while gathering her senses as Sylic touched his lips for silence. Deneska was staring at him, wavering back and forth. He knew she did not have enough senses to engage in any threat, so he crept into the open area and slowly placed the last wood on the fire behind his back. Deneska realized it must be a threat and steadied herself enough to rise and grab her spear, but she was dizzy just sitting on her knees, hoping it would clear as she backed up Sylic. Blakley was awake with his legs now making noise, trying to get a foothold to roll onto his belly, so Sylic was down to sight only, peering hard out into the darkness. He turned, found an almost burnt chunk of wood still holding a higher fire, then tossed it out onto a rocky area to see. Instantly, it outlined the silhouettes of two large cats with stripes and shiny white fur as they backed up quickly from the fire's threat to disappear against the night.

Sylic quickly crouched backward beside the fire, pointing with two fingers at where the cats were. Deneska was wide-eyed at the action, but still looked pale and sickly. Sylic showed big fangs beside his jaw, which Deneska immediately recognized as a sign that cats were stalking them. Sylic motioned for her to stay crouched and keep Blakley down, as the fire would keep them at bay for now. Deneska moved to calm the beast, lying down as Sylic again stood guard with two spears at the opening, keeping the fire in full view. If the fire held the night, they were safer, but not out of the woods. He knew the cats track their prey and had probably tracked them the day before. Luckily, the night continued uneventfully as the light crept back to begin the day just before the coals went out.

They searched the area carefully but found nothing but tracks everywhere, with the large indents poking the snow showing huge paws. Sylic gave the all-clear to Deneska as she brought out Blakley and loaded up, ready to travel. Deneska showed him she was tipsy and felt somewhat sick from not breathing deeply, so Sylic showed they would travel slowly and carefully, watching for the cats stalking them. Sylic had not seen white cats, only heard of them, snow cats, he recalled their name. Blakley seemed well enough to travel but could not easily hold Deneska on his back in this snow full of obstacles, so Sylic spent a great deal of time hanging back, overlooking any place where the cats may be hiding. The dark areas left too many voids, so he kept them in the light as best he could as they moved on. By noon, the winds were still calm. The clouds were breaking, and before long, they were above them. The sun was now fully beating down on them, making their breaks feel better. Blakley's hair thawed, and Deneska felt better with the warmer air, so they pushed on to gain as much ground as possible while seeking the summit.

By deep afternoon, they reached the summit horizon and rejoiced with a longer than usual break as all consumed fresh water in an opening in the thinner snow by a sunny rock face. Blakley was washing, so Deneska took the time to clean the wound and re-cover it with cloth and salves. Sylic foraged, finding massive pinecones with large intact nuts within them. They broke open the cones and ate nuts, then gathered more before moving down the long side, heading in the promising direction of their friends and family.

Deneska still felt sick but hid it as best she could from Sylic, not wanting him to worry about her while the cats were out there. Sylic checked on her often. She even held his hand on her face several times, showing gratitude for his care. She hoped they would make it to the others before the cats came, and they were not ready to fight such predators in their shape. Blakley was doing better, so hope was given to the descent where she would feel better in the thicker air below, but another night of camping was guaranteed.

Deneska motioned Sylic to camp early, gathering much wood to stand in a chosen place, to which he agreed. The team found a solid boundary of boulders too steep for the cats to get behind them, so they gathered branches to build up a wall in the opening, then got what sharper ones they could make to bolster the fortification. Much effort was taken as the two scattered across the valley to bring in supplies and copious amounts of firewood. Deneska spotted three cats higher up on a ledge across the shadow-covered canyon, having to flee back to Sylic to point them out. The two worked closer to the campsite while watching for the cats to appear once they left their perch. They knew they would be coming close tonight. Wood was stored high as an early fire was built as the last poles were set in place, pointing out with the wood pole gate pushed into brush and boulder to close off the entrance for the night using Blakley's massive trunk to secure the heavy barricade. Nothing could jump it, and nothing could penetrate around their back or sides now, so the wait began.

After more nuts were broken out, roasted, and consumed, the two sat warily against the warming rock face with spears at the ready. Winds were less this night, with sounds echoing across the canyon from the rivers running over rock, making the pair uneasy as soon as the sun set. The clouds had set high but brought more darkness to the deep valley, making the hair on their necks stand up. Blakley felt uneasy and stayed upright, but slightly dozed off at times. Deneska felt less sick but was still weak as she lay against the rock to warm her head, as Sylic, the best in health, awaited the inevitable. It was not long before they heard noises right outside their defensive barrier. First, soft steps came from various directions, then more clacks like jumping or stepping on wood were heard. Sylic was immediately on his feet, spear pointed toward the entry as Deneska got to her knees beside him, ready.

All at once the pouncing landed on the entrance branches, bending heavily from the unseen weight. Blakley jumped up at the ready, but the boards did not break nor reveal the beasts attacking. Again, they were hit but held firm within the brush and stone, wedged deep into both as predators attempted to break through. Sylic yelled at each attack with a loud bellow, but it seemed to have no effect. Blakley rumbled a low trumpet at times, threatening to charge them, and Deneska had to calm him down. Sylic threw several burning timbers over the entrance far enough away to not start a fire on their defenses to scare the cats, but it only worked briefly as they were back, scratching and cracking timbers like they were digging in. Sylic came forward during several long hammerings on the wall and thrust his spear into the gaps, trying to injure one, but no cry of was ever heard. The waves came and went with long pauses to give the group a false sense of ending before they returned.

Hours passed as the multiple directions of defense testing intensified. No rest was possible for anyone, so Deneska leaned heavily on the rock face, trying to conserve what little energy she had until needed. Sylic remained toward the entrance with extra firewood burning to bring against the beasts if they broke in. But soon, the cats were putting more effort into digging in every direction. Sylic used two sticks to throw coals over the boulder barricade to be sure they did not easily breach, which seemed to keep them toward the gate area only. After what seemed like hours, a large swath of brush and timber set against one side of the gate's front was drug out like they pulled it with their teeth. As the gap along the ground burst open, paws instantly flooded in. Sylic looked back at Deneska, as they realized more than three cats were now at the gate.

Deneska was sick from no sleep as she leaned on the rock for warmth, watching Sylic intently. Her adrenaline was spent as her breathing was harsh and shallow, still not getting recovery from the elevation they were in. Blakley was focused, so it took considerable energy to calm him down and return to guard duty. Then the louder noises began as Sylic looked at her fearfully, knowing more cats had joined the hunting party. His yells led to nothing, but his throwing of coals seemed to disperse those in the area for a time. But then the side of the gate collapsed, and Deneska sprung to life. At this point, her weakness would be nothing in death if she did not fight. Sylic was already heading for the breach with a fired log in hand and a spear in the other when she pushed off the face leading his way. She stumbled, realizing she had little strength to run as she headed toward him. As soon as Sylic was at the gate, huge paws with long claws shot out under it, scraping at the dirt. He threw the burning log directly on one pair as a piercing yowl rang out from under the timber as it jerked back and was heard running out into the valley. Another pair of claws took its place, landing a swipe right onto the burning timber, causing the same retreating effect. Deneska came beside Sylic as he speared the dirt, trying to make impacts on the paws as she joined in. Both raged at the beast's claws as they reached for them, pressing hard against heavily bowing limbs far too skinny to be a sure defense. Finally, Deneska extended her spear between the branch gaps and lunged it deep, making contact. As Sylic stabbed one paw so thoroughly, he stuck it to the dirt, Deneska speared it in the head, making it fall limp instantly.

There was no time for celebration, as many more were breaking through the surrounding branches. Sylic kept stabbing in the dirt as Deneska shoved the spear into the unknown, inciting giant growls and sharp rasps from the beasts as the points drove home. There seemed to be an unlimited number of cats to replace the ones they fought off, but blood soon poured under the timbers into the sands as they plunged and thrust. Once Deneska's spear was ripped from her hands as one cat clamped its jaws upon it to yank it out through the timbers, making Deneska grab the burning woods to thrust under the boards while Sylic grabbed for another spare spear stuck in the dirt beside him to rearm her. Deneska soon carried several boards over where the cats clawed more bottomless ravines in the land, threatening to be able to crawl under. The fires kept them out as random ripping of timbers by teeth was heard just inches behind the failing wood wall. Timber splintered as more branches began to snap, revealing the viscous teeth and faces of their enemy. Their spears were easily avoided once the cats could see their prey with long outstretched arms, keeping the imprisoned away from the wall far enough not to get good hits. They were just minutes from being overrun by the beasts with nothing but a fire behind them to ward off what they could, when Blakley pushed up against the back wall, realizing the sheer number of cats tearing through the wall.

Finally, Sylic yelled, "Fire! Fire!" as he motioned for her to light the entire wall up, beckoning Deneska to throw fire on everything wooden. Deneska was in shock, fearing they would have nothing to protect them if it burnt down. Then she realized that if the fire was just big enough and raged long enough, morning might come as spears could be brought to bear by throwing them. They had few but could build several more to get about ten to a usable form.

Deneska quickly stuck her spear in the dirt while stumbling toward the fire. She scooped up the largest burning logs she could carry, then hurled them directly over the wall, where they were seen lighting up the rearward darkness. Instantly, the many silhouettes of the cats were seen darting away as embers blew wildly, igniting the brush, flames leaping far into the night sky. She threw more to the sides then further out as great roars were heard as the cats darted away in all directions, some half on fire. Though, a few remained relentless and were caught by the fire, pressing against the last of the wall timbers. Sylic took advantage as he thrust his spear deep into the cat's back. It let out a tremendous roar that scattered the remaining cats.

Blakley could take no more, and he rushed the gate. Only slightly afraid of the fires he was used to, he burst right past Sylic into the center of the gate while lifting his low bent tusks into the air. Sylic flew sideways in shock as Deneska was pushed to the other side when Blakley stomped by. All at once, his tusks scooped up the sideways timbers, broken or not, then flung it all high into the air. The falling fire and coals peppered Blakley, finally sending him into retreat, and he stomped back toward the fire pit. Deneska was on her feet as she grabbed his reins to calm him. Blakley reluctantly stopped moving backward as he tromped side to side in his warlike stance but remained under his master's control. Deneska swept under his great trunk and then checked on Sylic, who remained on the ground, wiping bits of embers from his tunic. He was still shocked as Deneska reached down to help him, which he accepted. They stood together with spears in hand, simply watching the glow of the scattered fire searing the dead flesh of huge cat carcasses tossed around the entrance. The fire raged high into the night and re-routed the rest of the cat pack as they fled for their lives.

Soon, light started coming from the east as the three sat at the mouth of the entangled barrier splintered with charred wood. Ash kicked up with the early winds, rising when the two decided to venture out. Checking the perimeter, three dead cats were at the entrance, two more a distance away, appearing to succumb to wounds that delivered a slow death. The remaining cats were nowhere to be seen as tracks showed they scattered everywhere at night. The reluctant team of survivors patted Blakley down well for his surprising efforts that probably sent the final blow that broke the cat's spirits. They hurried to pack up, then left for better ground downhill.

By noon they had rested far less since Deneska felt better the more they walked. Blakley kept up, quickly going downhill as the ragged team fought their tired souls to keep going, hopefully away from the white cat's elevated hunting grounds. The nuts gave them energy boosts as they ate and walked, taking little breaks. Soon they began to see groups of large mountain sheep high on the canyon walls the cats hunted. The clouds were dropping and threatening moisture, so the group pressed on, within hours, encountering the first drizzles of the new storm.

They found taller trees thick with dry areas within, so they found another nook to set up a barrier defense. No tracks were this low, but they were not taking chances as they quickly designed the same spiked wall full of much more branches this time. Blakley easily pushed over several large trees, impressing Sylic anew, as Deneska smiled at his abilities, then lifted and placed them as she directed to make a strong fortification. Much leaf matter was accumulated with smoke piles able to be started in forward directions, along with fire piles set around the inside entry paths. The team pulled the last poles across the entrance again just before dark as the center fire raged.

Sylic was left guarding, but nothing came as the rains grew greater. The sky poured like they had never seen before, leaving little chance of hearing anything outside but washing away their scent from being followed. Deneska laid behind the fire nearer Blakley as Sylic took first watch. She fell asleep, knowing she would be better rested if the cats came. Blakley also felt at ease and laid down, stretching long as he drifted off.

Soon, a giant river of water cascaded down the valley they had just come from, bringing large rumbling sounds across to their camp as new paths were cut away. They were far from the lower levels of danger, so they settled down to the harmonious thundering of rampant water mixed with rain on leaves. Sylic awoke, realizing he had dozed off, but nothing but the rush of distant water and rain filled his ears. He re-stoked the fire and then thought of his team, Him encountering Deneska and Seldik magically surviving with who they hoped was her missing sister. Tired as he was, thinking of her kept him energized long into the morning, then he slept soundly.

When they rose, the fire was still blazing with white-hot coals. Deneska rose, excited to finally feel better, and Blakley following in almost a prance as Sylic stumbled up, happy to have gotten enough sleep. The rains continued but had thankfully not turned to snow, so they prepared themselves to be soaked to the bone and headed out as best they could. The clouds were thick as they worried about cats attacking, but their scent was erased in the rain so they made the best of it as they picked their way, avoiding the raging flooding waters lower in the canyon. The valley opened where they saw the first large lake far below, peering under the lowering clouds. Realizing they were out of the mountains and entering the lower lands, they were excited and had renewed energy, stomping the miles off as they pointed out things along the way.

The ground eventually changed from high, dense gravels to lower land soils that became soggy with sticky clays. Sylic and Deneska stopped as the rains poured, pointing to various options. Still, none were any good, leaving them to continue carefully along higher ridges that kept down the water content in the mud as they moved along. The more they chose a sideways path toward the lake's edge, the more they began to sink into the bog.

By mid-day, they were off the mountain fingers and clear of the valley, with only hours to the lake when they rested on the last rocky outcrops. As the rains refused to release them from their soaking, they decided to walk to the shoreline, hoping it was harder than the muddy terrain they were getting into. Far over the valley lip was seen the same soft soil. The point was to try heading northward when they reached the lake, and finally locate their split group so that this castaway journey could be ended. But no easy way was apparent and going directly down to the lake seemed safest. North or south provided only plains of mucky-looking land that may be bog or bottomless, which they were unwilling to confront. The soaked group decided to eat what little remained of their harvested nuts while trying to enjoy each other, keeping dry under a rough skin tarp that Deneska brought off Blakley in a roll.

Not long after they rose to wander down to the lake's edge, the repeated sounds of snapping trees came from behind them up the gentle slope of the mountains. Unlike the rushing wake of snow that they had both endured, nor the ash wave Sylic barely escaped from with his group, this sound was slow, steady, almost calming. Above them on the bottom of the cloud's misty edge, the noise continued to unfold, but it did not grow nor increase in intensity. It just cracked here and there as it continued to echo down the valley. Sylic motioned to Deneska that they best to be on their way now, so they picked up and struck out downhill at a safe pace, looking back on occasion as larger cracks echoed from above.

Nothing was seen as they traveled some distance, the ground staying fair underfoot. They made reasonable time to the flatter bottom but soon found themselves in softer soil that reached, then sunk, past their ankles as they stepped. Blakley, they realized, floated on the stuff, having a wide foot span that seemed fit for the task. He did not sink to the depth that their small statures did. They looked surprised at each other, shrugging, then continued, but soon their leisurely pace was tested as Sylic stopped them to look back at what he saw. Behind them, coming down where they had walked from, was what seemed to be the entire earth drifting down slowly. The two stared in awe at what was happening, while rocks and trees were all in place as the ground creeped downhill toward them. Looking as far as they could see along the entire mountain front, the same event was happening. Spotting a region over a round mound up the mountain that led to a gentle cliff, they watched in amazement as the ground surface slid as one entire blanket over it, then bent down vertically until the standing trees and suspended boulders plummeted to the valley floor.

They realized this thick wave was a wall of mud, slowly descending on them with deadly consequences if they got caught up in it. They quickly understood the danger, immediately ran downhill at the fastest rate they could. Deneska was pulling Blakley along, who resisted such speed, but they had to flee the impending flow. On the way, Sylic hunted for anyplace they could head toward that would shield them from this wave, but it was flat everywhere and slopped toward the lake with just enough angle to easily keep the mud flowing until it reached it.

Sylic realized they would be pinned against the lake. The mud certainly wouldn't stop as it flowed into the lake for a great distance, giving them no chance at survival. His frantic looks made Deneska take in what he was looking for when she realized what they were getting themselves into. From a simple, slow mud caused by heavy rains, they were locked into a location they could not escape. In all directions, the mud would overtake them if they traveled that way. Down was the only option until they hit the lake, where miles of muddy land would continue to flow, forcing them to swim until they perished from the hard, exhaustive effort. She realized Blakley would not survive that even for a minute but would be swept under the waters upon the mud.

The two pulled Blakley along, but near the lake, the relentless rains had created standing water on the mud as they sank deeper with each step. The lake edge was a distance away still as Blakley began to sink, making every footfall an effort, slowing his progress. Soon, the frontal flow of mud was within earshot. It was much higher than they thought. Some forty hands high towered over the terrain it consumed. Trees were toppling over as the slide flowed across the gentler ground, as both team members pulled Blakley's leash along to speed him up. Sylic knew there was no way Deneska would leave the elephant to his fate, so he would now finish his mission to help her by remaining by her side. Her frightful looks pained him to his core, so sad were her eyes with tears flowing freely, as she knew this was the end. They pushed on anyway, the flow now within a spear's throw from them as they hit the beach sands, allowing them to move faster toward the lake. However, Sylic knew this was no help, and they were out of options. Looking along the wavefront frantically, he saw it reaching the lake in all directions while giving them nowhere to run toward.

Deneska felt relieved, pulling herself higher on the sandy beach as Blakley followed. She was happy Sylic stayed with her so she would not die alone. She let go of Blakley's reins as she reached out, grabbed Sylic's arm, and hugged him tightly, awaiting the end. Only Blakley's continued roaring trumpets made them give a minute to their friend's wanting. Nobody would know where they went. The mud would cover them and dry up, hiding their bodies under the lake, leaving no evidence of their presence. Deneska shook in Sylic's arm as he held her tightly, her savior in death.

Chapter Thirty

THE SMOKING LAKE QUAKES

Aleelah and Seldik were the last to wake again. The others were already hard at work packing up. Unfortunately, the rains remained strong throughout the night into the day, and it was realized no break would be had from the soggy environment. The group untied the strung poles as they could not be carried in the muddy lands ahead, then headed south again along the river. Soon the next large lake came into view and swept a long distance around the valley. "Shall we build a better raft? It seems this lake may go on forever," Kolkesh said, looking at Seldik, who agreed.

The group made it to the lake's edge by noon. With the mud worsening, they realized the ground was moving downward from above. The speed of dragging timber down from higher sources commenced in haste, as more ground began to creep toward them.

"We will need the raft. This crazy land is crawling toward us as a mud blanket," Edeldon realized, pointing far up on the mountain flanks where trees flowed down, still upright.

The builders needed no other threat, and they quickly added more timbers to the layout as Kolkesh and Edeldon fashioned them together, lashing ropes around in intricate lacings that held them together. They soon had a working model, and it was hauled into the freezing water due to its more significant weight. Other logs were drug toward it as they lashed them rearward in a hurry as the first mud encroached onto their beach, ready to consume them all.

"We will build as we go. We have poles. Let's go!" Kolkesh ordered as they boarded and pushed off.

They sailed along the edge of the lake, watching the incredible sight of Mother's surface slowly flow into, then under, the water. They struck out further along the way as trees from above now stood in the lake, and the whole forest was moved along until no shoreline remained. They ran out of pole length quickly, going deep to avoid the obstacles. Then around a bend, they had to float along, since no bottom could be reached as the trees slowly tipped closer toward them. Nasok had fashioned more tips to several poles in time, which they used to paddle onward with some gains. Once around the curve, they could reach the bottom again, speeding up their journey.

As the day went on, they made good time, but there was no end to the mud flow devastating all the lands, leaving behind barren rocks high on the mountain slopes. The lack of visibility from the low-hanging clouds filled in by heavy rains kept seeing anything to a minimum, forcing them to row back toward shore several times after having sailed too far out. They drifted for an hour, making no small talk nor caring what others thought of the apparent drenched spirits. A meal was handed out to all as rowers broke to eat under tarps fashioned at an angle to huddle under.

Aleelah laid on Seldik's legs, tired from the pole pushing and rowing hard to keep up with the giant's more powerful pushes. She sweated as she lay there, panting with despair in her eyes.

"You think your sister and Sylic may be caught up in this?" Seldik asked her as he signed the elephant symbol, showing his hand to her jaw and then going toward the land to show her sister's motion. She nodded her head at the question.

"She worried?" Nasok asked, sitting closest to them. "It is a problem if the pass came out here. They may be above this mud or in it." Seldik said with a grim frown.

"I don't know how they could get out of it, especially the elephant," Seldik said, worried too.

"We seem to keep at the mud's edge. If they are out there, we'll find them," Kolkesh pronounced while making eye contact with Aleelah.

The day dragged on, but the rain refused to relent, the mud making little noise in its deathly march into the abyss. Aleelah returned to pushing the poles from the beachside and remained on constant lookout for her sister through the hazy patches of clouds. When they cleared, a shallow area ending beside a deep cove emerged as they rounded into it. Aleelah almost missed it, but a larger dark object seemed to move just before a puff of floating fog bank moved in front of it. She squinted hard, catching Seldik's attention. He followed the direction of her gaze and peered out, his eyes being higher and sharper than hers. Both stood for a long, hopeful moment before giving up. He glanced at her, knowing what she was going through, but the muds were clearly at the beach there, so what they saw was likely nothing more than a falling tree. He glanced back again to be sure, and as he turned, he saw the unusual shape himself. He immediately grabber Aleelah's arm and pointed at what he saw.

"Yes! Yes!" Aleelah cried out as everyone looked. There, as the misty bank cleared away, stood the undeniable form of Blakley with two people in front of it. Aleelah screamed as everyone quickly brought the poles to the raft's edges, heaving toward the beach. Aleelah yelled and jumped, waving her arms high in the air, but nobody on shore seemed to realize they were there. The giants might almost pulled the raft out from under Aleelah's feet as it shot forward, trying hard to make shore. As they approached, Blakley saw them, being the only lake-facing member of the stranded group, and he let out a fantastic trumpeting that did not stop. The group understood the danger as they approached as just behind them towered the massive mud wall. All Aleelah could do was crouch and hang on as the combined might pushed the raft inland with increasing speed.

Soon they were within earshot as Deneska and Sylic were just reaching the water with the mud upon them. Blakley paused just long enough, and the two spun around as Aleelah and the boat crew screamed at the top of their lungs to get their attention. Their wide eyes could barely comprehend the miracle before them, but they quickly grabbed Blakley's reins and led him into the water just as the raft beached against the shore. Seldik barred Aleelah's dash forward to stop her while the larger ones attempted a rescue as Aleelah fell to her knees, weeping, knowing she must wait.

"Grab the timbers around for a ramp!" Kolkesh yelled as Seldik and Nasok jumped over the sides, unlashing the timbers, trailing as Edeldon heaved the ropes toward the bow. Kolkesh was off in the sands holding the skiff firm.

The timbers were heaved upon the raft while the other end faced shore as they all struggled to lash them tightly together for Blakley's weight. Blakley did not relish stepping up on the boarding plank, so Deneska quickly mounted him and forced him forward as the others pulled on his tethers. Everyone was up on the back of the raft as a counterbalance, but Blakley pushed the nose into the sands below, tipping it downward. Aleelah, now useful, dashed forward and guided Blakley to the center as Deneska quickly commanded him to lie on his belly. Sylic was inches from the falling mud face as they all tried to push the raft off the beach before it could bury them. With groans, grunts, and bending poles, the overloaded raft finally gave way as it cast off the beach. Seldik, Nasok, and Edeldon kept pushing deep into the water and then held onto the makeshift ramp floating along tied to the raft. Cries rang out as Deneska and Aleelah grabbed each other and spoke their tongue, which the others smiled at as they hugged Sylic in greetings.

"You didn't expect to see us, land dwellers?" Kolkesh laughed as Sylic again hugged the big man.

"NO! It was our end of ends this time, for sure," Sylic rejoiced.

"Aleelah, I thought you were dead. I thought I was alone forever," Deneska cried and could say no more as she wept.

"I thought the same, that I had lost my sister. You are everything to me, Deneska," Aleelah, overjoyed, cried along with her as she patted Blakley hard on his trunk that was wrapped around them both as they knelt beside him.

"Good thing we brought enough wood. Let's get those boards on the side lashed up before you all freeze," Kolkesh ordered, smiling large.

"You, you surprise us all, Sylic. These stories will be told in the songs of our people and yours for all eternity," Edeldon proclaimed.

"I would much like to hear that sound, my friend. We were inches from a deep grave there with nowhere to go, then you water people saved us!" Sylic looked again, entirely grateful for the rescuers.

Large splashes were crashing all along the beach as the high mud flopped off into the water, pushing it, and sending wakes out to the raft. They all hurried to tie up the side timbers so they could climb aboard without the raft sinking below the top. Then the soaked climbed onboard as they began using the poles again to push the raft.

"The current is too strong, so we must continue south. We can't go deeper with this weight," Kolkesh pointed out as they pushed on.

The divided groups were once again whole. They watched the incredible power of the mudslide rush into the lake as the rains began to let up. As far as the eye could see, barren rock was exposed where a once beautiful forest existed, all descending into the valley where the lake consumed it.

"Deneska, this is Seldik," Aleelah told her sister as she introduced them.

Sylic was quickly introduced to Aleelah as Blakley was introduced to Seldik, who was fascinated by the creature they controlled. Blakley was not keen on the giants but maintained his stillness, knowing water surrounded them all.

Long talks in quick succession commenced as they resumed their push south. Deneska, upon learning some of her village survived, as did her mother, she wept again at the unbelievably good news. The group listened in horror as Sylic recounted their near demise at the paws of mountain cats and congratulating the two on surviving such a threat. Deneska and Sylic learned of the high lake and of the string of lakes attached to the one they were now on, reinforcing that their sailing abilities paid off this time as they traveled.

Night fell just as the clouds released their hold on the valley, so the group was put to rest as Kolkesh and Seldik remained, pushing the ores slowly. A slight moon cast shimmers on the lake top and the stars were finally seen again after what seemed to be months without them due to the ash that once blotted out their existence.

"You are still a boy, Seldik," Kolkesh spoke to him low, so the others were not awakened. "But you've grown up in a short time, like your father's vision foretold." Kolkesh paused, choosing his next words.

"But you are a man in all ways, a young explorer with the grit to survive the Netherweir!" Seldik stared at him, but the light refused to display his emotion.

"Without the Souls, Mumot, Sylic, and especially you, Aleelah and I would have been dead." Seldik earnestly mulled over his time within the land.

"A heavy price we all paid losing so many good ones," Kolkesh said, lowering his head. A pause on the topic was given in remembrance.

"What now, Kolkesh? I am afraid I am in love with Aleelah. My place is here, I think," Seldik turned to Kolkesh, knowing he would tell him he must return to CED.

"I know, Seldik. I know you're wise with a big heart." Kolkesh considered his following words carefully. "Yours is a heart that indeed belongs here with her. It was not by chance that this happened as it did," he said, leaving the thought open.

"I thought you may demand I come back to CED," Seldik stated in good faith. His friend took it as it should be, that they have a mission that is demanded by his father.

"I considered it, but speaking with Edeldon, we concluded this is your purpose in life, to be here." Kolkesh relayed an essential update to his quest for his Soul.

"What of my Soul Type?" Seldik asked. "Am I ever to find out what it is?"

Kolkesh stopped his pole pushing and turned to face to him.

"We are now sure that you have a Soul Type that we have never encountered. You are unique, Seldik," Kolkesh continued. "Now, what that type is still eluding us, young man, but it is important. We can tell you that." Kolkesh returned to his pole as Seldik did, and the two pondered the thought.

Sylic could no longer sleep and replaced Seldik, who joined Aleelah, lying beside her while her young sister slept soundly in her arms. Blakley slept well as the lap of water on the logs quickly lulled him to sleep. Kolkesh kept at the helm. A ship captain in his heart played equal to his War-Soul type, Seldik thought as he dozed off.

In the morning, they woke with the first intense sun shining down on the damp group. The raft bark had soaked up much water, wicking it into the layers pressed against it until all who were lying against it were half-soaked with cold clothes. Everyone awoke happy as Deneska had the best sleep in a long time as she jumped up, ecstatic for the day. Kolkesh was pointing to land where the lake ended with no sign of mud or tilted ground.

They quickly made landfall, then thoroughly checked the bedding, going deep up the ridgeline to ensure nothing else would come crashing down on them. An all-clear was given as they all got on the solid ground, and Blakley quickly rejoiced by stomping around a bit while trumpeting.

A large fire was set with the raft timbers as yet another river led away past where the eye could see. The camp was made, and fantastic food from the villagers was cooked and consumed. Wounds were tended to as others lazily sat and napped in the sun. The day was calm and warmer. The sisters walked long miles together with Blakley following behind and discussed what only sisters knew. As the night came on, everyone made it back to camp. As guards were set, the talks slowly gave way to sleep.

Early, the sun rose as they followed the fast-moving river south, where they ended on a large cliff face that looked far down into yet another valley full of water. The elevation drop to the next valley was unusual, taking a day at least to get down that far. Another irregularity was the vast smoke around the lake's edge. Aleelah quickly pointed as she spoke with Deneska on it, then motioned to Seldik some unrecognizable sign language they had not fully worked out. After completing her motions, Seldik looked again and consulted the rest.

"Aleelah is sure that is not volcanic smoke at the water's edge. It is steam from hot ground waters!" Kolkesh and the others looked at him strangely.

"She says they were at her home, too. They are very familiar." Seldik shrugged, intrigued by the thought of hot water steaming up from cold water. The others agreed as they started the long journey downhill. Conditions stayed sunny with no winds as temperatures rose the further down they went into the valley. It wasn't until dark when they reached the valley floor that the first long thrusts and shaking began on the ground as they traveled. They all stopped as the shaking rolled, then pitched along in steady waves followed by trembling endings that made everyone crouch down, anticipating it to worsen. The waves stopped as they watched Deneska calm Blakley down, who wanted little to do with it. They all stood motionless as they awaited more, but a calm settled across the valley with no more rumblings from Mother.

"I think we are all familiar with that feeling," Kolkesh said, reminding all of the volcanic eruption.

"Yes, but it is gentler, longer even," Seldik pointed out.

"I see no large mountain nor smoke, if that is steam at the lake, anyway." Nasok pointed again at the strange white clouds bellowing high from every part of the lakeside.

"We could go around, stay clear of the lake, but at this distance, if it was something that erupts, we will all be dead no matter what side we are on," Nasok said, pointing back. "And we can't go back that way for now," he finished, making them all realize they were here no matter what happened.

The group reluctantly pressed on, curving away from the steep mountain range they had survived several times, not wishing to tangle with it again. Instead, they headed east, trying to skirt the lake, but after not even an hour's march, Edeldon called them to a halt as he pointed toward the lake's edge. Everyone stood in shock at what they saw, and Aleelah tapped Seldik's arm, pointing to see what it was.

Below them on the beach lay a single sleek, black ship that resembled the Manoan's vessels. It appeared inactive, but two tents were set at a campsite further up the ridge, but no activity was seen.

"How in Mother's milk did that get here?" Kolkesh roared in disgust.

"That lake connects onward south to some other connected lakes. We did not see, War-Soul," Nasok said with further disgust.

"Well, if they are there, the lake is fine. That is not smoke," Seldik stated as he gave what information he could to Aleelah, who told Deneska.

"War, warriors, enemy," Aleelah reported, realizing they were not of his group.

"What do they want to do?" Deneska asked Aleelah, who just shrugged in response.

The group squatted down, considering their options. The only one they had was to march down to the camp and have it out with them. Kolkesh took the lead on the matter as the others agreed they must be interrogated about where they came from.

"It is our saving grace. We find out how they came, we take that boat, sail it back out to CED and finally bring our people here to this region without going over that hellish mountain," Kolkesh said, pointing to the tall mountain range.

"Agreed. If we are to return, we must find a better way out. There it is," Edeldon said, pointing out the obvious.

Nobody wished to ever go back over the mountain pass or toward the volcano area for some time. It was poisoned now for years to come. Aleelah was the first to grip her spear and hold it up. Deneska quickly standing to join beside her. As the others looked their way in astonishment, as Sylic stated the obvious.

"You guys might not have realized it yet, but they are both War-Souls themselves. We are in good company to do this." Sylic smiled brightly as he looked Deneska's way again. She returned the thoughtful contact by smiling brightly.

"Then we go." Kolkesh did not hesitate, wanting to circumvent the last journey's path with a clear intent to harm the enemy.

"I believe there might be more of them than us," Seldik mused. Kolkesh nodded in agreement but raised his steel tip spear in defiance of the thought, making sure everyone understood that the odds didn't matter.

The group formed up and filed down the hill, keeping the trees, rock, and brush inline to block their descent. They were close to the camp and in position to charge, holding their position behind mysterious rocks with water that flowed out of their tops, creating strange, rounded, white ripples on the rock's surface. Seldik sniffed, tasted the water, then promptly spit it out, whispering that it was salty. The attackers waited an extended period, listening for anything that may give them knowledge of how many there were in the camp, but no sounds were heard. A blast from a far-off geyser shot hot, steamy water skyward, and Aleelah smiled, excited to show Seldik she was correct. This was water only. Seldik was impressed with her knowledge, relaying that to Kolkesh in a whisper.

"I hear nothing. They may sleep. Let us walk right in, then fight whoever comes out of those tents," Kolkesh told the formed-up warriors. Everyone nodded yes as they started toward the camp, spread out.

Deneska mounted Blakley as she hushed him to a silent walk, Aleelah staying beside her in their usual fashion of attack. Seldik stayed beside Aleelah as Sylic flanked Deneska on the other side of Blakley. Both met, protecting their new loves. Kolkesh strode along in front as Edeldon remained directly behind with Nasok, all with spears at the ready.

When the group hit the camp, they split, entering the tents in a unified rush, but they were both empty. The split forces regrouped as they headed down toward the ship, eyes peeled, but no movement was seen.

"Where are they?" Kolkesh asked, all shrugging as they gave up looking around.

"The camp is abandoned," Nasok noted as everyone relaxed their stances as they approached the extended beach area.

"What is that?" Aleelah caught everyone's attention as she pointed toward the shoreline by the boat. Gazing, they all wondered what the strange-looking balls were. They were dark and poking out of the sands in a big, flat area.

"Rock?" Sylic asked, but Seldik shook no.

"Those seem to have hair," Seldik realized as everyone again drew up weapons in confusion.

They crept forward slowly, approaching the unusual sight, dark hair contrasting to the surrounding white of the beach, occurring only in that one spot. Nowhere else produced such a sight on either side. As they moved closer, they could smell the rot. Kolkesh stopped abruptly and held his hand up.

"THOSE ARE HEADS!" Kolkesh shouted, everyone now smelling the stench and covering their faces in disgust.

"Heads cut off?" Sylic asked from behind.

"They are all upright if they are," Kolkesh stated, more confused, then started to walk sideways as the group spread out around the field of rotting heads.

"They are buried?" Deneska asked Aleelah, who refused to step forward to see.

"Let me go forward alone. Stay put," Kolkesh ordered as he slowly shifted toward the nearest head.

He stomped the sand, but it was hard as stone, making an audible thump when his foot landed. He stuck his spear into the sand as he stepped, assuring it was familiar ground. Once near a head, he pushed on it with his spear, which did not move, showing it was still attached. He moved to more heads, testing as the others approached the grotesque scene to get a closer look.

"I count twelve heads, the amount probably needed as a full crew on one boat," Seldik stated as the others realized they missed that point.

"All dead and buried in the sand?" Sylic questioned, taking as close of a look as he could without throwing up.

"I see no wounds, only decay from flies," Nasok stated, seeing no reason to be buried here.

Seldik stepped back and pondered the entire scene. They were buried between their camp and their boat, with some tents sitting on the ground, not put up. Supplies lie around like they were unloaded but never got stowed, nor camp fully set up. Nobody liked the situation, so they pulled back up the beach to the camp to break while discussing their options. Kolkesh inspected the boat and returned, yelling that it was perfectly intact, ready to set sail.

"They have been there for weeks, maybe less," Kolkesh stated, knowing something of death.

"What put them there? Some force we do not know?" Edeldon worried this was the work of a wicked beast they could not fight off.

"It is a reason we should not stay here through the night. If something can do that to twelve men, it can do much more to the likes of our small group," Sylic pointed out. The girls looked worried as Seldik sat beside them, pondering all the information he gathered, trying to form his theory.

"Hey, they were all facing the boat, were they not?" Seldik stated, standing up quickly before pacing circles.

"Yes, I guess they are. Why?" Edeldon said, giving a question back to Seldik.

"So, they never set camp. The boat is fine. They were not injured, yet they are between the two, all facing the boat. Why?" Seldik looked around at the blank faces staring back at him.

"The beast buried them that way. It is a creature from the lake," Sylic stated, thinking of the unknown depths of water holding more creatures unseen.

"I don't think so. Those shakes we felt on the ridge. They were very strong and continued for some time." Seldik was connecting the dots now.

"You're saying the beast shakes the ground? It is so big?" Nasok questioned the thought.

"No, I believe the shaking caused it. I believe it continues on and off here in long events where if you were upon wet sands, they could turn soft like soup so anything on top of it would sink!" Seldik turned to the others as they sat, thinking of what he said.

"Like the snow as it flowed, the ash as water soaked in, or the mud we have seen turn into a wave. This shaking may make it like you are swimming in soup, just enough liquid to make you sink," Seldik continued.

"Then you sink below. They are up to their heads," Kolkesh stated, realizing it must not be.

"Not exactly. When you swim, you do not just sink, you are buoyant, but only some. The majority of your weight is underwater, and your head stays above easier," Seldik now had others making the connection.

"The quaking started when they were setting camp, so they ran to the boat only to get swallowed up by the sands?" Edeldon asked.

"Yes. On that flat sand area, very close to water height, I bet the water is just inches below the surface, easily turning the sand to liquid, whereas up here, it is harder." Seldik kicked the dirt around, showing it was dried as dust rose from his toes.

"You continue to amaze us, Seldik," Kolkesh stated, finally agreeing with the possibility.

"We stay clear of those lower sand areas, everyone. Stay up here until we decide where to go," Kolkesh ordered the group, who happily accepted.

Chapter Thirty-One

A NEW SOUL IS BORN

The group rummaged through the camp, finding many lovely items they took for themselves. They camped at the site, utilizing their new supplies as plans for the ship's use were developed. The only way to go was southward along the lake until more connections were made.

Aleelah asked Seldik if they were leaving too, but he informed her that they would not be going away with the others, to the girl's relief.

"We shall strike out south, find the waterways, fight our way to CED, then bring back reinforcements to set up here," Kolkesh finally spoke.

"Sylic and I will stay here with our new allies on land, head back to the high lake, then come back here when it warms more," Seldik confirmed as Nasok objected strongly.

"We should stay together. You are of the utmost importance, Seldik," Nasok stated.

"They will be fine. They will not leave their new loves, old Soul," Kolkesh interrupted.

"So, it is destiny. We will be divided again then," Edeldon stated like it was foretold.

"We have survived a perilous journey as the only survivors for a reason. I believe we are meant to stay here as we discover more of this land," Seldik stated in a new tone, exacting distinction among the Souls present.

The night came with slight tremors occurring regularly across the ground. None raised to the level they first felt on the journey down, but enough to keep everyone ready to not suffer the fate of the heads down by the lake. They realized they should try to float and lay flat, remaining on top of the ground until the quaking stopped if such an event caught them sinking in the sands. They surmised they suffocated. The sands were found tight against their bodies, just as Seldik predicted.

Fires raged as deep discussions brewed about the events they endured and the future for all. Nasok recorded now what he could on parchments found in the camp goods. Edeldon performed a ritual at the fire's edge of deep spiritual connection, seeking insight into the future they would all face. He tranced for long hours as the rest of the group found more entertaining things to do like sign more with the girls. Seldik had taught Aleelah as much as he could, then showed Deneska, who learned quickly. Soon, Sylic was directly communicating with Deneska as Aleelah coached her. He was entranced and now able to describe more to her. Seldik sat with Aleelah as they laughed at the two young love birds singing to each other. Kolkesh just chuckled as he watched the evening's events.

Edeldon began to pitch a higher thrumming from his lips that seemed to indicate he was at some apex of focus. Kolkesh quieted everyone, then waved for them to gather around the fire as he knew Edeldon would soon give his visions over to them. All Aquarionites believed in visions, one of the rarest gifts granted a Soul. They could see things others could not. The visions have saved Kolkesh alone countless times. Nasok passed around a bowl filled with a white paste that the group used to place thick lines down their faces. Aleelah wanted one, so Seldik carefully scraped one on her face and then kissed her lips to be sure. Deneska passed, but Sylic always participated, placing a line on his face as he sat near Deneska. Soon Edeldon was finished, then lowered his face as he pondered the unknown.

"I see the future clearer than I ever have. The lands cleanse my thoughts, the company purifying my heart." Edeldon spoke so eloquently that everyone was enthralled as they listened closely.

"You are a Soul of War. You have fulfilled your duty to this life here, Kolkesh," Edeldon spoke to a now slightly shaken Kolkesh.

"Of your journey with the Souls here, you have kept your vow to keep them safe," he said, continuing to promote Kolkesh.

"You are the Knowledge-Soul. You have witnessed these great events, and your words will echo across time itself of the deeds done in the Nether," he said, addressing Nasok.

Nasok rose and bowed profoundly, thanking the Soul for his kind future.

"Of my own accord, I see a dire future, one with pain as I always do, for my Soul's ending cannot be deduced by myself," he continued, now, speaking of his journey thus far.

"I am of the vision world, a place where Souls pass to their journey onward into new domains filled with more meaningful tasks we can never understand." Edeldon paused as he hummed chords from the connection he was having there. He then opened his eyes and made direct contact with Seldik to warn of his following words. Seldik felt a cold chill pass through him as Edeldon's gaze passed through his mortal body to the beyond, where Vision-Soul plays.

"Our journey ended so many times, young Seldik. Without you, we perished by the numbers until only a few..." Edeldon paused and pointed toward

Kolkesh and Sylic, "...only *they* remained," he said, hanging the words out raw, so everyone understood how much has been lost since they discovered the Netherweir.

"You alone saved us many times as your father had dreamed would happen, and as I have foreseen." Seldik was surprised Edeldon knew of his father's dream since he had been gone within the Nether for over a year. Seldik now felt bound to what was about to be said. *What am I if not a known Soul?*

"Do you not believe, child?" Edeldon now questioned Seldik, after seeing his shocked expression.

"Read to us your record of my vision as told before Seldik entered the Netherweir, Knowledge-Soul," Edeldon requested, looking to Nasok, who quickly came to an upright position and dug for his small journal that nobody knew was tucked within his beltline. He promptly flipped back as Seldik saw it was a book of pure golden pages, so thin they bent with ease as he turned them. In the firelight, Nasok squinted at the fine print inscribed on the pages until he found the passage he sought and began reading aloud. Aleelah and Deneska stared in amazement, as they had never seen noble metals.

"The day of equal sun and darkness in the year twenty thousand exactly, the beginning of the Great Year's Golden Era, a strong vision came to Vision-Soul Edeldon of CED City upon the bank of the long lake where he entered the Netherweir and where we retreat from again with losses in the interior that consumed so many men." Nasok paused, turning the page then continued, "It is hereby recorded for all time that from the vision came a clear image of a young boy of the King of CED, the mighty Chief-Soul Cedrin, coming to the Netherweir with no Soul announced as his destiny!" All were now gazing at Seldik, who sat with his mouth open at the reality of what had come to pass.

"It is further recorded that the vision showed a future where Seldik would succeed, where all others have failed. It is of the divine being that the boy will have with him a group of Soul's who will guard him on this journey where he will then be shown his true Soul, one never before seen in the world of man!" Nasok slowly closed the book and then returned it to his hidden pouch.

All remained quiet as everyone realized the vision described their journey. Seldik only coughed as he returned his gaze to Edeldon.

"As I have witnessed in the realm of the Souls, you have fulfilled this vision beyond the expectations of those Souls who passed this knowledge to me." Edeldon rose but pushed everyone to remain seated where they were. He approached Seldik now, Aleelah giving way to the event, moving away some for the two to be closer. Edeldon placed his hands atop Seldik's head, then hummed more for some time, chanting longer phrases in an ancient dialect unknown to everyone else. Finally, he convulsed slightly, appearing to almost fall. Then, when he spoke, it was frightening. It sounded like two pitches coming from the same mouth in a deep, rumbling tone that was not Edeldon's.

"Boy of CED, Son of King Cedrin no more, you are now a Soul bound to the Netherweir, bound to the mighty Aquarionites, bound to these Souls that bear witness to your rebirth." Edeldon jerked as his wicked voice commenced into high pitches so loud Aleelah covered her ears.

"The realm of man will rejoice in this time of the Great Golden Age, for upon the land and sea has come a new Soul never before witnessed since the dawn of man…" Edeldon trailed off into more gibberish but paused as he felt across Seldik's cheeks with his open hands. Seldik sat frozen from the ritual. All around the fire, everyone sat staring in awe at what was happening.

"We are the forefathers, the past Souls destined for new realms. We see all who travel between the void from their births to deaths." Edeldon spoke with the same deep voice, but was quieter now. The ancient tongue rolled from his mouth like many people within Edeldon wanted their words heard. A chill swept through the group, making everyone tremble as the smoke from the fire settled instantly instead of heading up and away. Absolute silence washed over the crowd, and nobody dared to break it by moving or breathing.

"You, Seldik of Netherweir, are of the War-Soul, but not a warrior. You are of the Knowledge-Soul, but not a recorder." Quieter now, the voice whispered, "You are of the Vison-Soul but do not sense by future. You are a Leader-Soul, but not one focused on just your people." Everyone looked sideways at each other as they tried to understand what that meant, including Seldik himself.

"There is another way you observe your life, one of witnessing, calculating, understanding all that occurs around you to work out reality in its orderly structure…." Edeldon continued in his trance-like state, pitching high and low notes as he spoke.

"You are the first Scientia-Soul!" Edeldon finally whispered in his multi-toned voice.

All the witnesses watched the great revelation, completely unaware of what it meant, including Seldik. As the great Vision-Soul returned to his seated position across the fire, all stayed quiet as he regained himself. Kolkesh looked at Nasok, who quickly stopped writing and spoke softly to the group as Aleelah returned to Seldik's side and wrapped her arm around his.

"A new Soul was born this day. You all bear witness to this incredible event," Nasok continued with a humble look. "There has not been a living witness to such an event for ten thousand years, it is told." Nasok again looked at his recorded script on the skin before him as flame light intensified the moment in everyone's thoughts. The ground again rumbled softly, welcoming Mother, ever-present, so the party would not forget her.

"The word Scientia is a new concept, born from a new thought of 'Sci' which proposes all we observe is not magic nor chance, but a multitude of constructs that work naturally in unison, a natural law." Nasok observed the group to assure he should continue.

"Scientia then means the active discovery of or investigating for the understanding of… well, that natural law!" Nasok looked to Edeldon to confirm his belief as Edeldon nodded his head yes.

"So, our newest, Seldik, the Scientia-Soul, sees the world differently than we do. He sees into the very fabric of the environment and situation, then concludes solutions based on that?" Kolkesh questioned in amazement.

"Yes. As we react well with our gifts to the environment, Seldik interprets the causes, then formulates the reason and thus the solution needed," Edeldon replied as Nasok quickly wrote down the statement.

"Seldik, you are now aware of your gift, your very purpose, in this realm. Do you see it now?" Edeldon now asked the final question of the ritual. Seldik pondered this new revelation in shock. He could see it as they had said. He had seen it all like that. His entire life, he questioned things others could not answer. During all he encountered, the ship combat, the whale attack, Mumot, and the Skagg fight, he looked only at the pieces of the reality that were happening. He would deconstruct it and understand what made it all fit together, then form conclusions based on that unseen information. Seldik was most impressed. He knew this was his Soul's destiny, which changed everything.

"Vision-Soul," Seldik rose to his feet and bowed to Edeldon. "This gift, I do see. I am a Scientia-Soul through and through." Seldik sat again to hold Aleelah's hand.

Many smiles and cheers went up around the fire as a new dawn of the Golden Age in the Great Year had commenced. The planets were aligned that night as the party rejoiced in their newest Soul. And after hours explaining what he could to Aleelah, who told Deneska, everyone finally drifted to sleep while decide their next steps.

The next day, everyone was finally well rested. Having healed wounds, they ate hardily, then ventured to the lake along higher ridges to avoid anything to do with the low flats where one could sink if Mother began to shake. Aleelah, Blakley, and Deneska quickly found a hot spring pool a short walk away that everyone piled into, enjoying a new healing power they had never felt before. Several days were spent along the lake, finding little food from the salty water of the unique lake. They all realized it could not last. A night's fire raged as the last of the wood was used to fuel it.

"We must take this new ship down the lake to find the way out to sea, everyone," Kolkesh said. "We will bring back troops to build a fort further away south, then explore northerly as the ash settles when the sun burns hotter."

"I must stay here. The Netherweir is now my home. I will return to the high lake to rejoin the village until spring, when we will come here to greet your return," Seldik proclaimed defiantly.

"We knew you would stay. As a Soul, you guide your destiny, Seldik. You have earned that right," Edeldon stated, unbinding him from the group of Souls he had traveled so far with.

Seldik felt the words like a knife stinging in his heart as he realized nothing now would be the same as it once was. He was of a land he was once fearful of. As he stared around the group looking at him, his expression of sorrow was palpable to all.

"There now, Seldik. It isn't like you're losing us for good. We will be back to greet you upon this shore if the stars have it as our destiny," Kolkesh spoke up first, having everyone quickly spirited on the topic.

"Then it is settled," Edeldon stated, but Sylic interrupted.

"Well, as fond as I am to you all, I will also be staying behind. This sea-fairing boy needs tending to by a real land lover." Sylic reached over as he joined hands with Seldik, smiling.

"We figured that out when we saw you and Deneska up in the snow, Sylic," Nasok said as everyone laughed loudly at his words.

"True, we knew not even a pack of snow cats could separate you two," Kolkesh laughed. Deneska got the hint, as did Aleelah, as both grabbed their men and held them tight. The fire died away by midnight as everyone turned in together for the last time.

By the sun's first light, Kolkesh, Nasok, and Edeldon packed supplies into the ship and then met Seldik, Sylic, Deneska, and Aleelah beside Blakley at the campsite. The sun sparkled as it brightened the sky, and Mother trembled to warn them that the hostile ground they stood near already captured prisoners that were now rotting on the beach below.

"We leave the humbling Netherweir in your formidable hands, Scientia-Soul, and you, Land Dweller." Kolkesh chuckled with his usual loud calling.

"We will miss you, Kolkesh, Nasok, and Edeldon, until we meet again. May your journey as Souls be gratifying." Kolkesh, not waiting, stepped forward and grabbed Seldik in his mighty arms to hug him tight. He released Seldik and then snatched up little Sylic in the same fashion, causing him to let out a mighty grunt. Seldik handed Kolkesh a letter for his father, asking him to tell him of his success.

Upon releasing the two, they accompanied the three to the ship, pushing it off the beach as Kolkesh pulled the main sail.

"We have this new technology we will be using in our fleet now. By the time we get back, you may see yet another amazing ship we constructed," Kolkesh stated while loudly slapping the sleek, little, black ship's hull.

"I hereby name this craft Blakley," Kolkesh resolved, making Deneska look up and laugh as he tapped the ship again.

The remaining couples held their significant other as they watched the ship sail across the lake, wondering if they would ever see them again. They knew the way home to the high lake would be dangerous, but they were together and with little concern for what they faced for now. Aleelah held Deneska's hand as they looked at each other, secure in knowing they were blessed with lovers who had dedicated their lives to staying behind with them. It was a new beginning to replace the tragic ending of their old lives from not long ago. Their different worlds collided into something extraordinary with a fresh start. As a final goodbye, Blakley raised his trunk high, then let out a mighty trumpet that the distant boat heard, and ores were seen raised high in the air.

Striking out above the lake, the group stopped as again Seldik found an encrusted stone outcrop resembling the rough outline of the Manoan ship. Aleelah and Seldik, with Deneska's help, carved into the softer tufa stack the accounts seen at the smoking lake along with the parting of friends whose life missions were far from over. Seldik pondered just how Mother positioned these seemingly familiar boulders that appeared to mirror the actual life events he witnessed in each location he drew knowledge from. He realized these events they endure were maybe foretold somewhere in the great beyond where these stones were cast upon the land from to commemorate what will happen someday. Maybe even the same place where the Vision Souls snatch their visions from the mystic air to reveal them in this realm before the events even happen. Either way, Seldik felt a sense of duty to write down the details of such events for all time so that they would never fade into oblivion.

The End

Dear reader,

I am pleased to have shared this story with you. Crafting it has brought me great joy. If you found it as captivating to read as I did to write, please consider leaving a review. Your feedback will invite others to join us in uncovering the ancient histories and stories of those who walked the land before us.

AuthorChrisHegg.com

Thank you!

Chris Hegg